CALLOWAY

Thad J.

Published by
NineStar Press
PO Box 91792
Albuquerque, New Mexico, 87199
www.ninestarpress.com

Print ISBN #978-1-947139-41-1
Cover by Natasha Snow
Edited by Jason Bradley

Welcome to the Township of Calloway! Home of the world-famous Daddy Cains' Foods Company, a staple for the local community.

No one knows this better than James (Jimmy) Cain, heir to the family business, and his father's pride and joy. With his limitless resources and a family that is always there for him, his life could not be more perfect. But that changes when he meets Benjamin Rei.

A determined and intelligent man, Benjamin is a junior acquisitions officers eager to close his first major purchase. His company has set Daddy Cains' between its crosshairs and will stop at nothing to get it. Although Benjamin has a simple enough task, people and forces outside of his control will test the limits of just how far he is willing to go to make it to the top.

For Billy.
There really is a difference between cowboys and country.

Prologue

"I CAN'T BELIEVE it. I just cannot believe that boy would ever do something like that. You'd better stop that lying, Cecily," Anna-Jean chided. She had known her girlfriend for many years and understood that exaggeration was something she couldn't help but do.

"Now you know I don't lie on people, Anna." Cecily sounded slightly flustered but too excited about her new gossip to take any offense. "I don't need to. Honey, you've spent just as much time as I have running off that poison clan that Daddy Cain made, so don't tell me you can't believe." Cecily flicked her hand.

Anna-Jean just smiled as she turned off the hose after watering her lawn and gestured for Cecily to join her. The two ladies waddled up the stairs to Anna-Jean's porch with Cecily assisting her girlfriend until the two plopped down into a set of twin rocking chairs.

It was a gorgeous Saturday morning, and the entire neighborhood had noticed. Taking in the sight and squeals of her grandchildren splashing in a small pool, with another doodling small crayon drawings on the sidewalk took her back many decades to a time when she had been doing the same. Spring days like these were always welcomed, and the sweet scent of Anna-Jean's azalea flowers mixed with the cooling cookies just out of the oven almost made what Cecily had said unfathomable.

"Cecily, I'm not trying to be mean, but it just doesn't sound right," Anna-Jean said sincerely. "I know he gets into all kind of trouble, but it's never anything serious. He's just a boy. I don't think he's older than what, eleven now?"

"Mmhmm..." Cecily grumbled while shaking her head.

"Are you mad at me now?" Anna-Jean teased.

"Oh not at all," Cecily said. "As old as I am, you know good and well I don't waste time with being mad at anyone. I'm just disappointed in you is all."

Anna-Jean went quiet when Cecily didn't offer any more but instead took off her glasses and pulled out a small handkerchief to wipe a perfectly clean lens.

Her patience grew thin, and Anna-Jean crossed her arms, waiting for Cecily to elaborate. "Well?"

"Hmm?" she asked innocently. "Well what, sweetheart?"

"Keep me near the cross," Anna-Jean said. "Cecily, you just said you don't waste time, so speak plain."

Cecily stopped cleaning her frames and set them down on the small table in front of their chairs.

"You sound just like that boy's father."

"How?" Anna-Jean asked.

"Just listen to yourself, Anna. 'He's just a boy.' 'He's so young.' Making excuses for him."

Anna-Jean was about to respond but noticed how stern Cecily looked so she let her continue.

"Every year, that boy gets worse and worse. First, it was pulling hair, then it was scaring people with his pranks, and now he's gone and taken a whole day of school from all of the other kids."

"Oh stop it, Cecily. No one knows who did it."

"I do. I caught him and that favorite cousin of his playing hooky out in Mr. Jenkins's field. Again. And they had poor little Kenneth-George with them. Charles just adopted him into their family and he's already being taught bad habits."

"So just because you caught those boys being boys, it's supposed to mean they were up to no good?" Anna-Jean asked.

"Exactly," Cecily almost screamed.

Anna-Jean held her gaze and placed a hand over her mouth as she let out a small laugh. She continued to chuckle as Cecily reached up to touch the small strands of hair that had shaken out of place from her outburst and then joined in while pulling her bun back into a presentable fashion.

"Cecily," she started, trying to appeal to reason. "He's only eleven. How do you suppose he did it? Made a bunch of those... what? What did you call them?"

"Stink bombs."

"Stink bombs then." Anna-Jean laughed that Cecily was even entertaining these thoughts. "And he snuck into every classroom and every office to set them off at just the right time. Just before Daddy Cain had to meet with his principal that morning?"

"I'm not sure how he did it, but I know he did." Cecily sounded agitated. "Everyone thinks that boy is an angel, but I can see past that cute smile. Someone has to help Daddy Cain raise him right with how busy he is."

Anna-Jean sighed and pursed her lips. "You still didn't tell me how he got those little bombs or whatever and how he got into all those rooms."

"Well, I obviously wasn't there, but I wouldn't put anything past him. That boy is smart as a whip, clever even. And he didn't get that stuff from anywhere. He made it."

"How in the world did he—" Anna-Jean stopped short of finishing her question when she noticed the look of disappointment on Cecily's face. The notions her girlfriend had put forth were absurd, but then so was all gossip. She knew that this was quite likely the highlight of her day, and instead of indulging her, Anna-Jean was dampening her spirits. Instead of trying to find more flaws in Cecily's reasoning, Anna-Jean simply asked, "How did he make that stuff, hon?"

Cecily picked back up, eager to show off her skills of deduction. "He's a Cain, Anna." A perplexed look remained on her face so Cecily happily explained. "What would you do if your father owned a factory?"

"I know one thing I wouldn't do; worry about the mailman being late with my Social Security check." Anna-Jean laughed.

"Tell it now," Cecily bellowed as they high-fived. "But that's what they do, Anna. Play with all those chemicals and such. Would you be willing to bet he hasn't learned a thing or two?"

"It's just vinegar and tomatoes, Cecily...but even they have some dangerous stuff there," Anna-Jean conceded.

"That's what I've been saying. I don't know how he got in that building, but I know he didn't want to go to that meeting. He can make excuses every day and twice on Sunday to Daddy Cain about his teachers but not with a principal." Cecily huffed and sat back in her chair, nodding to herself that she was correct. "That boy is bad as hell! But ever since he could pick up a pencil, he's always brought home straight As. That's how he fools everyone, you see. Believe me, when I talk to that father of his, I'm going to make sure he can't make any excuses for that boy this time."

"You are too nosy sometimes. You know that?" Anna-Jean laughed.

"I don't care." Cecily had her mouth open to continue when she was interrupted by a surprising question.

"So you figured it out?" a young boy asked from the end of the porch. "Ah shoot. What am I saying? Sure you did!"

The two women looked at one another, not sure what to do. They were talking innocently enough, but there were certain things that they would never want a child to hear. Smiling as warmly as they could, Anna-Jean and Cecily turned their full attention to the now-trio of boys standing there.

"Hey, sweetie," Anna-Jean said. "Did you finish those chores for me?"

Instead of answering the question, the boys started to move as fast as they could toward her. The first boy climbed up and over the wooden railing to vault up to the porch, which ran the entire length of the house. His slight pigeon-toe not impeding his stride in the slightest. The second child, who couldn't have been older than five, simply rolled under the railing in the gap that was formed between it and the deck. How he could see with such long bangs in his eyes surprised everyone. The last ran around to the stairs. He looked very much like the first only his stockier frame limited his physical flexibility. However, what he lacked in dexterity was more than made up for with strength. When all three of them reached the ladies, the first of the three spoke again.

"Lemme guess. Tea, right? A slice of lemon for you, Miss Anna, and no ice for you, Miss Sissy."

The two women once again looked at one another and Anna-Jean figured that the children hadn't overheard their earlier conversation. Relieved, she just smiled and motioned for him to come closer and then took him by the shoulders.

"Well, aren't you just sweet. We would love some, but did you finish?"

"Yes, ma'am, we sure did. Cousin Bryan even patched up that hole in your fence so you don't ever have to worry about those coons tearing up your garden anymore." James smiled.

Cecily raised an eyebrow but tilted her head with a look of approval. "Well, bless your heart. But hurry on in because the sun is on the move, and Miss Sissy is parched, honey."

James ran into the home and let the screen door slam shut behind him. Cecily and Anna-Jean started to turn around, but before they did, he came back out and apologized. "Sorry, Miss Anna." He looked down, ashamed. When Anna-Jean just smiled, he ran back in, taking the time to physically close the door slowly as he tiptoed backward into the house.

"Kenneth-George! Get up here and give Miss Sissy some sugar," Cecily called to the youngest child.

Kenneth-George almost tripped over his untied laces and baggy overalls as he ran over to jump into her lap.

"Oh you lost another tooth," Cecily said while trying to push his overgrown and unkempt curls out of his eyes. "When did he get so big, Bryan?"

"Beats the heck out of me," Bryan said. "I think he's part weed with how fast he's shooting up."

"He sure is growing," Anna-Jean said. "You spend a lot of time with your cousins, don't you?"

"Of course I do, ma'am," Bryan answered without hesitation. "Us Cain boys are like brothers, thick as thieves. And I swear Daddy Cain is the best uncle a kid can ask for."

Anna-Jean and Cecily just smiled. They didn't want to pry, but it was nice to know that Bryan had good people in his life, even if they weren't his immediate family. "Well, good for you boys."

Cecily appeared ready to speak but not before Bryan changed subjects. "Hey, KG, show 'em that new dance we taught you."

KENNETH-GEORGE JUMPED out of Cecily's lap and began entertaining the two ladies. As they watched and clapped on, Bryan looked through the screen door. His accomplice gave him a thumbs-up that his task had been completed, so Bryan knew they would only need to keep up the charade a little while longer. Just as Kenneth-George was finishing his dance, the door behind the women opened.

"Here you go, Miss Sissy. I made it just the way you like." His smile beamed as he handed her a glass.

"You boys have been working all morning. Are you hungry?" Anna-Jean asked.

"Are we ever—" Bryan began to say but then grimaced at how hard his cousin grabbed his shoulder near his neck. "Actually, we need to hit the road. Uncle Charles said he would pick us up at the store and take us to lunch."

"I don't think he will mind, Bryan. Miss Anna just made some cookies. How about you each have one?"

Kenneth-George looked to his big brother, but not even his young pleading eyes could persuade him.

"No thank you, ma'am. Daddy would tan my backside red if I gave KG any more sugar. He's losing those teeth faster than he's growing 'em back." James laughed. "Say, Miss Anna, do you need anything else? Anything from the store? I really do like helping out around your place." He looked down as if he were embarrassed. "We can get there and be back in no time before Daddy comes to pick us up."

"That's okay. Just grab your stuff and run along now," she said.

When the three returned from the backyard, they loaded up the bright-red Radio Flyer with all their tools. Kenneth-George sat in the wagon, pretending to steer while his cousin pulled him forward and his brother followed closely behind. When they got to the sidewalk, Anna-Jean waved.

"You boys stay out of trouble."

They all raised their arms and waved back. Just as the children were about to leave, Cecily stopped them when she noticed a small plastic bag that had just fallen to the ground from under the shirt of one of the boys.

"What is that?" Cecily asked angrily.

"Huh?"

"Don't you 'huh' me, Jimmy. I asked, what's that on the ground? By your foot, boy!" Cecily said, growing more furious by the moment.

James just shrugged. "It's nothing, Miss Sissy. We just can't throw this away in the trash. It's dangerous." He picked up the bag and started to push the wagon from the rear, encouraging Bryan to pull faster.

"Nothing, my tail!" Anna-Jean screamed. "The three of you get back up here right now!"

"Huh? What? Sorry, Miss Anna, I can't hear you. Been making too many of those bombs with those chemicals and such!" James said, almost at the end of the street. Bryan pulled on while Kenneth-George giddily bounced at the commotion.

"Jimmy! Jimmy Cain, you get back here!" Anna-Jean yelled while walking to the sidewalk. The boys were almost out of sight, but she kept on. "Jimmy, I swear when I tell your father and get my hands on... ugh!" She exhaled in defeat.

With a determined stride, Anna-Jean walked back toward her home to call Charles Cain. Her grandchildren were staring and so were the other parents who were out, but none of it fazed her. As she stepped onto her porch, Cecily intentionally avoided eye contact.

Anna-Jean faced her before entering and said one word, "Don't!"

Cecily knew how upset she was but couldn't help saying, "Didn't I tell you?"

Chapter One

"IS THERE ANYTHING else I should be made aware of? Have we covered everything?" Charles asked the department heads of his company. "Eugene?"

"N-No, sir, that's all," Eugene answered him timidly.

As he glanced around the conference room, he noticed uncomfortable looks on the faces of his entire assembly. Nothing brought up during the business discussions had troubled Charles, and no one had been put in the undesirable position of having to bear bad news. Most of the men and women who sat at the table had worked for him for many years, so Charles was at a loss as to why they would be reluctant to speak.

"Well then, I suppose it is time to adjourn this meeting," he said. Charles rose, and as he did so, everyone in the room stood twice as fast, rigid. Noticing this, he decided to ask once again, "Is everyone sure that there is nothing else?" Only this time, his voice projected through the entire wing of his home.

"Sir..." The plant manager started, but nothing more came out.

"What? Spit it out, son. I am all ears."

It seemed no one knew how to bring up the cause of all their distress. Charles Howard Cain was aware he had established himself as many things within his community. A philanthropist who donated to many causes, a leader in their local government, an active member of the church, and, perhaps most significant, an employer. The Cain family were some of the first settlers in America, starting in colonial Georgia. After helping to establish the city of Savannah, they remained in the local area as cooks and vendors. They would eventually start a small business that stood to this day, enduring the changing face of the country through its wars and social tides. Calloway, Georgia, was a small town not too far from the major metropolitan area, but there wasn't a person in the city who didn't at least know someone who worked for the Cains.

"Mr. Cain, if I could have a moment?" Eugene asked.

"Fine." He motioned him forward.

The entire room let out a collective sigh as they left the area, one whispering "good luck" before she disappeared.

"Sir, if we could just—"

"Hold on," Charles interrupted as he exited a double glass door that led to his massive garden. He motioned to one of his household staffers who brought over a glass that he then sipped from.

"Sir, it's a little early, don't you think?"

"For water?" Charles asked.

Eugene stammered something out, but it was too early in the morning for Charles to care about apologies only given to protect the offender.

"Never you mind." He drained his drink. "Now tell me, what is the problem?"

"Wait, sir, do you want me to shut up or—"

"Eugene," Charles yelled and dropped the glass, breaking it. He continued walking as custodians descended upon the glass without any instructions.

"It's about your son, sir, about James," Eugene finally spoke.

"When is it not?" Charles sighed. "Is he in trouble again? How much will it set me back this time?" He paused to stroke and smell his gardenias.

"Sir, I don't think you understand me. It has to do with the company. What he's doing or not doing is what I'm trying to say. I've tried to talk to him, but maybe if you did, he would listen."

Charles stopped admiring his flowers and understood why Eugene was so reluctant. There were many things he had to deal with concerning his company, and he would listen to everyone who had a good idea. But no one told him how to raise his children; it wasn't their concern. Whatever issues Eugene had with James had obviously affected his duties, and everything, including the people who worked at the company, was his job. Charles listened as his assistant voiced his concerns. When he was finished, Charles knew he couldn't delay dispensing some tough love.

"AND WHERE ARE you off to?" James asked.

"I really have to get going."

"Do you now?" James slid an arm around his stomach and flipped him on his back. "It's still early. Alls it takes is one phone call, and I can have a car drop you off anywhere you want."

It appeared he was about to answer, but James cut him off by cupping his head and massaging his neck. He kissed him, holding the affection so long that they both gulped down air when they parted.

"Don't go," James said.

James took his hand and kissed each of his fingertips lightly before saying again, "I won't keep you here too much longer, promise."

"But I should get ready..." he choked out.

"Ready?" James asked huskily. Flashing a smile that was more like a grifter's grin, James glanced behind him and then back just as quickly. "Boy, you're as ripe as a peach." James's hand reached behind his body and stroked him. "You sure are. Nice and firm, gives with just enough pressure, what do you think?" He quickened his pace.

"Jimmy..."

Without another word, James leaned in for a kiss. Instead of sitting up again, he pushed with his arms and shot his legs out, instantly repositioning himself between welcoming thighs. With his head so close to the conquest he held in his hand, James let out a warm breath before devouring him. He bucked and writhed uncontrollably as James slid his forearms under his thighs and held him down.

"No, you don't." James stopped and made his way higher on the man's body while tasting every part. "You may be ripe as a peach," he said while reaching down and using his middle finger to collect a small drop and lick it away. "But I swear your nectar is sweeter."

There was nothing more to be said, nothing either of them wanted to say.

"Jimmy..."

James was about to kiss him again but paused at how his name was said. "You sound like my daddy." He laughed.

"Jimmy!" Charles yelled once again.

James was still on top of the other man, but they both looked toward the source of the sound. Charles was framed by the double doors to the room, clutching his ivory cane so tightly it looked as if he would snap it in two. Several staff members came running toward the sounds of the disturbance, and hearing his father in such distress, Kenneth-George, snickering as always, entered the room also. They were frozen in the bed until Bryan finally walked through the door and, without skipping a beat, took out his phone and snapped a picture.

"Bryan!" James yelled.

"Don't even try to put this one on me." Bryan laughed.

"Out! O-U-T! You get out of my home this instance, boy!" Charles strode over, livid. He started to strike them both until they fell out of the bed, barely draped in linen.

"Wait, Daddy, please!" James tried but was knocked on the head with the end of his father's cane.

"I said out!" Charles yelled once again.

With each moment of repeating himself, the volume of his voice increased, and James flinched at how much louder his father had yelled. He could have sworn the windows shook.

"Can I get some help?" James shouted at his cousin and brother as he and his beau circled his massive room, trying to stay out of his father's reach.

Bryan and Kenneth-George looked at each other. With a shrug of his shoulders, Bryan started to move forward, but Kenneth-George placed a hand in front of him.

"Dang, I hoped you'd forgot. Ah okay, a bet's a bet," Bryan grumbled and gave Kenneth-George his money.

Bryan grabbed his uncle's cane while Kenneth-George softly patted his father's shoulder. While they attempted to calm him down, James found a pair of jeans and ushered his liaison toward the door where several attendants were waiting. After much practice, they had it down to a science how to extricate someone from these calamities, so James didn't say much.

"Call me sometime," James said as he left.

"You'll be lucky to hear anything once we are through, boy," Charles said. He pulled away from his other son and nephew and continued, "You have fifteen damn minutes, Jimmy. Put some clothes on your ass!" Charles then left without another word.

"I think you've done it this time, Jimmy." Bryan started to sit down on his bed but, at the last minute, sat on the sofa instead. Kenneth-George rolled over on a wheeled chair and sat backward in it while resting his chin on the top rail.

"I always *do* it," James tried to joke.

"I dunno. Uncle Charles is hot as hell at you right now."

James turned to his little brother who nodded. He couldn't remember the last time Bryan and his brother had agreed on anything, and that's when the worry set in.

"YOU'RE NO HELP." Benjamin scoffed at his phone. He tried zooming in and out as well as different configurations of the positioning and map application he was utilizing, but in such a small city, it was almost pointless.

He had just parked the rented vehicle in the lot of a small diner to orient himself, and after taking in his surroundings, he noticed how completely out of place he truly was. It was quite early in the morning so the many customers that made the commute to the larger city of Savannah were still having breakfast, but it lacked the hustle and bustle he was accustomed to. Deciding that his only options were to go back to the city or try to find where Charles Cain's offices were located, Benjamin headed for the entrance of the diner to obtain information the old-fashioned way.

Once inside, Benjamin did a double-take of his surroundings. The diner was classic in every definition of the word, but he couldn't tell if it was intentional or not. He didn't dwell on it and focused on finding someone to speak with, maybe asking for directions.

"Excuse me? Hello, good morning. Um, is there someone to seat us?" Benjamin asked a gentleman sitting on a bench near the entrance.

The gentleman folded his newspaper and turned to him. He gave Benjamin a once-over before smiling politely and answering. "Don't worry about it, son. She'll be over in no time."

Benjamin was about to ask him to explain when a loud voice eclipsed the din of the other patrons to address him.

"Hold on. Hold on now. Don't go anywhere, honey. I'll be right with you. Andy, hurry up with those eggs. Deacon Fairchild is waiting. Sandy, get over to table three! You know that man loves coffee."

In his entire life, Benjamin had never met a woman like this. He was expecting to encounter a quintessential older Southern woman, but not so soon. Smiling to himself, Benjamin realized that his new assignment in the South might prove to be more challenging than he cared to admit because of the differences in regional cultures, but it was something he wanted to accomplish nonetheless. Before his musings could continue, the woman, finally with a free moment, came to greet him.

"Sorry about that. Come right this way," she ordered yet again. He didn't have time to protest as she gently took his arm and guided him over to the service counter. "There you go. Have a seat. Now, what can I get for you?" Her gaze locked with his, a warm smile on her face as she rested her hands flat on the counter and leaned forward.

"You don't have a paper or pad, though... Cecily is it?" Benjamin asked while pointing at her name tag.

"Ha!" She laughed along with the people flanking Benjamin. "Honey, Miss Sissy remembers everything. Ask anyone."

Benjamin had so many questions, but his train of thought had been broken by Cecily's latest outburst. Everything she said was very loud, almost like it was the only level her voice was set to. Still, she was just being nice, so he figured this too would be a challenge in his assignment.

"I'm not hungry, thank you."

"Oh, coffee? You want something to drink?" she asked, grabbing a pot.

"No. Thank you again, but I don't drink coffee."

"Well, what? Tea? Some water? Oh, I know. It's a bit early, but one of my peach pops will put a spring in your step."

"No. No thank you. I'm fine."

Cecily didn't appear to be upset but simply unsure how else to phrase her question. "Well, if you're not hungry or thirsty, baby, then what in the world are you doing in my diner during breakfast rush, taking up a seat?"

"Good question," Benjamin answered to give himself time to think. One of the skills he had learned as a junior acquisitions officer for his corporation was to carefully ask questions. Depending on whom he was with, the questions could be broad. But if Cecily's ability to ask direct questions applied all the time, then he decided that he would need to tread lightly. "I'm a little lost and need some information."

"Oh well, if you need a map or something, you can ask anyone. Half of the boys in here are truckers anyway," she said.

"I'll be all right in that department... I meant information about Mr. Charles Cain."

Cecily's expression instantly turned suspicious. "Information doesn't come cheap," she said with a small amount of heat while putting her hands on her hips.

Benjamin glanced around for a menu and then up to the one posted on the wall. He didn't want her to be gone long so asked for something simple. "Water?"

"I don't charge for water," she said.

"Orange juice?"

"Orange juice what," Cecily said more than asked, with even more heat in her voice.

"P-Please?" he added. She still didn't move so he asked the question a different way. "May I please have some orange juice, Sissy?"

"Miss Sissy."

He started to speak again, but she just smiled and walked off, grumbling to herself. "Damn kids these days. Not an ounce of home training. I blame all this new-age parenting with 'time outs' and 'stress cards' or whatever they call them..."

When Cecily was out of sight, Benjamin exhaled. It was very difficult to get a read on her, and she didn't seem to have the patience to deal with his feigned naiveté. His first impression was that Cecily was a direct woman, and if experience taught him anything, it's that he would have to respond in kind.

She returned with his beverage, and he spoke before she could get out her comment. "Thank you, Miss Sissy. Can we talk about Mr. Cain now, if that's all right?"

Folding her arms on the table, Cecily said, "That depends."

"Nothing inappropriate, I assure you, ma'am. My name is Benjamin Rei," he said and extended his hand.

"Ray? Oh that's so sweet," Cecily said, clasping her hands in front of her mouth. "You know I have grandbaby named Raymond."

"No, ma'am. Rei, it's Filipino."

"So you're from *Filip*?" she asked.

"Miss Sissy."

"I'm sorry, honey. Go ahead."

Benjamin was about to ask his questions but decided to be cordial. "I'm from Chicago, ma'am. I work for a corporation up there that owns many of the chain restaurants you're familiar with. I'm a junior acquisitions officer, and I go around the country to see firsthand if the products companies make are something that we can purchase. It's not always a purchase, but usually after our deals are made, both parties are more than satisfied."

"Well, that's a fancy title and job, but what do you want to know about Daddy Cain?"

"Things like that, ma'am. I didn't even know that was a name he went by," Benjamin said while making a note on his phone.

"Oh it's nothing formal. Just something the people around here call whoever runs the plant. Aside from that, I'm not sure how I can help you." Cecily sounded confused.

"Do you know anything about his business?"

Cecily once again put one hand on her hip while the other tipped down her glasses to look over them at Benjamin. "Now are you telling me that you came all the way down from Illinois without doing your homework?" she asked suspiciously.

"Not at all, Miss Sissy, but maybe you can help fill in the gaps. In general terms, anyway."

"Well, everyone knows about the Cains in the area. Their family makes the best barbecue sauce, rubs, preserves, seasonings, and such that anyone has ever tasted. They make and bottle it at the plant not too far from here, and everyone buys it. Stores, restaurants, schools, you name it. Folks even buy it on their computers. They've been in business since 1751 and won't be going anywhere anytime soon. The factory even has a small restaurant and cafeteria that people go to on the weekends when it's open. If you're around you should try to make it over there. You haven't lived until you try all of their *Big* sauces."

"*Big* Sauce?" Benjamin asked.

"Their oldest and most popular line of barbecue sauce. Every Daddy Cain over the generations has created their own recipe. Number nine belongs to Charles, and just so happens to be my favorite. But don't you go telling him that," Cecily said and winked.

"That's a proud legacy," Benjamin started. "But I meant can you tell me things about Mr. Cain himself?"

Cecily chuckled. "I can write a book on that man in volumes. He's certainly a character. Always walking around with that cane and old pipe in his hand, dressed in his Sunday best ever'day like he's so important. Which he is, mind you, but for those that are close to him like me, it just seems a bit extravagant. But everyone loves him. All the kids say he reminds them of a big-bellied granddad who curses a little too much."

"And what does he like? How does he treat his employees—"

"No!" Cecily said with an even louder voice than normal, causing many of her customers to stare.

"Miss Sissy, I only wanted—"

"Oh, I know what you wanted, Mr. Rei," she said while crossing her arms. "I thought you were one of those big distributors, but I own a business too, so don't think I don't see what's happening. You want me to tell you all his secrets so you can play him like a piano."

Benjamin tried to come up with a way to reassure her, but now that she knew his true motives, it was pointless. Instead of trying, he picked up on a topic Cecily had mentioned.

"You're wrong, ma'am," Benjamin said.

"Goodbye," a customer sitting next to Benjamin said as he got up to leave. The other doing the same without a word.

There was no going back, so Benjamin pressed on. "I told you what I do because I don't waste time by lying. With or without anyone's help, I am going to meet with Mr. Cain. In the short time that we've been speaking, I've learned much about the people in this area, and I want to make sure I give Mr. Cain the same respect."

Cecily just stood with an impassive face but didn't interrupt.

"Ma'am, I said I was a junior officer. I get my assignments and I work my butt off to complete them. What my bosses do is not my concern. You're a business woman, so I know you understand that. But any information you can give me or answers to questions you are comfortable with would be much appreciated."

Benjamin thought he had miscalculated until Cecily uncrossed her arms.

"Sit down. I'm gonna go get you some breakfast."

"But I'm not hungry."

"Boy, what did I say?" she snapped. "Sit down at the counter and eat your breakfast. Then we can talk. Maybe."

Thankful for this break, Benjamin did as he was told. He figured he would have to go back and forth with Cecily for a few more rounds to see if she was willing to part with anything useful. Although she might not have said anything of worth, he was always of the opinion that it was better to try and fail than not to try at all.

"OW!" JAMES SHOUTED while rubbing the top of his head. "Dang it, Daddy, stop hitting me!"

"I will. Do you think I enjoy this, son? I will stop just as soon as you learn your lesson. To think that a child of mine..." Charles trailed off. "This is not the first time, and every incident is more horrific than the last. Did I not tell you to put on some clothing?"

"I got on pants," James said while rolling his eyes. "What side of the bed did you wake up on this morning?"

After cleaning up, James met his father downstairs in a kitchen that was built exclusively for James. Although James had wanted it for his own use, his cousin and brother were usually there waiting for him to wake up in the mornings. Once his father had gotten wind of this, Charles always sought out James there, and it had become more of an unofficial gathering place. A small spot in their massive home that made them all slightly less separated.

"Sass me again, boy, and I swear I will break this cane off in you sideways," Charles threatened.

"Uncle Charles, all Jimmy was saying is that you're getting mad over nothing."

"Nothing?" Charles asked. "How many has it been this week, Jimmy? I am not aware of how many incidents there have been because I have stopped counting. The Williams's boy, Eddie's nephew, the damn Carver twins!"

"I didn't mess with them at the same time, though." James tried defending himself.

"Is that supposed to make it better?"

"Now if I say yes, I just know you're gonna hit me again." James smiled, but his father's expression remained sour. "You want me to swear off boys till I'm hitched then?"

Kenneth-George was drinking from a carton and snorted hard enough for a drop of juice to fall from his nose. Bryan pulled a rag from his coveralls and wiped his brow while seeming to suppress his laughter.

"Please, son, I would not even wish that upon my worst enemy." Charles scoffed. "With all of your shenanigans, you would put that poor man into an early grave, or drive him to the bottle. Possibly both."

James threw up his hands. "Then what do you want from me?"

"I want you to act like you were raised with some damn common courtesy. Carrying on like that. If I did not know better, I would swear that you are doing your damn best to turn my home into a brothel!"

"If you want me to move out, just say so," James said tiredly. "I'm twenty-five and know how to take care of myself."

James turned from Charles and walked to the stove to prepare something.

"You mean you know how to spend my money is what," Charles said.

James spun around and almost dropped the ingredients he was using. "I've been working for you damn near a year now. I spend what you pay me, and if you want rent, you can take it outta my paycheck. The one you sign since I work for you."

Bryan suddenly stood and motioned to his younger cousin before saying, "Let's take a walk, KG." They left the kitchen to Charles and James.

"Do not try to change the subject. You know that I am speaking the truth. Did you even get that boy's name from this morning?"

Only slightly less upset, James answered, "No. We met right outside of the Army base, and they all look alike."

"It is stitched on his damn chest, for heaven's sake!" his father cried.

"But I didn't want his name. I just wanted to taste his tadpoles."

"Damn it, that is exactly what I am talking about. Using such foul language at the table!"

"Okay, just calm down."

"I will not calm down! And I will not be spoken to in such a manner. Not inside of my own home!"

"Daddy, please." James noticed his father turning red, as he often did when angry, so he brought over a cool towel. At first, his father swatted him away, but James wouldn't be moved. Eventually Charles gave in and let his son dab away the small beads of sweat that had formed on his temples. He cupped his son's hand over his brow while James leaned in to rest his cheek upon his father's crown.

"I didn't mean to get your pressure up," James apologized.

"You never do," Charles said while taking the cloth from his son and placing it behind his neck. While Charles breathed more steadily, James brought over his breakfast and waited quietly as he ate a bit before trying to talk to him again. "I do not want you to move out, son, not unless you want to."

"It's always appreciated, but why do you have it out for me today?"

Finished with his meal, Charles brought up the issue that had soured his morning. "Eugene took me into his confidence this morning. He spoke of your work attendance, or lack thereof, son."

"I'm there when I need to be. Shoot, I'm heading over there this morning right after I stop by the bank."

Charles laughed a little and took his son's face into his hand. "You need to be there all the time. What the hell am I paying your annual salary for if you are not?"

"What about plant operations? Safety? All that's up, including sales since I've been in charge, and we haven't had one safety violation or accident since you put me in the big chair. Not a one," James said smugly. "Those aren't exactly small potatoes."

"Yet, your department managers need to speak with you at your earliest convenience, which is now in case you were wondering."

"For crying out loud, we're damn near a score into the new millennium," he said, taken aback. "Daddy, I got phones to answer my phones, and I don't even know how many mailboxes, electronic and metal. If they have something to say, I'll listen, but you pay them to oversee their sections. What the heck do I need to do besides say yes or no when they ask?"

James turned from him to call a member of the house staff. He had learned much by following in his father's footsteps, but despite his accomplishments, it never seemed to be good enough. Even with six years of formal business school, his father just didn't seem comfortable entrusting him with the family business.

The staff member arrived with the materials James had requested, and he carried the small jar of pomade and mirror with him as he returned. James saw his father light up when he pulled his comb from his back pocket, knowing how much he enjoyed this time together when they could have it.

"Just do me a favor and talk to them this morning. Have a meeting."

"I will," James said while combing his father's hair back and styling it just the way he liked. "I told you, I'm on my way there this morning after the bank."

"Is everything all right?" Charles asked, lifting his head, which was immediately returned to the position James needed it to be to finish his father's grooming.

"Yeah, don't worry. I just need to go over some reports that don't look right. It's funny 'cause I done told them how I want 'em, and for a few weeks, they're fine, but then I get stuff like this so I gotta head down there."

"I shall avail myself should you need help, son. I realize that I am getting up in years and have been busy these past weeks with Mayor Ferguson, but I can make the time and there is not one part of our company that I do not know."

"Except how much money you make," James said while holding up the mirror.

"Now see, if you are cooking my books, you are not supposed to tell me," he said.

"Not cooking, I got those sales down in Pensacola—Navy, he was in the Navy!"

"Jimmy..." his father said deliberately.

"Yep, money makes that blood cool down." James smiled. "That's why I was down there. I wasn't showing my tail or anything, for the most part. I locked on being a vendor to those grocery stores I mentioned a few weeks back."

"That is an impressive accomplishment son, which stores?"

"The only one that matters, but seventeen in the chain. They're going through at least five pallets a week. Hold on, lemme bring up the bill," James said while he searched his phone.

"That's okay, son, just bottom line it. How much?"

"Offhand? I figure about two hundred to two hundred thirty thousand dollars a month. They're stocking wholesale and don't wanna wait for the winter months when our prices go up. I'm actually still working on the main base, though." James was about to continue when his phone rang. He spoke for a few seconds and, when he hung up, started to run around the kitchen. "Sorry, Daddy. I gotta go. KG is getting restless. Love you."

After kissing his father's forehead, James headed for the elevator. He thought he was finally free to go about his day but received one last chide.

"Jimmy, put some clothes on."

WITH THE EARLY morning breakfast rush over, Cecily took the time to help clear and clean some of the tables as Benjamin followed closely behind her. She had answered his questions, which he restricted to mostly the history of the business itself, and he was glad that she was at least talking to him. Benjamin wouldn't leave however, and even after she made him do small tasks such as carrying plates back to the scullery or restocking condiments, he remained.

"Don't you have to get on to work soon, Benji?" Cecily asked.

"Not today, ma'am, no," he answered promptly. "I got here early so that tomorrow, when I go in, I'll have an idea of who I'll be working with."

"That's smart, honey. I wish you could work for me."

"And I wish you could tell me more about the Cains."

"If you mean Jimmy, don't waste your time. He's spoiled through and through," a handsome man said as he entered the diner.

"Ellsworth Thomas Ferguson," Cecily yelled. "Don't you come into my diner and talk bad about my godson like that."

"Apologies, Miss Sissy," he said while walking over to kiss her cheeks. "You raised me better than that." After he finished his greeting, Ellsworth turned toward Benjamin. "What do you care about Jimmy?"

"Hello, I'm Benjamin Rei." He extended his hand, and it was taken cautiously. "Excuse my confusion, but you don't seem to care much for Mr. Cain. I thought everyone in town liked him."

"I'm not talking about Daddy Cain, I meant his sorry—" Ellsworth held his tongue when he noticed Cecily listening in. "I'm talking about his boy. He's—"

"Better than butter melting on top of Miss Sissy's pancakes." James spoke over Ellsworth as he and his family walked over to the table she had just set up. Kenneth-George and Bryan sat while James went to the kitchen and brought out a tray with all the foods they had called ahead for. With his brother buried in a bowl of oats and Bryan working on his eggs, James tried to eat, but his plate was snatched from in front of him. "Miss Sissy?"

"Don't you *Miss Sissy* me. Jimmy, you don't rise before noon, so if you're up, your daddy's pissed. Which boy did he run off this time?"

"Tell me something. How come I had to be with some boy last night?" When every customer in the diner stopped eating and looked at James, he rescinded his question. "Never mind! Now c'mon, I'm hungry."

"You didn't get your fill of meat this morning, Jimmy?" Ellsworth asked, walking up to him.

James set down his fork and flashed a smile at Ellsworth before saying, "You cannot keep my name out of your mouth, can you, Ellie?"

Ellsworth slammed his hands down on the table in front of James. "You wanna say that one more time?"

James just turned his palms upward and replied, "Tell you what, let's cut a deal. Just lemme finish my breakfast, and if you ask real nice like, we can head over to my office and I'll let you watch me and—dang, I lost track of who the last one was."

Before James could insult him again, Ellsworth hoisted him out of the seat by his shirt. The other Cains stood, but James gestured them to remain calm.

"I'm gonna make you hurt, boy!" Ellsworth whispered.

"Sure you will," James egged him on. "Excuse us, everybody."

James removed Ellsworth's hands and walked through the kitchen to the back exit. Ellsworth followed as Bryan and Kenneth-George exited to the front. Benjamin had seen the entire altercation and wasn't sure what to do.

His inaction was getting the better of him until Cecily touched his shoulder. "Here's your chance to learn about the Cains, Benji."

"C'MON! C'MON, JIMMY, let's go!" Ellsworth hollered.

James circled Ellsworth until his back was toward the building. There wasn't much out there save for a few crates on the loading dock, along with some stacked-up pallets and a few large dumpsters. James seemed unaware that he was being watched by Benjamin.

"I'm right here. Come get a taste of the Sauce Boss." James motioned him forward with his hand.

Benjamin was entranced by both men. This childish rivalry was the stuff of movies, and he couldn't believe people really did such things. Ellsworth was just as lean and defined as James, only he was slightly taller, matching Benjamin's frame more closely. Ellsworth's crystal-blue eyes shone with fury as his opponent continued his taunts. Ellsworth dashed at James only for James to step to the side.

"Someone's a slowpoke." James laughed at him.

"Get over here! Or are you turning yellow?" Ellsworth said as he continued his assault, each blow missing its mark.

James danced around behind the building until finally ending up near the dumpsters. One particularly large and cylindrical white one caught his attention so James ran to it. "Try to reach me."

"Dang it!" Ellsworth screamed and grabbed the lid of the container. He and James circled it several times until James's back was pinned against a wall. "Quit running and fight like a man! I don't have time for this!"

"Me neither," James agreed.

He pressed his back against the building and brought his legs up. With all his strength, and before Ellsworth realized what was happening, James pushed the container with his legs until it toppled. Ellsworth tried to move out of the way, but once it hit the ground, the reservoir storing all of the used deep-fat frying oil exploded. Enveloped by the many gallons of the viscous liquid, Ellsworth lost his footing and flailed about in a mixture of grease and sand.

"Wow, Ellie, you sure look good with some color on your skin." James slapped his knee and doubled forward, laughing. "Good luck with that smell, though."

"J-Jim... Jimmy!" Ellsworth snarled while trying to stand. He continued slipping and finally gave up, taking a sitting position.

At the same time, a loud diesel pickup truck came skidding around the building. Kenneth-George was driving with Bryan standing up with his head out of the sunroof as his cousin spun the vehicle around James several times until perfectly positioning the passenger-side door in front of him.

"Gotta go. You get yourself cleaned up."

"I swear, I'm gonna make you pay for this!" Ellsworth said, once again falling after trying to stand.

"What in the hell?" Cecily yelled at the two men.

"Don't worry, Miss Sissy. I'll have that fixed up for you in no time." James said as he straddled the open window of the truck. "Get some haul ass, KG!"

With an unnecessary amount of dirt being kicked up from the rear tires, the three men took off.

Benjamin was so stunned he couldn't move. Several people went to help Ellsworth up, but Benjamin returned to his car. He drove for a bit, then pulled over onto a wide dirt shoulder that was the beginning of a frontage road. Benjamin hadn't noticed, but his hands were shaking. He felt his heart racing within him and, when he noticed himself in the mirror, could see small trails of perspiration.

"What just happened?" Benjamin asked himself but knew the answer. He had just witnessed one of the most exciting things in real life that he could remember. He wanted to exhale but was still exhilarated. Instead of dwelling, he started to pull out but was cut off by a loud blur that sprayed dirt on his windshield. "What the—"

He stepped out of his car to see the Cain boys in the truck from earlier. They had driven off the road and were making stage-coach rotations around Benjamin, bringing the circle in tighter with each revolution. Benjamin instinctively backed up as the exhaust from the large truck choked him. He bumped into his car and then opened the door only to have Kenneth-George bring the passenger side up next to him.

Still hanging out of the window, James just smiled and asked, "Wanna tag along?"

Chapter Two

"OH CRAP!" BENJAMIN said while trying to swerve around another large piece of debris the Cain truck had kicked up and sent straight for his window.

"Ben, what is it? What's wrong?"

"Nothing, Clint, it's just... Crap," he yelled once again.

The Cains were ahead of Benjamin by at least three car lengths, and his modern compact sedan struggled to keep up. He snorted to himself, not able to comprehend why someone would ever own a vehicle like the Cains' truck, let alone invest in making it even more dangerous. Makeshift steel handles were welded to its side so that anyone could grab on; the tires were of a radius usually reserved for large forklifts, and of course, it was lifted higher from the ground with dual smokestack exhausts spewing black clouds as the driver accelerated even faster.

"Are you okay?" Clint asked once again, his voice carrying through the speakers of Benjamin's car.

"I'm working right now. Can I give you a call back?"

"I just wanted to make sure you got here, but take care of your business," Clinton said, giving him the focus he needed. *"And don't talk on the phone and drive. It's dangerous."*

With the call ended, Benjamin turned his attention back to the truck in front of him.

"WELL, WOULD YOU look at that," James said. "He's actually keeping up." He leaned his head out the passenger window and waved to the car behind them.

"Why'd you want 'im along anyway?" Bryan asked.

James ducked back into the truck. "Just trying to figure out why he was staring at Ellie and me playing around back there."

"All you had to say was that you wanna get into his pants, cousin."

James wore a guilty grin on his face. He didn't argue but instead said, "Let 'im catch up."

Kenneth-George slowed the truck and moved into the left lane, allowing the other car to pull alongside it. When the driver rolled down his window, James once again leaned out of the truck.

"So, you decided to take me up on my offer?"

"What...what offer?" he said.

"The one I'm about to pitch. Don't worry none, I—" James cut himself off and started to cough and curse loudly as Bryan pulled him back in. While trying to catch his breath, the other car swerved, but the driver righted himself quickly.

"Smooth one, lover boy," Bryan said.

"You choke down a handful of gnats and see how you feel!"

"Look, we got work to do so enough with the romancing for now."

The truck pulled forward again. After a few miles, Kenneth-George took one of the numerous backroads that ran through Calloway. It led to the main path to their family's factory entrance where he parked and they all exited, then waited on the other car to catch up.

BENJAMIN REACHED THE three men quickly. After parking next to their truck, he approached them at the entrance gate, upset at how reckless their driving had been earlier.

"You want to explain what that was back there?" Benjamin asked.

"Who in the hell do you think you're talking to?" Bryan asked. Kenneth-George placed a hand on Bryan's shoulder and held him back.

"Don't mind Bryan. He's quick blow his top," James said.

"You almost made me run off the road."

"Did I scare ya?"

"No," Benjamin said sternly.

"You sure? You're looking a shade or two paler than chalk."

They all began laughing at him, and Benjamin's patience wore out. Interesting as this morning had been, he didn't have time for games.

"I think I've made mistake," he said and turned to leave.

"Whoa, hey, slow down there." James followed. "We didn't mean any offense there, Mister..."

"Benjamin. If you could remind your father about our meeting, it would be helpful." He reached his car and opened the door, but James held it firmly.

"I don't know anything about a meeting," James said. "But you can tell him yourself. I'll take you over right after I finish my rounds."

"I don't have time to do...this," Benjamin said while waving his hand.

"You don't have time to take a walk with the man in charge of this here factory?" James asked him.

"I'm listening."

"Well, first off, smile," James said with a grin.

"That's it? That's your way of convincing me to join you?" Benjamin opened the door to his car.

"No, but a boy as pretty as you? It doesn't look right unless you smile."

Benjamin closed the door of his vehicle but didn't say anything. James waited while scratching his head and chewing his bottom lip a bit. There was nothing impressive about James's manner of dress. Worn boots that had seen better days, jeans that were so broken-in he probably refused to wash them unless required, and a tight-fitting white shirt with a wider collar. He also noticed the button-up shirt tied about James's waist at the sleeves he hadn't seen earlier at Cecily's diner. And yet despite how underwhelming the attire he wore, James was very handsome. His deep green eyes were brought out by his strong jaw and the soft cleft in his chin. James's hair was cut short but just long enough to curl in places. The healthy glow on his skin was most likely from working outside.

"I have other things on my schedule so I can't follow you around all day long."

"We'll be in and out," James said, stepping into Benjamin's personal space. "Cross my heart. Time to make it up to you for almost making you run into a ditch."

Benjamin didn't move even as James inched closer. He was about to stop him when he felt James's breath on his face, but he didn't have to when they were interrupted.

"What's the hold up?" Bryan shouted at them.

"Can we please get to it?" Benjamin asked, a complete professional. He walked around James yet again and made his own way to the entrance.

"WHAT THE HECK is his problem?" James asked no one. Benjamin was still ahead of them as they headed to the plant.

"That is what we call striking out." Bryan laughed. "Guess those charms don't work on city boys, huh?"

"You know dang well I can sell a blind man glasses for his dog." James accepted the challenge. "What do you say, KG? Wanna take some of this action?"

Instead of answering, Kenneth-George just snickered and took his brother's hand.

"When they all reached the door, James opened it for Benjamin. "After you."

"I have no idea where I'm going."

"Good point." James led the way until they reached the hallway that led to the main bottling area of the plant.

"Don't worry, this here's the part where I like to show off, so stay with me now," James said to Benjamin as he passed hairnets to the three men. He was speaking louder to be heard over all the equipment.

James was eager to share the many aspects of modernization he had made to his family's company. While the large brick building barely looked like it made the turn with the century, inside steel and conveyor belts dominated. The bottling facility was state of the art with computer-monitored gauges, and everyone appeared to do their reports on electronic tablets. James even showed Benjamin the highlights he was proud of, including an antiquated kettle he kept for his personal use, and allowed him to taste various sauces.

"And here we are. I saved the best for last," James said as they entered his personal office.

"There's something even better?" Benjamin asked.

"Don't sound so surprised."

"Actually, I am Mr. Cain."

"Please, call me Jimmy," he said warmly.

"Only if you call Ben."

"Nah, I like Benji better."

"You're not the only one. Honestly the tour has been incredibly impressive, but it's still a distant second to the products you make. This was my first time sampling them, and I can't imagine what could top what I've already had."

James walked over to a kitchenette in the corner where a small pressure cooker sat on a burner. He broke the seal on the lid and spooned some of the contents into a small cup before returning to Benjamin.

"Get a taste of this." James held the spoon close to Benjamin's mouth.

"Thank you." Benjamin took the spoon from James.

"I'm still working on—"

"What is this?" Benjamin asked, clearly surprised. "I've never tasted anything like this." He took the cup from James.

"It's always worth it for that reaction. *You're gonna want some meat for this sauce.* What do you think of that slogan?"

"Catchy."

"I'd like to think so."

James took a moment to appreciate Benjamin, who had to be around his age. But that was where the similarities ended. His Pacific Islander features were unique in Calloway, strong and symmetrical. Benjamin was a few inches taller than James, and his build was slightly stockier, which James hadn't noticed until just now.

He was about to introduce Benjamin to something else he was proud of, but a knock on his door stopped him.

"Yes."

Eugene entered with Bryan. "Sorry to disturb you, Mr. Cain, but we could use your help in going over these reports. We're both finding too many inconsistencies, and another pair of eyes would help before we go to the section heads."

"That's all fine and well, Eugene, but get started on it without me. I'm talking money right now."

"But sir."

"Make sure I'm not disturbed now," James said, ending the conversation.

When the two left, James gestured for Benjamin to take a seat at a small coffee table while James sat adjacent to him.

"So? How am I doing so far?" James asked.

"Despite how the morning started, very well."

"And I'd like to do even better. There's a lot more I can show you when I'm off of work. Calloway and the best parts of Savannah."

"Unfortunately, I may not have the time. But I wanted to talk about your father—about his company particularly and an opportunity I'm sure will make many people very happy. If you could facilitate that meeting earlier than scheduled, I'd be in your debt."

James perked up at the suggestion. "What do you have to talk about? I told you I didn't know anything about it."

"I remember," Benjamin said, considering. "James, if he hasn't told you, then maybe it's best I don't discuss the details. This is a family-owned company, but I don't want to presume anything. Your father may well have kept information about the meeting from you intentionally."

"Suppose you're right." James clapped his hands together. "So lemme ask you, who do you think all of this goes to when my daddy leaves this earth? My sisters have their own families and other plans. KG? He just ain't the type, and Bryan works for me."

"That may be true," Benjamin said, trying to change topics. "But as of right now, your father is in charge."

James stood in front of Benjamin and just smiled. He placed both of his hands on the armrests of the chair in which Benjamin sat and leaned in as if he was about to kiss him.

At the last moment, he went to Benjamin's ear and said just confidently, "I'm the one in charge of this here plant. My daddy owns everything you see in here, but there isn't a purchase or sale without my say so." He stood back up and looked down at Benjamin. "You're not too good at distribution, are you?"

"No," Benjamin said, standing up. "I'm not good at it because I'm an acquisitions officer."

"Ac... You're a...a what?" James asked as he backed away, looking angry.

"It means that I—"

"I know exactly what the hell it means! Acquisitions, procurement. Down here, though, we keep it simple, purchasing."

"That's correct. James, you seem upset?"

"You think?" James turned on him, growing red with anger. "You don't wanna make a deal or anything. You wanna try to make my daddy sell his company!"

"I'm going to do a lot more than try. Your father is a business man, and once he sees all the benefits my corporation can offer, I will succeed."

"Well, kiss my ass." James threw up his hands. "And you figured the best way to get your hands on *Daddy Cain's* was to go through his baby boy?"

"'Wanna tag along?'" Benjamin reminded James. "Sound familiar? It should because it wasn't even an hour ago. I told you I wanted to speak with your father, and I meant it. You were the one who asked me here."

James turned from him and activated the intercom on his desk. A second later, Bryan and Kenneth-George were back with security as well. "And now I'm asking you to leave." He turned to his security. "Please make sure Mr. Rei gets back to his vehicle in one piece." He turned to Benjamin. "Any damage I've done will be taken care of. Just let KG know. I'll get it fixed for you."

Benjamin was about to speak again when Bryan and the two other guards grabbed him to show him the door.

"HE'S COMING DOWN right now, Mr. Rei."

"Thank you." Benjamin sighed after waiting what seemed like hours.

After his rude removal from the Cain plant, he decided to check in with his offices in the neighboring city of Savannah. Although he was still upset by James's grossly inappropriate and aggressive flirtations, what was most off-putting was James's presumptiveness. The idea that he would instantly fall in lust with him. In his business dealings, Benjamin had met many people like James. It didn't matter which region they were from or even what continent, they were all spoiled. And if the young Mr. Cain had proven anything, it was that he was a man who was used to getting what he wanted.

"Benjamin?" a stout man asked as he walked up to shake hands. "Clinton Jackson. Nice to finally meet you."

"You as well, Clint," he responded, sounding noticeably lighter. "It's nice to finally be back to some semblance of civilization."

"I gather you're not too fond of the South?" Clinton asked as they stepped into the elevator.

It was true that Benjamin did prefer the metal jungle that was the city of Chicago, but even he found the historic city of Savannah breathtaking. The historic district was vast—its elegant ironwork and revered taverns a beautiful and yet sobering reminder of the nation's darker antebellum period. Cultures and ideas fused on the riverfront where visitors were able to take in everything from street trolley rides to museum tours. He had also made a mental note to visit one of the oldest Baptist congregations for the descendants of slaves, not for any spiritual purposes, but to simply stand in awe of history.

"Let's just say that it's not on my list of places I want to retire," Benjamin said, letting out another long sigh. "I know it's not like this everywhere, but with the type of morning I've had, the memories will be more than enough."

Clinton didn't say anything more and waited until they reached the floor that their corporate office was leasing for their southeast division. After exiting and navigating the maze of cubicles to his office, Clinton offered Benjamin a seat and closed his door.

"It's a good thing you don't work today, you look like you've just gone ten rounds."

"Feels more like one hundred. I took your advice about researching Mr. Cain by trying to meet with him early, but that didn't exactly work out."

"You did what?" Clinton asked, surprised. "One on one?"

"No, not him," Benjamin corrected. "Jimmy, his son."

"Oh..." Clinton smirked. "I met him not too long ago when we first started after *Daddy Cain's*. So did he turn on the charm?"

"Aggressively so. He used food. That's cheating." Benjamin shook his head.

"Not your type then?"

"What? No, that's not it. He might have had a shot if it was under different circumstances. Namely, him not being him." Benjamin finally smiled.

"Don't give him a second thought. From what I hear, the kid is harmless." Clinton looked away at nothing before adding, "But word is that they redefined some stalking laws and invented a stronger mace because of him."

"You're exaggerating," Benjamin accused.

"Sure I am, but not by that much." Clinton stood to exit his office and walked them over a few steps to his subordinate's cubicle before speaking again. "I'm not trying to scare you, but Jimmy has always played the perfect season if you catch my meaning. We sent a few interns over there to get the lay of the place and they all came back telling the same story."

Benjamin finally laughed at the idea of literally beating James off him with a stick. He was thankful that Clinton had been assigned as his point of contact for getting adjusted to his new work environment. This was the first time the two had met in person, but after the many video conferences and multiple collaborations on accounts, the two felt like old colleagues.

Clinton was originally from this area in Georgia and slightly older than Benjamin but, after completing his studies, had moved north to work in the faster-paced world of New England. After gaining the experience and position he wanted, Clinton had returned home to Savannah.

Benjamin made a tight fist and flexed the muscles in his forearm. "Thanks for the advice, but I think I can handle myself. I'm just glad that I won't have to deal with any more Cains after tomorrow."

"And how many have you dealt with today?" the stern voice of a woman asked from across the room.

Clinton and Benjamin looked toward the sound in unison to see a striking middle-aged woman approaching them. Her pace was that of a seasoned professional who took the adage of time and money to heart. But each step she took was so poised, so powerful that her presence was nearly palpable. As she came closer, Benjamin took note of her classic curls pulled up into a trendy design along with the skirt and smoky stockings, which completed her ultra-modern power suit. The woman stopped just short of them and seemed to pose; the gold trim of her clothing in addition to the expensive jewelry about her almond skin gave her a commanding and borderline-intimidating aura that was pulled off exceptionally.

"Ms. Harvington?" Benjamin asked nervously.

"I am aware of my name, Mr. Benjamin. And I am most certainly aware of who you are, but that was not an answer to my question," she said impatiently. "Now for your sake, I suggest that you do not make Ms. Laura repeat herself."

From the way she spoke, Benjamin could tell that Laura was definitely from this region, however her accent was much more refined. Not at all surprised that the chief procurement officer for their company's Mergers & Acquisitions Department would have an extensive educational background, he once again retold the events of the morning to her. It had been his intention to recite the entirety of the events, but once he got to the part about bringing up the meeting to James, his boss took on a different persona.

"You did what?" Laura shouted.

"Ma'am, I saw an opportunity…" Benjamin never finished as she walked past him and, after a few steps, snapped her fingers for him to follow into her office.

With the door shut, Benjamin said, "Ms. Harvington, I understand that—"

"Let me make one thing perfectly clear, Mr. Benjamin," she started while offering him a seat. Laura remained standing if only to assert her dominance over him. "If—and rest assured that it is, in fact, a very big 'if'—I want your excuses or explanations, I will ask for them. Do you understand?"

"Yes, ma'am." He gulped. As he sat, Laura circled him several times with her arms crossed before speaking again.

"Tell me something. Why were you sent down here?"

"T-To help with the acquisition of Mr. Cain's company, ma'am." He looked at her reluctantly.

"Avert your eyes!" she said, causing Benjamin to whip his head forward. She walked over to a personal library filled with many law books, running a finger along the spines of noteworthy volumes before continuing. "Your sole reason for being down here is because I requested it. Do you know what that means?"

"I don't, ma'am."

"It means," she said, articulating each syllable precisely, "that your purpose is to fulfill the obligations and tasks that I assign to you. If I am thirsty, then you are to bring me water. If I am cold, then the shirt off your back is mine to have. And if I say jump?"

"Then I say how high," he said, controlling the unpleasant emotions he felt at this moment.

Laura surprised Benjamin when she chuckled. She walked over and, leaning forward, patted his face a few times before saying, "I thought you were supposed to be smart. That is why I requested you." She stood up straight and turned her nose down at him, a sneer snaking across her face. Anger changed her deep eyes into horizontal slits. "If I say jump, you do not say a damn thing, you just start jumping." She seethed.

"Ms. Harvington, I was just—"

"Not paying attention to a thing I just said. I need you to convince one Mr. Charles Howard Cain to sell his business to us. I have approached him from every angle, and I assumed that some new blood may just be able to appeal to him. I did not tell you to play with his family or meet the neighbors. Now if this is something that you do not think you are up to—following simple instructions that is—then that is a short conversation we can have right here and now." Benjamin remained quiet. The silence was stretched out for almost a minute before Laura sat and said, "We are finished here."

BENJAMIN LEFT, SHOVING open her door, and Laura didn't give a second thought to his reaction. She opened the scheduler on her planner to adjust certain meetings and was satisfied that her plans were still on track. Even if they had been slightly altered by Benjamin's eagerness. There were other matters that required her attention, but before leaving, she took out another phone from her desk to place a call. A phone that was simple, cheap, and most importantly disposable.

"Where are we at?" she asked immediately once connected.

"Same place we were yesterday, Governess."

"We are not in the same place, or have you not realized that James knows of our meeting tomorrow?"

"So what? It's not like he can stop it."

Laura pulled the phone from her ear to stare at it. Her scowl deepened as she took long breaths to compose her response. The device shook violently in her hand as her grip constricted the plastic so tightly the unlit indicators on the screen started to bleed over. Satisfied that her screams wouldn't be heard throughout the office, she addressed the person on the other end of the line.

"Listen to me, child, do not just wait for me to stop speaking and then agree. Everything must go exactly as I have planned. This is no mere backwoods feud, the likes of which you people are so accustomed to. This is the real world. And in the real world, people go to prison. Are you able to understand me?"

"Yes, ma'am." The person on the other end swallowed.

"I do not believe you."

"Governess?"

"I said that I do not believe you. I do not believe that you do understand, but I suppose that cannot be held against you necessarily, all things considered. But know this. I have come too far and have worked tirelessly to ensure this goes off swimmingly. And I shall not have my plans uprooted or altered simply because you all are not capable of following instructions." Her voice changed from superior to threatening. "If the authorities come and ask questions, I guarantee that I will serve you up to them on a platter."

She didn't wait for a response. Ending the conversation, Laura dropped the phone on the floor and crushed it beneath her designer heels before leaving her office. She made sure to leave a note with her personal secretary to have her office cleaned while she was out and all of the trash taken to their industrial incinerator.

"BUY YOU A drink, stranger?" Clinton asked as he sat down on a stool next to Benjamin.

"Lucky number two, it is," he said, sulking into the empty glass.

After leaving Laura's office, Clinton had sent Benjamin home for the remainder of the day to get settled into his new loft. It was located only a few blocks from the office in which he worked and on the riverfront as well. The building was very new, and while the lower floors were being utilized by multiple shops, restaurants, and the very bar that the two were in, the upper floors were leased to young professionals who worked in the business district. Their corporation was paying the rent and utilities for Benjamin, so he was thankful that he only had to purchase personal incidentals. Spirits being his choice at the moment.

"I just wanna say sorry about earlier. Ms. Harvington can be a real pain in the you-know-what sometimes."

Benjamin could tell she was a tough boss, but he still couldn't understand why she was so upset. "Do you think I messed up?" he asked Clinton.

"C'mon, Ben, I know I'm technically your boss, but do we have to do evaluations right now?"

"I just want to know," Benjamin said, even more resolved.

Clinton sighed. "Look, I understand why you wanted to get a jump on things. Although when I said research, I meant to study his past business practices. Trying to meet with him early was pretty darn aggressive. That's a trait that gets you noticed in this industry."

"But..."

"But the fact of the matter is that you did tip your hat—our hat." Clinton set his drink down and looked at him. "James didn't know about the meeting, and now that he does, he'll probably bring it up to his dad. When that happens, well, everything can go to hell in a handbasket."

"You guys and your metaphors." Benjamin laughed.

"They work," Clinton shot back.

"Okay, I get it. Jimmy talks to his father about the meeting, but so what? He gets brought along? Whines about how he wanted the company? We're about to buy them out, and once they see the zeroes, I'm sure he'll stop complaining."

Clinton just smiled into his drink as he said, "Not everyone cares about money, Ben."

The two continued to drink in silence for a few minutes until a pretty young waitress came back to their table. "Can I get you guys anything else?" she asked pleasantly.

"You can make your way over here and give Big Daddy Cain a hug," an older gentleman, who must have been Charles Cain, said, walking into the bar with his entourage. The waitress gestured that she would be right back and went to greet them.

"I believe that you quite enjoy calling yourself that." Mayor Ferguson chuckled. "No one could tell me that you weren't planning to have your name put on this building after you closed the deal."

Charles ignored his oldest friend and continued speaking to the young waitress. "My goodness gracious, look at you, sweetheart. Just as pretty as you can be. The Lord is being gracious to my eyes, yes indeed!"

"Oh, Daddy Cain." She laughed and brought them to a private booth.

Benjamin was starting to realize how eccentric Mr. Cain was. He was sure that Charles was only a harmless flirt, but that didn't stop him from coming off as a dirty old man. As he sweet-talked with even more women, some of whom were at least four decades younger, Benjamin's face broke into a light smile when it occurred to him that perhaps James was exactly like his father, or at the very least, he knew where his mannerisms came from. Feeling confident in his knowledge that perhaps Mr. Cain and his son shared similar personalities, he prepared to stand.

"Don't," Clinton protested.

"I just want to bring up the meeting. Don't worry about it. I'm not going to bring up serious talks." He left before the other man could stop him.

Benjamin wasn't even within ten feet of Mr. Cain before his bodyguards were blocking his path. While being escorted away, Benjamin kept shouting Charles's name until he finally looked up from cupping the face of a random young lady to answer.

"Who is that? Does he work for me? If so let him pass. Never let it be said that Daddy Cain does not listen to his workers."

Now free from the guards, Benjamin said, "Mr. Cain, thank you for your time. I work for Ms. Harvington, and I just wanted to remind you of our meeting tomorrow, and to thank you on behalf of our company for allowing us to work for you. I'm sure that—"

"Careful there, son, I think I see something of mine on your nose." Charles laughed while lighting up his pipe. "So how's about you go get yourself washed up, and I shall see you all tomorrow."

"Sir, I was just..." Benjamin started but didn't know how to recover.

"You just what, son?" Charles asked while spreading his arms out wide. "You just thought that you would come over and talk business, while I am enjoying myself and entertaining my company?" He pinched the thigh of a girl next to him.

"I just wanted to thank you."

"Of course you did." Charles laughed. "You just keep right on digging that hole." With a lift of his cane, the guards moved Benjamin back.

Clinton came to take Benjamin away, and instead of returning to their table, he led them both outside. Benjamin started to pace up and down the street, running his hands through his dark hair and trying to figure out his next move.

"I told you not to do that," Clinton chided.

"I-I'm sorry," Benjamin said nervously.

"No, I am, I should have stopped you, but I didn't. And now you might have just singlehandedly cost us this account." He slowed Benjamin down and faced him. "Ben, if this goes south, I'm going to have to put it in my report."

Panic filled Benjamin. He had never wanted to bungle an account, and this would not be his first. There was no way he would get to Mr. Cain again, so he decided to go for a different one.

"Do you know where Jimmy lives?"

"With his father," Clinton said. "Everyone...no! You've already messed up twice, and I'm not taking you over there."

"If you don't, then this deal is through. The only thing Mr. Cain will remember in the meeting tomorrow is me tonight and how much I pissed him off. If he talks to his son about it and our meeting at the plant is brought up, then we can kiss it all good-bye."

"What makes you even think he's home?" Clinton asked. "He's probably off doing something or someone."

"I'll tell you on the way there." He tossed his keys over.

The drive to the Cain residence wasn't very long, but during the short trip, Benjamin reiterated how James knew nothing of the meeting. He reasoned that James would be at home waiting for his father and that he would put off personal plans. Clinton, on the other hand, took the time to explain to Benjamin everything he had done wrong in his approach with Mr. Cain. He was about to go over more etiquette when Benjamin turned from him suddenly.

"That's his home?" He gasped.

"You thought that was just a picture on their bottle labels?" Clinton asked, surprised.

In the late evening sun, Benjamin held his breath as they drove down the long cobblestone road that was the entrance to the Cain Plantation. Massive oak trees mirrored one another like standing sentries as the Spanish moss infecting each one almost touched their trunks. The gray-and-white home had been restored beautifully, with its splendor on display for tourists to see in passing. The lamps were classical, and the stanchions supporting the roof towered over the groundskeepers while they attended their duties. As they neared the mansion, Clinton took a frontage road slightly off that of the main toward a small building where visitors checked in.

"I'm sorry, but Mr. Cain isn't here, and no one has informed us that he is expecting guests," the muscle-bound guard said without looking up at them.

"If you let James know that I'm here, I'm sure he'll want to see me," Benjamin said.

"If he wanted to see you, then he would have given you a way to call him directly."

Clinton moved to leave with Benjamin, who appeared dejected until he heard the voice of the person he wanted to see.

"Mr. Eddie," James said, walking from the back office door. "I just wanna apologize to you again about last week. I didn't mean for you to catch us like that." He extended a hand. The two shook, but not before James did a double-take at Benjamin. "You!"

"James...Jimmy," Benjamin said. "Can we...that is, I would like to—"

"Eddie," James said dryly and walked past them all to the exit.

The guard stood, but Clinton and Benjamin put up their hands and left without any need of force. As they headed back to their car, the door to the guardhouse creaked open, and James exited. He headed toward one of the security gold carts and sat down, seemingly doing nothing in particular.

Benjamin was just about in his vehicle when he asked Clinton, "You said it's all about respect, right?"

"Huh?" Clinton asked, not following.

"Southern mentality—it's all about respect? Doing right by people or whatever?"

"I know what you're going to do, Benjamin. You're persistent, I'll give you that." Clinton sighed again. "Yes, that's a part of it. But be humble. And apologize."

"For what?" Benjamin asked angrily.

"Do you want to get within five steps of him without having security swarm you or not?"

Benjamin took a deep breath and jogged toward James.

JAMES WAS LYING across the driver and passenger seats of the cart when he saw Benjamin jogging toward him. Not caring for arguing anymore, he rolled his head to the side and reached to pick up the radio when Benjamin shouted.

"I'm sorry."

James sat up and furrowed his brow. "I told you good-bye, Benji, and I'm not known for being the patient type."

"I know that, but I still wanted to say it...to your face...man to man," Benjamin added.

Skeptical, James walked closer and asked, "What exactly are you saying sorry for?"

"E-Everything, I guess. It was unprofessional of me not to let you know exactly who I was when we met. I didn't want to disturb you at your home, and I'll take myself off this assignment if you want me to, so I won't even be at the meeting tomorrow."

James took a long pause and held Benjamin's gaze. Earlier, Benjamin had said the meeting was inevitable so there really wasn't a point in being angry with him. James had been called out for only asking Benjamin to the plant for personal reasons, so he decided to accept some of the blame.

"It's already forgotten," James said, grabbing Benjamin's shoulder and shaking him lightly. Benjamin exhaled and turned back to his car but James stopped him. "And don't worry about the meeting tomorrow. I'll take care of that."

"What? I thought you didn't want your father to sell his company," Benjamin said, returning with a spring in his step.

"See there, look at that. Too darn pretty when you smile." James grinned.

"Jimmy..."

"It's called a compliment." He laughed. "And I don't want him to sell. You just don't have to worry about tomorrow because there won't be a meeting. Not after I talk to my daddy."

"Do you think even you can persuade him like that?"

"Won't be any trouble at all," James proclaimed proudly. "But I was being serious. It's not happening tomorrow. I'll have him push it back, give you a little more time to get it together."

Benjamin appeared stunned. "Thank you."

"Don't thank me just yet," James said, serious. "I told you that I didn't know anything about this meeting so this isn't just for you."

"Thank you anyway. You probably just saved my career," Benjamin said. "But a little advice, bring your A-game, because I'm about to get to work."

Chapter Three

"ALL RIGHT, THAT'S all of it," James said as he finished stirring the ingredients in the kettle with a long paddle. "Lock it down, cousin."

"You got it," Bryan said while lowering the large lid. "Which batch number is this?"

James held up a hand for Bryan to stop speaking as he made some notes on his tablet. He wanted to make sure that he annotated every detail, no matter how minute, of the changes he had just made to his recipe. While everyone who had sampled the sauce critiqued it as tasting delicious, James still found the flavor to be lacking in some way.

"Sorry about that, but I had a light bulb blow up in my head last night and didn't want it to slip my mind. Here's to hoping this batch will be lucky number seven," James said without looking up.

"Has it been that many already?" Bryan asked.

"Sure has, but it'll all pay off in the end."

James started to walk away with a quick step, and a confused-looking Bryan tried to catch up after a few seconds. On the way to his office, James gave stern instructions to several department heads before reaching his office and again burying himself in work.

"What is it?" Bryan asked with a concerned voice.

"Huh? Oh it's nothing, I just got a lot on my plate today." He sat down at his desk.

"I bet you do." Bryan laughed at him. "Are you going on a work binge just so you can get off early and spend the next few days in the wind?"

James glanced up and threw a pen at Bryan. "Hush up. I just have things to take care of today." He shook his head.

"You mean that Benji boy?"

James furrowed his brow. He had told his cousin about the visit from Benjamin and how their conversation had been civil. However, James had intentionally left out how he still felt uneasy about the entire situation. He wanted a different perspective, so he motioned for Bryan to pull up a chair.

"It's not really him. It's Daddy," James said, now aware of his own frustrations. "Why does he wanna sell?"

"You're asking me?" Bryan pointed at himself. "Shoot, you two never really talk about your business stuff around me anyway, so to be honest, I don't have a clue."

"Me neither, and that's what I don't like. He tells me everything, so I don't understand where this is coming from."

"He's not hurting for money, is he?" Bryan asked skeptically.

James snorted. "No. Nothing short of actually giving it away would cause that. But that's what I'm saying. Why is he even giving these people the time of day?"

"Exactly who is 'they'?"

"I'm not too sure on that one either, but that's why I gotta bite the bullet and ask."

"You're gonna talk to that Benji boy again?" Bryan asked. "Well, I wish you would have thought of that before you had me toss 'im out on the street."

"No, not him—Daddy. I had KG go remind him of the fact that he was growing up. Alls it takes is a little nostalgia to butter him up and loosen those lips. Still, he got nothing, so I gotta take care of this myself. I figure I'll ask him—"

"What is it?" Bryan asked. He appeared worried at the way James cut himself off.

"Oh dang it, I'm gonna be late," James shouted. "Daddy is gonna tear me a new one for this."

"I believe that we can forgo any tearing this time, Jimmy, or at the very least, postpone it," Charles said as he walked into his son's office with several personal assistants and lawyers.

"Uncle Charles," Bryan said gleefully. "What are you doing here?"

Charles turned to his son, and James started to explain.

"I forgot that we're having a brunch meeting with that company that wants to buy us out."

"You forgot?" Charles asked, more to himself than James. "Or did you not wish to attend because you do not want for me to sell my company?"

"I was working," James defended himself.

Charles laughed slightly and shook his head. He nodded to several of his assistants who left the room. Charles then called to one of his lawyers and held up a waiting hand until a folder was placed in it.

"I am not upset with you. We have our meeting not too long from now, and I simply wished to take a ride with my children. That is, unless you did not want to know the details of where all of this business about selling is coming from?" He held up the folder and shook it in James's direction.

James hurried to his father. As he looked over the folder contents, James's personal assistant entered his office with a perfectly pressed suit.

"Thanks. Where are we off to?"

"The Club House," Charles answered him.

"Oh yeah!" Bryan shouted, causing the other two to smile. "And when we get done, we can all get in few holes."

James was about to concur when his father chimed in.

"Unfortunately, Bryan, you will have to sit this one out. This is strictly business, and your cousins and I are not having lunch at our usual retreat on the golf trails."

James made a confused face. "Well, where then?"

"The Club House located at *my* country club, son," Charles said with obvious caution.

"Please, no." James groaned.

"Very well then, I suppose we could skip it and commence with that aforementioned 'tearing' you spoke of." Charles placed his cane directly between his legs and both of his hands on the handle while he glared at James.

James once again groaned, only this time it was at having to attend what he thought would be a pleasant meal.

"I hate that place. It's so stuffy, and everybody there gets all quiet when I come around. I wish they would just say what they're thinking so I can tell 'em about themselves."

"No one is concerned about you in that manner," Charles said reassuringly. "And even if they were, it would not matter. I own most of the property and, to a lesser degree, the tail ends of practically all of the members."

James didn't seem impressed, so Charles went on.

"There is an ulterior motive for my conducting the meeting there, son." He grinned.

James thought for a moment, and his eyes began to shine as he mirrored his father's smile. "Shock and awe? Oh that's mean."

Bryan interrupted by raising his hand and stepping forward. "You two are doing that thing again where you are the only ones in on the joke."

"We're making them play defense. They're gonna try to impress us, wine and dine and all that. Our meal was always gonna be at the country club, right?" James asked.

Charles nodded.

"But we're taking it up a notch by inviting them to break bread with us in a place only a very few can go." James laughed to himself a bit as his eyes became hooded in a devilish grin of anticipation. "They're not gonna beat us at this game. Shoot, I don't think they realize that they aren't even players."

Charles walked over and tousled James's hair. "That's my boy. Now make haste getting changed, son. Your brother is in the car, and I worry when he is left alone to his own devices for too long."

"Think you can hold down the fort, cousin?" James asked Bryan. "You're in charge while I'm gone."

"Well, I was a little upset, but I think I can handle it," Bryan said with a mischievous smile.

"DO WE HAVE those projections?" Benjamin asked Clinton. "And what about the cost-saving analysis we performed the other day? I don't see them."

"Hey, take a breath," Clinton said. "Don't worry, everything is here. You should really try to be more organized."

"Not to sound clichéd—"

"But you have a system." Clinton cut him off.

Benjamin looked at him and took the breath that was suggested. With the time that James had provided by convincing his father to push back the meeting, he and several of his associates had been able to produce much more detailed reports, which were invaluable. Charles Cain had initially given them a very small window to make their pitch, but because of his actions, Benjamin had made their chances of success much more likely.

"Just a few more days left, but the progress we've made since you arrived has been incredible."

"Thanks," Benjamin said with relief. "This is really important, and I've already almost screwed up twice with Mr. Cain and his son. Thank goodness for small miracles, huh?"

"I am not so sure, Mr. Benjamin. Although I am a woman of faith, I sincerely doubt that divine intervention has anything to do with our impending purchase," Laura said as she entered Clinton's office.

"Ms. Harvington! I-I..."

Laura turned to Clinton with a displeased expression and sighed. "I would have thought by now that you would have instructed him to never interrupt Ms. Laura."

"Of course, Ms. Harvington, was there something you needed from us?" Clinton asked neutrally.

"As a matter of fact, I do." She turned to Benjamin. "You see, although I may not have been pleased with Mr. Cain postponing our proposal meeting, I most certainly cannot deny the fact that, because of your action, we are much better positioned to seal this deal. And I am quite appreciative of our new position."

Benjamin remained silent.

"That was a compliment, child," Laura said expectantly.

"T-Thank you, ma'am," Benjamin stammered out.

"Yes, well, you seem to have developed quite the rapport with the Cain family, and it has benefited us all. As such, you will be accompanying me to brunch."

"What?" Benjamin and Clinton shouted at the same time.

"And here I thought stereo was an outdated technology." Laura barely smiled. "Myself and several other board members have invited Mr. Cain to join us for a small gathering. And I am of the opinion that it would be most advantageous for you to join us."

Benjamin was still silent, only this time not nearly as intimidated. Laura had shown kindness and, of all people, toward him. With her praise, he finally felt as if she took him seriously and was eager to impress her yet again.

"When do we leave?" Benjamin asked.

Laura raised an eyebrow and turned from them. "Be downstairs in five."

As she walked away, Benjamin and Clinton stared at one another. Clinton moved first and ushered Benjamin to his desk to grab his coat. He walked with Benjamin down to the garage where Laura's driver was waiting for him with an open door.

"Make or break time. Are you scared?" Clinton asked.

"Only because Ms. Harvington keeps referring to herself in the third person. That can't be healthy." He chuckled.

Benjamin entered the limousine. As he took in the vehicle, Laura entered as well and sat adjacent to him. She didn't say anything, and once they were moving, she silently reviewed her notes.

"Ms. Harvington, I just want to thank you again for this opportunity. It means a lot to me."

Laura didn't respond. Instead, she quickly darted her eyes up in his direction, then back down to her notes.

"I also would like to say, uh..."

Laura looked up and crossed her legs and arms. "You wish to say 'uh'?"

"N-No, ma'am. It's just that... I'm a little nervous. Out of my element." Benjamin exhaled. He was expecting a very harsh reaction from his boss.

"You know, you and I are not so unalike in certain aspects," Laura said patiently. "I took the liberty to review your personnel file. An extremely modest background, a simple family, you even attended public education no less."

"I did, ma'am, but for graduate school... I didn't mean to interrupt you again, ma'am."

"So he can be taught," Laura said. "My point, child, is that I do not care about your humble origins. You are here now, and you will conduct yourself in a manner befitting your position. We are about to be surrounded by some of the most elite of the elite, so do not, I repeat do not, embarrass me."

Benjamin swallowed hard and nodded. Laura looked down again and had returned to going over her notes when he decided to hazard a question. "Are you humble as well, Ms. Harvington?"

She looked up at him. "Excuse me?"

"Your origins, you said you and I are not so unalike."

Laura closed her folder and set it to the side. She reached to the left and pulled a small glass from the bar and poured a drink. After swallowing the shot, she locked eyes with Benjamin for some time before finally speaking.

"Let me be absolutely clear on this subject," she said in a low growl. "The only reason we are speaking of this is because I opened the door.

As such, I will tell you that you are correct. Although I never wanted for anything, I was raised in a home that valued the ideas of humility and charity. But I wanted more. So much more. And now I am where I am today because of my actions. My tenacity. I do what it takes to succeed, and if you need proof of that, you need simply look at our current situation."

"Trust me, Ms. Harvington, when I tell you that I understand," Benjamin said with conviction.

"You may not be a lost cause yet, child." Laura cocked her head. "I requested you because your file impressed me, but make no mistake, that *you* have yet to do so. Rough around the edges does not even come close to an adequate description, however you do have potential."

They both were quiet as their vehicle entered the gates of the secluded country club. Benjamin wasn't as overwhelmed or in awe as he was when he saw Mr. Cain's plantation, mostly because the former home was larger. Still, he felt prudent to ask one last question before they exited.

"Anything else, ma'am?" Benjamin asked.

"Oh there is so much more, Mr. Benjamin," she said with a deep inhale. "But for right now, here is a bit of good advice. I understand that you are not from this region, however in the future, do show a bit more class and do not enter a building, or a car for that matter, before a lady does."

"KENNETH-GEORGE!" CHARLES admonished. "My word, son, it is a good thing this is a private dining hall." He motioned for a waiter to bring him a towel and clean up the drink his son had just spit out.

"What's wrong with this stuff?" James took a sip from his glass and grimaced. "Okay, Daddy, you can't be mad at him. Who mixes juice and champagne together?"

"You speak as if you have never had a libation."

"Oh, so you're saying this stuff is for alcoholics who need another excuse to drink before banks open up?"

Charles silenced his children as he saw several of his guests approaching to greet him. After many handshakes, they took their seats at the ornate table, and Charles gestured for more attendants to pour drinks. When everyone had settled, he raised his glass to offer a toast that was halted by one of the board members.

"One moment, Charles, we have two more joining us," he said.

"Is that so?" Charles asked with insincere surprise.

"Making Big Daddy Cain wait isn't exactly smart, especially after he went through all this trouble for the lot of you," James said smugly and saw a few of the members shift uncomfortably. "Why are we here again, Daddy?"

"These fine ladies and gentlemen would like for me to sell my company to them, son," Charles replied just as smugly.

"They do?" James turned to his brother and said, "Well, shoot. They must have a whole stash of money to waste your time by making you wait. Seeing as how they're one and the same."

They all took a sip from their glasses and set them down, shifting uncomfortably or clearing their throats. The delegation was starting to look even more nervous when the head of the group finally replied to James's accusation.

"That's not true, Jimmy..."

"*James*," he corrected quickly and sharply. "My apologies, sir, but I don't recall us being friends or anything like that."

They all became silent once again. James was content to let them stew, but his father had other plans.

"Hmm, well, this has been a very interesting morning. And I thank you all for this invitation, but I am a very busy man."

"Wait, Mr. Cain, please don't leave just yet," a young executive spoke up.

"Don't worry none. We aren't," James said and heard them all let out a sigh of relief. "My daddy is the president of the *Club House,* and you're his guests. Guests that just overstayed your welcome."

LAURA WAS WALKING toward the breakfast table when she saw Charles stand, as did all her associates on the other side. He lifted his cane, and a concierge joined them who gestured toward the exit for them to leave. They were all shaking hands so hadn't noticed her, so Laura called out in a most elegant voice that stopped anyone from proceeding.

"Now who says that chivalry is dead? Why I simply cannot recall the last time that so many men have stood for me," Laura said as she approached the table with Benjamin in tow. "Charles, it's been much too long!"

She walked over to Charles and hugged him lightly, smiling to herself at how stiff Charles held himself as his breathing increased. After a moment, he hugged her back and placed small pecks on each of her cheeks. Laura then did the same to a confused Kenneth-George, and when she finally turned to James, her smile became even larger.

"*Jimmy*, is that you?" she asked. "You have grown up so handsome, the spitting image of Charles. Come, give us a kiss," Laura almost ordered.

James quickly glanced at his father and then acquiesced to Laura. As she held him, James glared over her shoulders to a baffled Benjamin and mouthed a curse.

"Mr. Cain." The head of the delegation spoke much more confidently. "I would like to introduce you to our chief procurement officer, the lovely Ms. Laura Harvington."

"Oh, no need to be formal. Charles and I go back some time," Laura said. She turned to a clearly upset James and said, "Jimmy, you're slouching."

James looked up at her slowly and said, "Yes... Governess."

Laura smiled but decided to use her intimate knowledge of the Cains to her advantage more so than she already was.

"Oh my, you look flustered. Perhaps you should excuse yourself to freshen up a bit. Benjamin, why don't you escort him?"

Laura almost smiled as James left the table without another word. When Benjamin looked to her, she nodded for him to follow after him.

Without James to work in tandem with his efforts, she turned her attention back to Charles. "Shall we get to it?"

"I shall wait for my son to return, Laura, but this is a most fortunate opportunity for us to catch up a bit," he said and gestured for them to leave the table.

Laura joined him, and they walked off to a more secluded area of the lodge. Out of earshot, the two put on their most joyous faces as they said through pseudo smiles what they were both truly thinking.

"What the hell are you doing here?" Charles asked angrily.

"Let us not do this here, Charles. After all, you would not wish to make a scene."

"I believe a better scene will be your removal from whatever position you claim, once I have you tied up in litigation for breaching the terms of our agreement!" he threatened.

She laughed at him. "Now you and I both know that is not something you are prepared to do. That would require you to clean all of those skeletons out of your closet."

"I will ask you again, why are you here?"

"Why, this is simply business. Your business to be exact. My company wants it, and I was assigned to get it."

Charles turned from her, clutching the head of his cane so hard his knuckles were turning white. "Despite what transpired between us in the past, that is where it belongs. We had an agreement when you left."

"One I have honored." She jutted her chin at him. "Do not be so vain as to think that this is personal. Is that what you believe? That I have some sort of vendetta?" Laura shook her head. "Once we are finished here, I will go back to work in Savannah and stay as far away as you like."

"You cannot possibly believe that I will sell to you now." Charles hissed. "I should end this farce this instance."

"But you will not—cannot rather." Laura motioned for him to walk with her back to the table. "Jimmy will not be coming back to join us. We both know that."

"My son—"

"Is that all you can think about? Your legacy?" Laura suppressed her own anger. "He hates me with a passion, and nothing will make him happier than leaving this place at once. But you, you cannot just shut down this meeting. No, Charles, you may have influence, but bad business practices follow you for life. Snub these people, and it will hurt. Think of your children."

She walked to her seat.

"JAMES... JAMES," BENJAMIN shouted after James while trying to catch up to him.

James expertly navigated the hallways and finally exited to a veranda where no one else was present.

After catching his breath slightly, Benjamin repeated, "James."

"Take one more damn step toward me, and I swear I'll beat the brakes off you, boy!" James screamed.

Benjamin froze, more confused and concerned with James than his words. "James... Jimmy. Don't ever threaten me again. If you do, I won't play around with you like that Ellsworth guy. I can see that something is wrong, and I followed you to see if you were okay, but if you want to be left alone, just say so."

"You and that woman," James shouted. "I should have known the minute you stepped foot into town, but listen up good—"

"No, you listen, damn it! God, of all the assignments, I get stuck with an overgrown man-child!" Benjamin rubbed his temples. "I don't know what you're talking about. You and your father are still very much strangers to me, so how could I? Whatever that was back there with Ms. Harvington doesn't matter to me. She's my boss. End of story."

"You know, you could've just smacked me and told me to get a hold of myself." James sighed and stepped closer. "I'm sorry. You don't know any of us, and it wasn't right to blow up at you like that."

"I'm still trying to buy your father's company," Benjamin replied with a soft smile. The words had been spoken to James, but Benjamin also felt as if he was speaking to himself. Seeing this as an opportunity to build a relationship that could influence James in his favor, he took a chance and asked, "Do you want to talk about it?"

"Not really," James said while crossing his arms. "What makes you think that I'm gonna stand here and tell you all about my business?"

"Because I know what you've dealt with or have a general idea anyway." Benjamin looked around and saw a break in the veranda. There weren't many of the club members outside so he gestured toward a long and empty cloister. "Let's take a walk. We can compare notes."

James smiled and grabbed Benjamin by a shoulder. "Sounds like a fine idea."

"Hands," Benjamin warned, and James innocently placed his arms behind his back. "But are you all right? You were pretty shaken up just a minute ago."

"I am." They both started to walk. "There's just too much bad blood between Governess and my family."

"That's the second time I've heard you call her that," Benjamin said with a light laugh. "Remind me what year this is again."

"Can I finish this story please? And yeah, she's old-school like that. My second sister was born happy and healthy, but Momma Cain didn't make it through the delivery. It hit my daddy pretty hard so he kept all of us really close to his chest for a while. Ms. Harvington was hired as our tutor and stayed with us for a nice spell."

"I'm sorry about your mother," Benjamin said solemnly.

"Huh...oh no, I appreciate that, but both of my sisters are older than me. My old man eventually started to live again and found company with whoever carried me."

Benjamin made a face.

"What? I never met her," James said.

As the two men walked, they passed several open quads and eventually made their way back to the main building of the country club. Since James had accompanied his father, he didn't have his own vehicle and had to call for a chauffeur. Benjamin and James were escorted to a private lounge where they waited, so James continued the conversation.

"What did you mean by you having an idea of what she's like?" James asked.

"What's that? Oh um..."

"Don't worry, my lips are sealed." James nodded.

"Thanks, but over these last few weeks, she's been the boss from hell. Yelling all the time, cutting me off, talking down to me. And as much as she does that, she flips script and can be an almost decent human being."

"You didn't grow up with her," James shot back.

"No," Benjamin conceded. "I just have to do everything she says now because my livelihood and career aspirations depend on what she says. Besides, no matter how strict she is, I can see her being a good teacher."

James shuddered. "You say that, but you might wanna look up her title again. You're telling me you didn't have a teacher growing up who was out to get you and always on your case no matter what?"

"We all did, Jimmy."

"Yeah, but mine lived with me." James grimaced with his last words. He might very well have had many not-so-fond memories of Laura, but that still didn't explain why he was so upset.

"Is that all there is to it? She brings back bad memories of when you were a boy?"

"She does, but that's not why." James stopped and looked Benjamin in the eyes. "I appreciate you listening to me, but I don't know you from *Adam,* so I can't say I'm exactly okay talking to you about this."

"Who's he?" Benjamin asked and took out his phone to make another note.

James burst out laughing and tried to nudge Benjamin, only he wouldn't move. "Don't worry about it, but if you see 'im, tell 'im I want that twenty dollars he owes me."

Benjamin didn't understand the phrase but could tell when he was the butt of a joke. "Believe it or not, I'm talking to you right now because I want to. Ms. Harvington told me to check on you, not follow you."

"All right, I hear you."

"Good, but how about you take it easy on the accent for me?"

James nodded.

"Thanks, but you don't know me, and I'm not going to be down here forever. Even if you just want to vent for a second."

"Nah, I don't have a chip on my shoulder or nothin'—er, uh—anything. It's just that she makes my daddy mad, and that makes me mad."

"Why? Mr. Cain, I mean," Benjamin asked.

"I don't know, and even if I did, it's not my reasons to tell. But in a nutshell, as I grew up, I saw how much she got under his skin. He would be fine, but then she would show up and I could just see how much she upset him. It was worse when she would yell about my studies or me playing around too much."

Benjamin started to ask more, but the driver arrived and led them to their vehicle. Once inside, James asked, "Where are you going?"

"Me? Oh, I guess I should head back to my offices in Savannah."

"Works for me. I have some business to take care of over there anyway." He nodded to the driver, and they started to move. "So?"

"What?" Benjamin asked, confused.

"It's your turn. Tell me about yourself."

Benjamin shrugged and looked up at nothing. "There's nothing really special about me, Jimmy. I'm from Chicago via Subic Bay and a purchasing officer. Lived with my mom over there until I got a scholarship on a student visa and came to the States."

"Wait, really?" James asked sheepishly.

"Yeah. It's a bay over in the Philippines," Benjamin started to explain.

"In Zambales, right? What did I win?" James asked a surprised Benjamin.

"Okay, well, as I was saying, once I saved up enough money, I brought her over here and that's pretty much it."

"Are you two close?" James asked carefully.

"Yeah... Why are you talking like that?"

"Like what?"

Benjamin didn't answer immediately as he thought over what he had said to James. None of the information was private or sensitive, but something about their conversation had changed. As he stared at James, who didn't break eye contact, Benjamin noticed how closely James mirrored his own posture and body language from their conversation earlier.

"Do you want to ask me something?"

"I thought we were just talking, but since you asked, sure. Do you have any siblings?"

"No," Benjamin said flatly.

"Well, what about your daddy?"

"What about him?" Benjamin caught himself and James leaned back. He was about to speak, but James held up a hand and rolled up the divider between the two of them and the driver.

"So, are we ready to put our cards on the table?" James said emotionless. "Unless you wanna keep on with the getting-to-know-you dance."

"You were working me?" Benjamin asked angrily.

"No, I was getting to know who I would be working with."

"My business is with your father, not you."

James lifted his hand and wagged a finger in Benjamin's direction. "Now see, that there is mistake number one, or didn't you notice who was at the head of the table with him? I did want to get to know you. Shoot, you've known that since the day we met. But in all seriousness, at the end of the day, you want something from me that I don't wanna give up."

"Was that entire story a lie? Just to get my guard down?" Benjamin almost shouted.

"Keep it together now. If there's one thing I can't stand in this world, it's a liar. I told you all that because the Governess really did upset me. You gave me your ear, and I gave you mine."

"I—"

"Don't sit there and tell me you weren't gonna use any of that stuff I told you to help yourself out when you talk to my daddy again. Cards on the table, man."

Benjamin was still slightly upset but more shocked that James could see his other motivations for accompanying him. He did genuinely want to know about James, but any information that he could use was also a perk.

"Fine. You're a legacy with a sense of entitlement and some mommy issues. Probably because of your relationship with Ms. Harvington. You're obviously your father's favorite, and he places a great deal of trust in you. I thought that was because he wanted to keep it in the family, but I can see that you do have an idea of what you are doing."

James lifted his chin. "Why thank you, Mr. Rei, and just so we're clear, I wanted to know about you too."

"What'd you learn?"

"That you're driven as hell. You're smart, calculating, and cool as a cucumber. I'm guessing that's 'cause you know where you wanna go in life but also 'cause you wanna do right by your mom."

Benjamin was finally feeling uncomfortable but didn't stop James. "You opened up to me, so go ahead."

"Considering where you come from, you're a pretty tall and big guy. I'll drop it if you want, but you don't seem too keen on your daddy none either."

"An absent parent is something we share," Benjamin said.

"Was he even there at all? Subic Bay is nice and all, but a lot of our sailors and marines go there all the time. It doesn't take much to put it together and see the son of a working woman who was taught everything he needs to know by a deadbeat who wasn't there 'cause he was just passing through."

Benjamin was speechless. Not only was James very observant, but he was also well traveled. He didn't want to speak about the intimate details of his family, but in the span of only a few hours of speaking together, James had surmised Benjamin's origins almost to the letter.

"Mind if we switch topics?" Benjamin asked.

"Not at all. I didn't mean any offense. It's never easy when somebody sees something about you that you don't want 'em to."

"It's not that. Not entirely. I just don't think we should continue with this."

James slid closer to Benjamin. "And what exactly are we doing?"

"Nothing, or at least I'm not. Look, I can see that you're interested in me, and I'm kind of flattered."

"Dang it, I hear a 'but' coming," James said and slid back.

"But I don't get involved with clients. It's too much of a distraction, and to be honest, since your father is the only person I really have to deal with, I can't risk anything unprofessional."

"My daddy can't tell me who to spend my time with."

Benjamin didn't respond. He looked out of the window to discover they were approaching a municipal building. James rolled down the divider and instructed the driver to drop them both off in the front of what was a smaller annex for the city's ancillary operations.

"Why are we here?" Benjamin asked. "I thought you said you were taking me back to my office."

"And I will, but I told you I had business to take care of today. Besides, if you can't wait, then just go ahead and beat feet. Your building is just over there a few blocks." He pointed to the larger building towering over the others in the distance.

James walked ahead and into the building before Benjamin answered. As soon as the door started to close behind him, Benjamin entered as well and quickly caught up to James. While still walking, and at a very brisk pace, James turned to smile at Benjamin who smiled back without any hesitation.

"Don't worry, this won't take long. And once I'm done here, lemme treat you to some, um, what is it you city folk like? One of those crazy coffees or something?" James stopped in front of an office door and knocked.

"I think that's innocent enough," Benjamin said.

A voice instructed them to enter, and James opened the door. Benjamin followed to find a striking man with a stern visage sitting behind a desk. He appeared to be the same age as Benjamin and had a frame that was comparable to James's, but that was where the similarities ended. His impeccably styled red hair shone as if it were ablaze. And while his eyes could have been softer, at the moment, his brow was furrowed, offering an expression of annoyance.

"How's it going, Maynard?" James asked while extending a hand.

Instead of taking it, Maynard stood and walked over to Benjamin. "Maynard Winchester." He crossed his arms in front of him.

"Um, hey, I'm Ben."

James stepped between the two and stared Maynard down with a patient smile. "I'm just here to sign off on your inspection. Just show me where to put the X, and we'll be outta your hair."

"I bet you will be," Maynard said. "But now that I think about it, we should go over some of the discrepancies again."

"Oh c'mon now, don't be like that," James whined. "I already know what I gotta fix."

"If you knew what you had to do, then you wouldn't have had a problem in the first place," Maynard said.

As Benjamin listened, he could sense the tension between the two. The familiarity of their tones and in the way they used their given names was more than enough evidence that these two had a falling out in their history.

"Fine then, I'll play this game with you. I didn't know you missed me so much," James said and winked at him.

"Get over yourself," Maynard yelled.

"You're the one making me sit with you for a few hours."

Maynard scoffed and walked over to open his door. "Not me. I'm actually meeting Ellsworth in a few minutes. You get to deal with my assistant."

James rolled his eyes and gestured for Benjamin to leave. As Benjamin stepped out of the office, Maynard intentionally blocked his path and stared him down for a moment before moving aside.

When James walked around him, he called out, "You know, Ellsworth and I have gotten pretty close since I started working down here."

James turned to him and looked very confused. "Congratulations...?"

Maynard closed his door in James's face, causing him to jump back.

Benjamin tried to maintain a stoic face but couldn't help snickering.

"What?" James asked.

"You know, I want to take you up on that offer for drinks just so you can explain what the hell just happened in there." He finally laughed.

"Don't go there," James warned. "And I'm sorry I can't go with you today. That boy is gonna have me tied up all afternoon."

"Rain check?"

"What happened to professional?"

Benjamin shrugged and said, "It's just drinks, and besides, you actually took the time to listen to me."

"You gave me your ear too. I have plenty of people to talk to, but you listened to me, so thank you." James stood in front of him and took one of Benjamin's hands into his own.

Benjamin patted the hand on top of his and gently removed it. He looked back at James, who chewed his bottom lip a bit and then left. Although the morning had been tiring, Benjamin walked back to his office with a light spring in his step. James really was a nice, albeit persistent, man.

Chapter Four

"THERE YOU ARE, Jimmy. Where the heck have you been?" Ellsworth asked as he leapt off his all-terrain vehicle and walked over to a shirtless James.

James quickly spun around. "Oh hey. Were you looking for me?"

Ellsworth tried to peer around James but couldn't see what was at his foot. The two were currently behind a large shed on the farm they were visiting this morning. Before he could ask another question, Bryan and Kenneth-George came running toward them both, one carrying a scarecrow and the other a large melon. When Ellsworth noticed them, they slowed their pace and tried to hide the items behind their backs.

"What are you three up to?" Ellsworth asked suspiciously.

Instead of answering, James patted Ellsworth on the back and led him to his four-wheeler. "We just headed over here to grab some supplies, man. It might be a long day for us all, and it wouldn't make sense to keep running back and forth—"

James was cut off when a small explosion surprised them all. While everyone crouched for safety, Ellsworth pulled James down with him and slightly covered him with his own body. He was again about to ask James what they were doing, but the smoldering bust from an old *Daddy Cain* advertisement fell from the sky and landed in front of them.

"Oops." James giggled. "Guess I didn't put that wick out all the way when you walked up."

Ellsworth pointed to the slumped sack of fertilizer and asked, "You three are making your own fireworks again, aren't you?"

"No—maybe," James said while looking to his family. They propped up the next things they wanted to destroy.

"Why didn't you call me?" Ellsworth shoved him lightly with a smile on his face. "You know I'm better at making 'em than you."

"I remember, they say during the winter when they turn the heat on, you can still smell something sour in the schoolhouse," James said.

Ellsworth pulled James along as they went over to help Bryan and Kenneth-George. He looked over what they had made, and once he was satisfied they wouldn't injure themselves or set anything on fire, he turned back to James.

"We need to get back over to market. Daddy Cain sent me to come and find you," Ellsworth said.

"Oh shoot, is it time already?" James stole a look at his phone where Ellsworth knew there were multiple missed calls. "Can you give me a lift? I won't make it back before they start."

"Didn't I just say your pops sent me to find you?"

James ran past Ellsworth and hopped on his four-wheeler. "Shotgun."

"No. No way am I riding chick with you!" Ellsworth yelled but still smiled.

"Hop on already. You can fight me or argue, but if either of us is late, then we both have to deal with our old men."

Ellsworth thought of the prospect and immediately got on. As the mayor's son, there was much expected of him by way of public appearances. Raleigh Ferguson and Charles Cain had invested a lot into their current project, and he knew that letting his father down in such a manner would hurt deeply, particularly for such a noble cause.

As James drove down the dirt access road to the farm, pushing the modified engine of the small vehicle to its limits, Ellsworth grabbed James about his shoulders to steady himself. He thought that he could maintain his balance, but that was before James leaned farther into the steering column and swerved on the road. The sudden turns almost threw Ellsworth to the ground, so he moved his hands under James's arms to cross them slightly but snuggly around James's chest.

"Hang on," James warned.

Ellsworth didn't have a problem with the orders. He tightened his grip into a bear hug and leaned forward until his chin was resting on James's shoulder. James stole a quick glance and smiled at him before returning his attention to the road. As they neared the market, the wind changed directions and suddenly blew directly into their faces.

"I wish we didn't have to work today," James said even as his voice was mostly lost in the wind.

"And I wish I took my dang shirt off before I came to find you," Ellsworth grumbled softly to himself.

Even the tight tank top he wore was too much fabric for Ellsworth as he closed his eyes and let his senses overload from all the stimulation. The shudder of James's back and thighs from the growling engine against Ellsworth was euphoric. A slight musk emanated from James's skin from his earlier childish tasks. It filled Ellsworth's nose and made his lips part while he let out a slow breath on James's skin.

James slowed, and Ellsworth gradually lifted his head to see a small crowd of people already gathered at the market. After James pulled off into the parking lot, he jumped off the vehicle and ran to Bryan's truck to retrieve his clothing.

"Thanks for the lift," James said while getting dressed. "Dang, I didn't realize how much I miss tearing up those dirt roads till just now. It's been a while."

"And here I thought you only liked playing with Bryan and KG like that." Ellsworth chuckled nervously.

"Hey, I'm always up for it. I guess we all know what we're doing once our daddies turn us loose, though." He looked at the time again. "We still got a few minutes, so I'm gonna go wipe off a bit."

James slapped Ellsworth on the shoulder and ran off. Once James had his back turned, Ellsworth opened his mouth and slightly raised his hand, then brought it down into a clenched fist.

"That is so damn sad," Cecily said while walking up to Ellsworth.

"Miss Sissy?" Ellsworth blurted out, embarrassed. "I-I... Where did you come from?"

"Oh you wanna change subjects, honey? That's fine. It is a lovely morning."

Cecily walked past him slowly and deliberately. Intentionally holding her large purse up by her wrist as she sauntered to the market.

"I already know you heard everything, so just give me my lumps," Ellsworth said, crestfallen.

"I don't have to, Ellsworth. You've been beating yourself up over it since you two were in diapers. It's such a shame, though." She shook her head. "One is as blind as a bat, and the other is as yellow as a duck."

"Ducks aren't yellow, ma'am." He tried to defend himself.

"They are when they're babies. I guess you just never grew out of your color. But you two aren't kids anymore. Maybe it's time you stopped acting like one with him."

Ellsworth opened his mouth, but nothing came out. Instead, he grimaced slightly and then ran to catch up with Cecily and escort her into the open market.

"IT'S ABOUT TIME, Jimmy," Mayor Ferguson said, "I thought that Ellsworth was unable to locate you, and it would have been such a shame not to have you here today because of your other obligations."

James had just come from making himself more presentable when Mayor Ferguson stopped him. As he walked over to his godfather in the center of the market, he noticed that many of those attending the grand opening had taken up positions so that they could see the podium, where their mayor was standing.

"No, sir, Mr. Mayor," James said warmly and hugged him. "I'm free all day and wouldn't miss this for the world."

"That is wonderful, son, but I have watched you grow and know how easily you can be...*distracted*." James started to blush, and Mayor Ferguson went on. "And that is not to say there is anything wrong with that, mind you. I suppose I am used to always having an eye on Ellsworth and knowing his whereabouts."

"And I for one believe in a little thing called autonomy," Charles said as he joined them. "What are they calling it now, *Free-Range Parenting*?" Charles used the same tone his old friend had to address James.

James smirked and slowly backed away from the two gentlemen. He did a quick scan of the area, and when he saw Ellsworth releasing Cecily, James waved him over. As Ellsworth came within speaking distance, James placed a single finger over his lips and gestured toward their fathers. They both started to snicker.

"We are on a tight schedule, Charles. I was simply suggesting that you keep Jimmy close. With how much work has been put into this project, I am sure that your son is a bit overwhelmed. But there is no need to worry, my friend. Ellsworth just passed his exams and is a licensed physician's assistant now."

"Well, congratulations, my boy," Charles said and shook Ellsworth's hand. "Jimmy may well be in need of your skills. After securing all of those accounts down in Florida, and well, after his bonus, I'm sure he will be on cloud nine and in need of some pure oxygen." Charles patted a beaming James on the shoulder.

Charles Cain and Raleigh Ferguson continued to bicker, so James and Ellsworth walked over to the podium. Just as James was about to speak, his phone chimed, and he smiled at the screen showing Benjamin had sent him a message. His excitement was short-lived, however, when he read that he and Laura had just pulled into the parking lot.

Ellsworth tapped the microphone a few times and, once he had everyone's attention, informed the crowd that they would be starting within the next few minutes. This made Charles and Mayor Ferguson halt in their attempts to outdo one another. They both took up positions behind their sons, and James shook off the upsetting news.

"G-Good morning, everyone," James stammered but then composed himself to speak in the manner he had been raised to when introducing his father. "I hope ya'll are having a nice time trying some of the best food our new market has been able to provide." James attempted to settle the crowd and the stragglers making their way to the speech.

Ellsworth took over.

"And while there are a whole mess of people that deserve credit, me and Jimmy would like to take the time to thank our daddies for putting up the funds to make a lot of this happen. They've expanded the farming acres, purchased the newest equipment, and renovated and built many of the buildings here."

James and Ellsworth paused as a short round of soft applause greeted them. When it stopped, James finished.

"So without further ado, it's my honor to introduce the men who have done so much for Calloway, Mayor Raleigh Ferguson and my old man, Daddy Charles Cain," James said and stepped back.

Charles moved forward, waving to the crowd with Raleigh at his side. "My goodness, son. You embarrass me sometimes." He joked. "Thank you, everyone. While it is true that Raleigh and I were the principal backers of this endeavor, we should not take anything from those who put in the legwork to make this happen. It is because of them, that we are all here today."

Another soft round of applause came, and before it subsided, a different person spoke up.

"I could not have said it better myself, Charles," Laura said and continued to clap. Benjamin was at her side and doing the same only in a much slower manner.

Charles stared at her and kept his face as neutral as possible. James moved to step in front of him, but both Mayor Ferguson and Charles placed gentle arms in his path. When James calmed, Mayor Ferguson took the microphone and addressed Laura.

"Thank you for that, Ms. Harvington, and we will be delighted to speak more with you, after our dedication is complete." Mayor Ferguson was smiling, but the tone of his voice left no ambiguity in his intention for her to stop talking.

"Oh of course, Raleigh," Laura said and waved her hand. But when the mayor of Calloway was about to speak, she interrupted again. "But I would also like to donate something to this glorious morning that the good Lord has given us."

Mayor Ferguson inclined his head for Laura to speak, and instead, she walked through the crowd with Benjamin and took up a position between Charles and Mayor Ferguson, with Benjamin standing back with James and Ellsworth. One look at James had to have told Benjamin how angry he was, but Benjamin appeared just as agitated and embarrassed.

Laura started to speak but closed her mouth suddenly and touched a hand to her neck. She cleared her throat lightly and looked back to James who glowered but went to an aide to have a small cup of water brought to her.

"Such a gentleman," Laura exclaimed as James walked away, and the crowd chuckled softly. "But that should come as no surprise to anyone. He is the son of Daddy Cain." She turned to address the crowd. "You know, when I first received wind of this project, I wondered to myself, what are those two thinking...by not asking for help. Because there is always so much more that can be done." Laura looked to Charles and winked. "You should not take it all upon your own shoulders.

"And in the spirit of today, I feel obligated to give in any way that I am able. Now I realize that the buildings are completed and the fields are being tended, but what of the days after this ceremony is over? What of tomorrow?" she asked and received many nods from the crowd.

"With this in mind, I took it upon myself to secure a sizeable donation from several different banks and corporations, including the one I work for. This is in addition to a generous amount from my own purse. My purpose? To set up an even larger market. One where we will be able to provide wholesome and nutritious produce to those unsightly food desert zones that are popping up over the country. One where we can continue to provide long-term jobs to the workers that have made this endeavor a reality, and even a place that will provide education and therapy to all those who wish to donate their time. Be they exceptional family members, or our wounded veterans who need assistance in transitioning," Laura finished.

A thunderous round of applause erupted from the crowd this time, and with their attention on Laura, Charles graciously escorted James away from the podium even though his face contorted to anger once no one was able to see him clearly.

"Daddy, what—?" James tried to ask.

"Not now, Jimmy," Charles yelled at James. "Just remove yourself from our sight."

"But," James shouted, the hurt in his voice clear.

His father didn't speak to him like this, or rather he had forgotten the last time he had. He locked his gaze on Laura.

"Go," Charles said and walked back to the podium.

"Now," Mayor Ferguson said and nodded to Ellsworth.

James clenched his fist and shook slightly from anger. Ellsworth took him by his shoulders and gently turned them around to walk away. Neither of them wanted to make a scene in front of their fathers who were suddenly treating them like strangers.

"HEY, ELLSWORTH, WHERE'S Jimmy?" Bryan asked while still approaching him with Kenneth-George in tow.

Ellsworth pointed to the bed of Bryan's truck where James was buried in one of the side-mounted storage boxes, which contained many items his cousin used on his farm. James's family tried to get his attention, but James remained focused in his search for the tool he wanted.

"He's been like that for the last few minutes," Ellsworth said to Bryan with a grimace. "I hope you don't have anything dangerous in there. Something tells me he's gunning for his old nanny."

"You think?" Bryan asked. He shook his head and walked around his truck to James. "Jimmy, listen, I know you're pissed right now."

"That's not the word," James said sharply without looking up.

Ellsworth joined them and said, "Just tell us what you want us to do. You want us to leave?"

James looked up to find all eyes on him. Kenneth-George entered the truck bed with his brother and placed a hand on his shoulder. After a few seconds, James relented.

"No, no, I don't want you guys to do that." He pulled his brother in. "Oh, there it is."

"Where what is?" Bryan asked, and James held up several bungee straps.

"I changed my mind, cousin. I wanna go back to the shed. And then I wanna take that scarecrow, pretend it's Governess, and get you guys to help me pull it apart into four pieces."

The three of them stared at James, openmouthed, until Kenneth-George slapped him on the back and jumped down from the truck bed, sprinting off.

"KG?" James yelled at his back. He turned to Bryan and Ellsworth. "Where's he going?"

Kenneth-George ran over to the four-wheel vehicle James and Ellsworth had used earlier and hopped on, waving for James to come over. He didn't stay on it long, however, and soon jumped off to return to his normal place as the driver of his cousin's truck.

"Get a move on," Bryan said and entered the passenger side. "You two need to bring that back over anyway."

James got out of the bed and walked over to the all-terrain vehicle. When he tried to start it unsuccessfully, he whipped his head toward his brother and shouted. Kenneth-George didn't pay any attention and smiled along with Bryan as they both left.

"WHAT HAPPENED?" ELLSWORTH asked.

"He flooded the engine," James said. "I'm gonna kill that boy when we catch up to 'em."

"Just cool your heels off for now and give it a few minutes." Ellsworth sat down and leaned against the vehicle, then patted the ground next to him.

James took a moment to remove his shirt and ball it before sitting down and draping it over his head. He didn't say anything, but after letting out a long breath, Ellsworth figured he had calmed down enough to talk about earlier.

"I'm sorry you had to go through that," Ellsworth said. "I know it wasn't the easiest time with her, growing up."

"Nah, I appreciate you even more, taking me away from there and all," James said softly. He turned his head to Ellsworth and rested his head lazily on his shoulder. "You're a pain in my butt most times, but I know I can count on you when I'm in a jam."

Ellsworth brought his arm up behind James and grabbed the base of his neck with a soft clap. "I have to."

"What? Why?" James asked and lifted his head.

Ellsworth tried to answer but lost his train of thought. James's face remained puzzled, but he didn't break his gaze. While trying to find the words, Ellsworth continued to be distracted by the steady rise and fall of James's breathing as his hand remained on his neck.

"Speak up now. Cat got your tongue or something?" James said and slapped Ellsworth's stomach.

"No one likes running their mouth more than me."

Ellsworth swung his arm, and James flinched. Instead, Ellsworth softly patted his stomach and rubbed James's shoulders while once again shaking him but bringing him in closer.

"I just meant that I'm the only one who's allowed to get under your skin."

"And you're proud of that?" James asked.

"I know what I said." Ellsworth's other hand was still on James's stomach, and he stopped patting and wrapped his arm around James's waist.

"Can I help you with something? You're not blind so you don't need to touch me to know what I look like."

"I know," Ellsworth said and continued. "What's wrong? Am I making you turn red or something?"

"A little bit," James said.

"James, James," Benjamin yelled from the other side of the parking lot.

"What in the hell is he doing here?" Ellsworth growled. James had an even bigger smile on his face at the sight of Benjamin approaching than the one he'd had only seconds earlier.

James jumped out of the embrace Ellsworth held him in and ran to meet Benjamin. "I told you—call me Jimmy."

"I know, but this is the second time Ms. Harvington has ambushed you," Benjamin explained. "The timing is just too convenient, and honestly I'm getting tired of pissing off my client, well you're not but..." Benjamin grinned.

"Then maybe you should leave," Ellsworth interrupted once he joined them.

"Excuse me?" Benjamin asked and turned to Ellsworth.

"No, I really don't think there's an excuse for you." Ellsworth turned to James. "C'mon, let's get to it."

"Now hold on there. Benji is the one who gave me a heads-up about Governess."

"But a phone call was too dang much? Now let's go," Ellsworth shouted and then grabbed James's hand, which was quickly pulled back.

"What just got into you?" James demanded.

"Bryan and KG are waiting on us. We had plans for today."

"Had is right." James guided Benjamin to the all-terrain vehicle. When they were both on, James was able to start it and then said to Ellsworth, "You're the worst damn best friend a guy can have. You know that?"

The two took off, leaving Ellsworth alone. He threw his head back and closed his eyes while screaming a curse in a long, drawn-out way before bringing his head back down. Tears of anger and anguish formed in his eyes, so he kept them closed for a bit longer to catch his breath.

"Ellsworth, what am I going to do with you, sweetheart?" Cecily said as she walked past him.

"Please, Miss Sissy, not now," Ellsworth begged while blinking away tears.

"Don't worry, honey. I have better things to do than babysit you two all over again. But here's some advice."

"I didn't ask for any...ma'am."

Cecily opened her purse to rummage through it and kept talking as if Ellsworth hadn't said anything. "Mmhmm, but as I was saying, you can't fight for someone unless you're there."

Ellsworth didn't say anything.

"Go after them, boy, or wave the white flag and move on. It's not healthy to keep putting yourself through this, and it's definitely not fair to Jimmy."

"What are you talking about?"

"The way you're as sweet as candy to him until another boy comes around and suddenly you can't stand either of them. Why it's as plain as day to everyone except the only person you want to notice." Cecily finished and finally found what she was looking for in her purse. "Oh and do me a favor. Give this to Kenneth-George." She handed him money. "And I thought I knew everything about everyone, but still lost a bet on you and Jimmy."

"OKAY, YOU CAN let go now," James said while trying to pry Benjamin's hands from around his torso. "C'mon, Benji, knock it off. I can't breathe, and you're stronger than me."

"Yeah, sorry about that." Benjamin released James but remained seated on the vehicle.

"I wasn't driving that fast."

"Yes, you were. On a dirt road, hitting every pothole you saw, and with no helmets," Benjamin chided.

"Fine, I'll make sure I have one for you next time."

"Next time?"

"Oh yeah. I'll even get you some knee pads, and if you're real nice, I'll show you how to use 'em." James grinned.

Benjamin's mouth fell open, and he couldn't help but laugh. James motioned for him to follow, and once he caught up and composed himself, he tried to talk to James again.

"So you decided that charmer wouldn't work and you switch to vulgar?"

"I'm running out of tricks here." James spread his palms. "But I wouldn't have to if you'd stop playing hard to get."

"I'm not playing."

James stopped walking and crossed his arms across his chest, before turning to face Benjamin. James's family gestured for them to hurry, and eventually escalated to annoying taunts.

"What? What is it?" Benjamin asked.

"You. C'mon now, we've already played cards in a manner, so I'm just gonna ask you flat-out. What's wrong with me?"

"Nothing, you're...nothing," Benjamin said carefully.

"I'm not pretty enough for you?"

"Jimmy."

"What? Is it my accent? Or am I too country for you?" James grinned.

"Take a breath. Anyone would be lucky to spend time with you," Benjamin said and was slightly surprised that he meant it.

"I'm listening."

"Incredible," Benjamin said in a low voice. "Is this your first time being rejected?"

James just stood there in silence.

"Okay, hound dog, I don't have a problem with you. And in truth, if we met back in Chicago or even down here without any strings, I wouldn't be so guarded. But no matter what, until this deal is complete, I can't risk anything."

"So you're saying in a few days, once all of this is over?" James asked.

"Not even then. Call me old-fashioned, but I would at least like to get to know you a bit better first."

"Now that's something I can definitely do, so let's go before they come over here and get us," James said and started to run.

Benjamin took off after James and, even though he was able to match his pace, still lagged behind slightly. He was about to make a small joke, but as he stared at James from behind, Benjamin was left speechless.

With each labored step as they ran through the soft, uneven soil in the field, Benjamin was entranced at the metronomic way James's body moved. The tightening of his torso from his rapid breathing, how his muscles shuddered with each dull impact his feet made with the ground. So lost in the sight of what completely filled his view, Benjamin didn't register in time that they had reached the other men and James had stopped.

"Jimmy, watch out," Benjamin tried to warn him but collided with James and sent the both tumbling to the ground. It wasn't painful for him since James broke his fall.

Lifting his head from the ground slowly, James spat out a few blades of grass and dirt before looking over his shoulder. "How is this old-fashioned again?" He smiled.

"Yeah, about that," Benjamin said, embarrassed. "Are you all right?"

"Don't worry none. I can take a hit. But two hundred pounds lying on top of me while I'm chewing dirt isn't something I do regularly."

"Oh, sorry." Benjamin started to push himself up, but James grabbed his forearm.

"I didn't tell you to get up," James yelled.

Benjamin shook his head and moved off James until he was propped up on both knees. When James rolled over, he crawled over to meet Benjamin, and both remained kneeling. Without saying a word, Benjamin brought his hand up to wipe away a dark smudge of dirt from the corner of James's mouth. He wasn't at all surprised when James turned his head and his thumb gently brushed against James's lips.

"Okay, we can all see where this is going, so me and KG are gonna find someplace where you two aren't," Bryan said while laughing at his cousin.

"No don't." Benjamin was unable to break eye contact with James. "I'm not sure why Jimmy brought me out here, but I might as well see." He stood and walked over to Bryan. "But to be clear, our relationship is strictly business."

"And pigs can fly," Bryan said dryly. "I don't think we should blow anything else up, guys, too many people are at the market and could hear us."

"Well then, I guess we'll just have to show Benji how to ride then, won't we?" James patted Benjamin on the back.

"We will?" Benjamin asked.

"Yeah, we actually have a few mounds of dirt piled up on the other side of the shed. Wanna jump 'em?" James asked.

"Absolutely not." Benjamin didn't yell, but he was serious. "I don't have a problem taking a break with you guys, but I'm on the clock and who knows when Ms. Harvington will call me back."

"She probably won't even need a phone. I can hear her yelling now— Mr. Benjamin!" James laughed.

"You do that well. I guess all those years... Who is that?" Benjamin pointed to the access road.

Someone sped up the access road on a motorbike. As the driver got closer, Benjamin recognized Ellsworth, who skidded to a stop in front of him with the engine still running and its tires kicking up dirt onto his shoes.

"Hello again," Benjamin said, but Ellsworth rolled past him.

Ellsworth moved himself over to James while sitting on his bike. "Jimmy, we need to... Can I talk to you for a minute?"

"Looks like you cooled off." James grinned slightly. "How about later? We're about to go riding. Well, actually we weren't. Benji doesn't know how and isn't interested."

"That's a shame," Ellsworth said to Benjamin. "I really could've shown you a thing or two. Guess I'll have to save all my tricks for Jimmy."

Benjamin stared at Ellsworth and then turned to James, who looked oblivious to what was going on with this exchange. It was then he realized whatever affection Ellsworth held for James was one-sided, so much so that it had never been brought up.

Although Benjamin knew he wasn't looking for anything in particular with James, he was beyond annoyed at the fact that he had become the lightning rod for Ellsworth to take his frustrations out on. And on a selfish level, he did want to be the one James chose.

"Actually I wouldn't mind a small lesson," Benjamin said to Ellsworth.

"You wouldn't?" everyone asked Benjamin in a surprised tone. James even more so.

"No, I wouldn't." Benjamin walked over to Ellsworth. "James's four-wheeler is a bit much for me, but I think I can handle your little bike."

"It's not little," Ellsworth grunted back.

"I guess it's just me then," Benjamin said. "Your offer is still good, right?"

Ellsworth gripped the throttle of his bike hard and stared Benjamin down. "I'm a man of my word." He revved the engine loudly.

"That's good to know. I—" Benjamin was cut off when Ellsworth revved the engine again.

"Sorry about that, boy. What was that?" Ellsworth asked.

Benjamin tried speaking again only for Ellsworth to rev the engine over his voice again. This happened several times, and at first Benjamin smiled. But after no time, everyone was tired of the silly game, and James spoke up.

"C'mon, Ellie, stop being a jerk," James said.

"I'm not," Ellsworth said while still revving the engine. "He needs to be able to hear us when he rides, in case he gets away from us too far."

"Sure you're not." James crossed his arms and walked over to them. "And speaking of getting away, ease up on that throttle."

Ellsworth looked at James angrily. "I know what I'm doing!"

"I never said that you didn't," James shouted over Ellsworth revving the engine again.

"Let's just watch." Benjamin turned to Ellsworth again and placed a hand on James's shoulder, to which he received a large smile in return. "I'm sure he didn't ride all the way out here just to pick a fight."

Benjamin held Ellsworth's stare while the whine from the bike's engine grew louder. Ellsworth still held down the throttle and suddenly, the bike shot away from them. Ellsworth traveled a short distance over the bumps and holes of the uneven dirt before he let go of his bike, as it surged forward, and fell back onto the ground with an audible thud.

"Ouch," Bryan said. Everyone ran over to check on Ellsworth except for Benjamin who walked.

"Really, Ellsworth?" Bryan hovered over him. "You still don't know how to stop a whiskey throttle?"

Ellsworth groaned in a low voice, so James pushed through them and knelt by his side to help him sit up. "Are you happy now?"

"I'm in pain, so the answer to that would be no," Ellsworth snapped. He looked at James who didn't move and continued to cradle his head. Immediately he closed his eyes and let out a sigh.

"It's your own fault, but can you stand?"

James threw Ellsworth's arm over his shoulder and supported him while they stood. Ellsworth almost slipped from James's grip a few times when the sweat on their bare torsos combined, but Ellsworth leaned onto James even harder.

"This isn't exactly how I saw this moment," Ellsworth said weakly.

"Me neither, I thought we would be riding by now."

"Wow," Benjamin said, astonished, while running his hands through his hair. He looked to Kenneth-George who shook his head.

"Sometimes I think my cousin is a bit slow," Bryan said.

James glanced over at the three before shifting to help Ellsworth stand up straight. "I'm gonna let go, all right?"

Ellsworth's disappointment showed in his eyes, but he nodded. When James let go, he took a small step toward him but was claimed by vertigo and almost collapsed in front of him. He would have hit the ground if James hadn't quickly caught him.

"I think you should go get checked out. You probably bumped your head a little too hard," James said.

"Too bad mine isn't as thick as yours." He chuckled.

"If you say so." James turned to his family. "Can you two see to it that he gets back okay? Take your truck so he can lie in back, Bryan."

Bryan turned to Benjamin and then back to James. "You got it." He laughed.

"Why can't you take me back?" Ellsworth demanded. "This could be the last time you ever lay eyes on me."

He was rewarded with an odd stare from everyone.

"You'll be fine, Ellie," James stammered out in surprise. "They're just taking you back over to your daddy. And this way, me and Benji get some alone time to practice riding."

"Sounds like a plan," Benjamin interrupted and stood at James's side.

"Get me outta here, Bryan." Ellsworth said.

As Kenneth-George and Bryan took Ellsworth from James's support, James stood silently as they all walked to Bryan's vehicle with Ellsworth glancing over his shoulder. It was intense. So much so that James almost called to ask him if something was wrong, but instead let them leave.

"Is this standard in Calloway? Dirt bikes, and farms, and mild concussions?" Benjamin asked.

"Oh, nope, I'm not gonna say it." James laughed. "But you seem a little bit more touchy since we got over here. Am I finally wearing you down?"

"I made myself clear on that." Benjamin lifted Ellsworth's bike and brought it over.

"What?"

"I still would like that lesson on how to ride, unless you want me to wait for Ellsworth to come back," Benjamin said.

"I don't think we have to worry about any more interruptions for the day." James sat on the bike in front of Benjamin and smiled when he felt Benjamin's arms wrap around his stomach. "You might get a better grip if you take your shirt off."

"No," Benjamin said quickly.

"It was worth a shot." James started the engine. "Don't worry, though, I'll cool my jets."

Benjamin took one hand off of James's stomach and placed it over James's hand holding the throttle. He squeezed gently and said, "That's good, because our proposal meeting is only a few days away. Succeed or fail, I'm off this assignment after that, and it'll be a few days before I leave."

"So?" James asked.

Benjamin leaned in to whisper into James's ear. "So let's see where it goes."

Chapter Five

"AHH!" JAMES SCREAMED as he was jolted back to consciousness. "Daddy!" He tried to yell but received another pail full of ice-cold water.

"Are you awake yet, son? It's only twelve forty-five in the afternoon, and I know how much you need your beauty sleep." Charles motioned for another one of his staff to throw more water onto James.

James stood up from his bed and took a stoic stance with his hands on his hips as they continued to drench his naked body. When his father realized that he was no longer being affected, he motioned for them to stop and made his way past his son to sit at the table on the balcony.

Charles picked up a newspaper. "Do not keep me waiting."

James didn't even dry off before pulling on his favorite jeans and joining his father. He called for something to eat, which was cancelled by Charles, and waited in silence until he set down the paper and lit his pipe.

"What'd I do now?" James asked.

"Why are you not at work?"

"My weekend starts on Friday. Perks of being the boss and all that."

Charles sighed. "Son, I thought we spoke of this only a few days ago. Or were you so wrapped up in your rendezvous that you forgot?"

James shot up from the table. He walked to the edge of his large circular balcony and faced the eastern sky. It was a hazy, humid day with the sun blazing. And in the manner in which he had woken, he was in no mood.

"I'm well past sick and tired of this," James said angrily.

"Of what?" Charles asked calmly. "Tired of me caring about your welfare? Sick of me ensuring that you do what is right, because believe me when I say I do know what is best. Or is it me trying to make a decent man out of you through hard work?"

"Who I spend my time with isn't any of your business," James said.

"It is when it affects my business."

Charles walked closer, stood next to his son, and spun him around.

"I could make you punch a time clock every morning. Make you send me reports and check out with me before you leave, but I do not. So how is it too much to ask that you are at work when you are supposed to be?"

"For the same damn reason you can't ask me what I was doing first," James answered him. "I didn't see any boys in my room this morning. Any of 'em."

"Am I supposed to be impressed that you went a single night alone?"

"No, but I thought you'd be proud that I wrote some formulas that'll balance our books and give us projections at least five times as accurate. I also got with some third-party logistics people so we're saving on shipping too."

"We are?" Charles asked. "I will not withhold credit where it is due, but are you saying that is why you were not at the office this morning? Even for a modest appearance?"

"Yeah," he said, confused. "I stayed up all last night working on these plans and such. Do you know how much typing I had to do? I've been busting my tail for the last three days, and the only thing you can do is try to baptize me again." James slapped the side of his head, trying to empty the water from his ears.

"And in that time, you have not been with Bryan or your brother?" Charles asked in a worried voice.

"No. I just said that, what's wrong?"

Instead of answering, Charles led his son back inside. He allowed him to get cleaned up and, once he was presentable, called down to have his son's car made ready. The two walked toward the west garage, but his father took a detour through his garden. Although the weather was hot and his father wore an expensive suit, he couldn't have looked more comfortable.

"When did you last speak to Kenneth-George, son?" Charles asked as their stroll took them deeper into his organic retreat.

"Me and KG talk all the time, you know that," James answered him. "What is it? Tell me?"

Charles sighed.

"The other night, I received a call from the sheriff concerning your brother. It was nothing serious, I assure you, however his shenanigans are starting to skirt the edges of misdemeanors. His latest actions may very well have been a serious offense, if not for the sizable donation I provided to the department last year."

James sighed with relief; he thought it had been something serious. "Please don't scare me like that again."

"You are not listening," his father said. "This is not the first time something like this has happened."

"He's seventeen years old, Daddy, just a kid. Getting in trouble is his day job. You used to call that finding your way."

The two stopped exactly where James knew his father was taking them. In the center of his ornate garden, there was a raised dais with a marble memorial to his first and only wife at its center. The simple square pillar had a single gardenia placed upon it, one that was cut fresh every day by Charles.

"Trouble is one thing, but trying to get caught is another. When the officer asked him why, he just said 'I dunno.'"

Trying to defuse the tension, James said, "I used to raise all kinds of hell growing up."

"I know. Who do you think he gets it from?" James appeared to be getting angry again, but Charles spoke before he could. "It is not my intention to assign you as the guilty party, son. And while I am positive that is not the case, it does not exculpate you of your responsibilities."

"Daddy..."

"James," Charles returned just as forcefully. "Kenneth-George looks up to you. He always has. You are his elder brother, and I know in my heart that he wants to be just like you. One way or another, he is going to find that way you spoke of. I am just asking that you help to set him off on the right path."

"If you want me to talk to him, I will, but why can't you?"

Charles laughed. James didn't know what to do so he let him continue until his father turned his head toward the memorial and spoke.

"You were always so much better with children."

"I'll talk to him, right now as a matter of fact. I'm heading over to Effingham County to see Bryan anyway, so he can help us with the chores."

"It is a start," his father said. "Ensure that he understands the seriousness of this matter. I promised the sheriff that, as a punishment, Kenneth-George would be at his grandson's game later today to help with ushering. See that he is there, and on time, no less. I would myself, however I am headed over to the mayor's mansion and will be occupied for some time."

"I will, but since we're doing favors for each other, how about you go over my activity reports from this week," James asked.

"Is that still giving you a headache?" Charles asked, concerned. "The people I brought in summarized that the main problem was simply a formatting issue. That the numbers were off most likely due to a lack of attention to detail."

James shook his head. "No... I don't know. Something just doesn't look right. It's not the typing or anything this week, and all the numbers are good, but I just don't know. Every time I get one like this, I take Eugene and Bryan over to the section to roll some heads. That fixes it for a while, but it keeps happening."

"Is this a safety issue? Is anyone hurt?" Charles asked impatiently.

"It's not the people... Can you just look 'em over? I don't care if your people do. I just don't want anyone from the plant. We got that state inspection any day now, and I want all my bases covered."

His father nodded, and after kissing him goodbye, James made his way to the garage to depart.

"BREAK TIME, FELLAS," Bryan said to his cousins.

"Nice timing." James wiped the sweat from his brow, then took off his work gloves and headed toward a nearby tree for shade.

James had arrived at Bryan's farm and found that his brother was already there. The two helped their cousin with his normal routine of maintenance and repairs with Kenneth-George primarily behind the wheel of a tractor to haul away the many bushels of pecan nuts that his cousin grew.

While the farm itself remained the property of his father, Bryan had taken over the primary duties once his father could no longer keep up because of age and injuries. The job might not have been glamorous, but Bryan held on to it for the simple fact that it was his.

Bryan tossed James a bottle of water before saying, "I appreciate your help, but won't Uncle Charles be pissed that you're not at work?"

"We already went at it," James said. "Besides, he's all up in arms over that meeting he's got with Benji in a few so he let me be."

"Dang it." Bryan snapped his fingers. As he did so, Kenneth-George flipped down from the branch and came over to collect his money once again. "You're sending me to the poor house."

"You two need a new hobby," James said, only slightly perturbed. "What was that one about anyhow?"

"Nothing," Bryan said carefully. "KG just figured that you're kinda sweet on that boy is all."

"I'm not sweet on anyone," James said defensively.

"And a Yankee to boot, don't that just beat all?"

"You're seeing what you want to believe," James said sternly. When his family members only smiled harder, he gave up trying to convince them of anything different and instead switched to making them answer questions. "How come you think that?"

"Who the heck is *Benji*?" Bryan asked, grinning.

"That's his name."

"And you just let him come to your house at night to talk?"

"That was business. Anything else," James asked.

"Well, you could explain why you're playing defense like you're back in school now that we're talking about 'im."

"We should get back to it. This work won't finish itself," James said while turning from him, the flush in his face making him even hotter out in the sun. "Ya know, I don't recall ever giving either of you a hard time for all the girls you chase after."

"Yeah, but Jimmy Cain always gets his man. I saw the way you were looking at him back at the market."

"You act like I don't have a good reason," James said with a devilish grin. "That right there is something you bring home to make the family jealous."

"So you're gonna come clean now?"

"It's nothing serious. I just like looking at him. What's wrong with that?"

"And talking to him," Bryan added. "Makes sense, though. He wouldn't stop going on about you neither."

"And when did this happen?"

"I'm not too sure. My memory is a little fuzzy."

"Don't you go holding out on me. I wanna know everything that boy—"

"What?" Bryan asked when James cut himself off.

"When?" James replied. When Bryan didn't say anything, he delved deeper. "When did you talk to him? And why the heck was I on your mind? I don't need you to shoot arrows for me."

Bryan grimaced because he knew how James would react. But James already had an idea, so trying to change subjects wouldn't work.

"Last week, when you had me show 'im the door. We didn't talk so much about you, but he was going on, so I just let 'im run his mouth and listened. Only spoke up like a few times."

James was so livid he walked away. When he got close enough to a basket full of the pecans they had harvested, he kicked it over.

"First me and now you? I'm getting damn tired of him trying to go around the only person who can actually sell them anything!"

"Jim—"

"No!" He cut him off. "Don't even try to make an excuse for him. I know he was trying to fill your head up with all kinds of nonsense. All that time we spent talking, I knew he was working me."

"He only said nice things."

"So he wasn't carrying on about you talking to me? Trying to make me listen and to talk to Daddy?" When Bryan didn't answer, James knew he was right, but more so, the embarrassed look on his cousin's face shocked him even more. "You want us to sell?"

Bryan looked toward Kenneth-George who took up a position alongside his brother and crossed his arms.

"I told you he was just talking. Saying how much more money you guys can make if you work with 'em."

"We do fine by ourselves," James said, and Kenneth-George nodded at his point.

"I can see, you must be doing okay since you have the time to waste in the weeds with me," Bryan said and walked from them to collect the basket James had kicked.

James and KG paused from Bryan's words and then ran to catch him. At his side, James said, "It's not even like that, and you know it."

"Don't worry about it. My mouth just got away from me." Bryan returned to pick up his crop with their help. "Still, though, you love staying out all night and waking up when you want, and you know that. You hate it when Uncle Charles rides your tail, so why not hear 'em out?" Bryan stopped for a moment to look at James. "You're already lucky to have your life, so why not try to make it better if you can?"

"It's not luck. It's blessings," James said while pulling him in. "You know it's not my call to make, though, right? If Daddy wants to sell, then I can't stop 'im."

"I just said listen to the guy is all."

"A little too late for that now," James said while helping him to lift the basket.

"We know where they all are," Bryan said with a smile forming on his face. Kenneth-George draped his arm over James's shoulder, jingling the keys in front of his eyes.

"You two wanna crash Daddy's meeting? I don't even have a good one for that," James said, and his brother ran to pull up Bryan's truck, ready to go.

"Sure, you do. Just say you wanted to see 'im," Bryan said as he entered his vehicle.

Not able to think of any more excuses why he couldn't, James climbed in, knowing that his cousin was, in fact, correct about him wanting to see a certain person.

"FINALLY HERE, BOYS, I can't believe we made it. And with time to spare," James said as they approached the entrance to the offices where Charles was having his meeting.

"I can't believe we didn't get a ticket. You're riding in the back if you drive through the city like that again, KG." Bryan shook him.

They walked into the entrance foyer where a young receptionist blinked quickly before smiling and greeting them.

"Good morning. May I help you?" she asked.

"As a matter of fact, that lovely smile of yours already helped to make my day ten times better," James said. He reached out and shook her hand and, before she could take hers back, placed his other hand on top. "James Cain, but you can call me Jimmy." He winked.

The receptionist blushed but recovered quickly. "And how can I help you, Jimmy?"

James released her hand and crossed his arms before leaning on her table. He started to speak but then turned his head down and chuckled. He glanced back at his cousin and then to the receptionist again with an embarrassed expression.

"I'm uh…" James lowered his voice to a whisper. "I'm kinda in a bind and was hoping you can help me out, Miss…?"

"Amanda," she answered.

"Amanda," James repeated. "That name's almost as pretty as you."

"T-Thank you. I'll do whatever I can." Her voice lowered in response to his.

James moistened his lips before making eye contact with her. "Well, ya see, I'm running late for a meeting my daddy, Mr. Charles Cain, is having right now. I didn't wanna be rude by calling him or anything, so me and my family are trying to tiptoe in and hope they don't notice us."

"Oh, well, I'm not sure how I can help." She didn't with his gaze.

"This may be little backward, but you could escort us to the office. I don't mind hanging on your arm."

"I know where the meeting is being held, but Ms. Harvington asked not to be disturbed."

He flexed his shoulder muscles and lowered his voice. "I hear ya, almost as bad as those professors back in school when you were late."

"Absolutely."

"I was hoping to take some time off soon, but missing this meeting is gonna keep me all wrapped up. Bet I won't have any time to meet new people like yourself."

"I-I..."

"Look at me," James said. "You're obviously a million times better at this stuff. I mean, you work, go to school, and still find the time to keep everything perfect." He finished while looking her up and down hungrily.

She shook her head and reached for a slip of paper, then scribbled something quickly on it.

"I hope everything works out." She handed the note to James.

"As long as this is your direct number along with the office line, it will."

James walked away before she could answer.

When they were out of earshot of the receptionist, Bryan whispered in his ear. "One day you're gonna teach me how to do that."

"SO AS YOU can see from our projections and the target segment data that we've collected over the last several months, by allowing our company to purchase *Daddy Cain's* and to market it under the same banner, we can take your brand international. Imagine, small fast-food restaurants all modeled off the kitchen in your factory. *Daddy Cain's* will become a household name that has the potential to become an American standard," Benjamin said proudly.

"And that's in addition to the lump sum for the purchase of your property, Mr. Cain," Clinton added. "It wouldn't be permanent, but as an added incentive, we are authorized to negotiate a certain percentage of royalties that you are due from specific sales."

Charles looked over the business plan and models with interest and nodded. He spoke quietly to his assembly of lawyers and Eugene who was also present.

After an extended silence, he sat all the papers down and stood. "Thank you for your time, gentlemen, but I am afraid I must decline."

"Sir—" Clinton started, but Charles waved a hand at him.

"Do not misunderstand me, son. This is a most generous offer. And you presented it in a manner that has made me feel most welcome, of which I'm quite appreciative of," he said, inclining his head toward Benjamin. "But I do not wish to sell my company. Maybe one day you can try again, once it is no longer in my control. However, at this time, it is, and my answer is final."

Clinton and Benjamin shook Charles's hand. As they turned to leave, Charles wasn't shocked to see who entered.

"Charles. How lovely to see you again," Laura said.

"Laura," Charles replied evenly. "I did not know you would be a part of our discussions today."

"Is that so?" Laura asked coldly. "Well, I suppose I shouldn't be surprised. You never were the best at noticing the important, finer details of any matter."

"Ms. Harvington—"

"Spare me the excuses, Mr. Clinton. I am already aware of what has transpired during this meeting." She pointed at the intercom that was recording the conference. "And while your tactics may have been sound, they ultimately proved untenable. Therefore, it is time I stepped in."

"You are wasting both our time," Charles said in a tone he had never used toward any of his employees. "I have made my decision, and nothing short of the hand of God will change my mind."

Laura strode over to him and defiantly jutted her chin out. She smirked and then turned to take a seat with Clinton and Benjamin.

"You are, of course, correct, however your cooperation is no longer required."

Eugene stepped forward. "Mr. Cain's business is sound. You can introduce as many products to compete as you want, but as you've said, our customers know us and know quality."

"Sound as it may be, you are in no way different from any other company." Laura leaned back in her chair and crossed her legs, speaking in soft but serious tones. "I have already made deals or bought out all of the local shipping companies. Your suppliers as well. Now of course you can shop around, but I have also ensured that the only ones available will triple your overhead at the very least. Times are hard, Charles, and if you start to pass those costs on to your customers, well, you see where this is going."

Charles raised a hand, but Eugene was already making calls to verify her claim. He confirmed with a nod, and Charles started to shake with anger. "I don't know what the hell—"

"Please, Charles, do not embarrass yourself," Laura said with a wicked grin.

"She's right, Daddy, that's what I'm for," James said as he burst into the office. He and Kenneth-George went to their father's side while Bryan brought over some water. "Have you lost your mind, Governess?"

"Jimmy," she said. "You were always such an impudent little boy. Run along now. The grown-ups are talking."

"Let's go," James said while taking his father's hand.

"Yes, run along now, and keep in mind what I said. I shall be along in a few months when your company is so broke that you will not have a pot to piss in or a window to throw it out of," Laura yelled, sounding much less dignified.

CHARLES CAIN AND his entire assembly had just left the conference room where Laura leaned back in her chair, a satisfied look on her face. She rocked lazily back and forth a few times before turning to Benjamin and Clinton.

"That went better than expected," she said.

Neither Benjamin nor Clinton said anything. Several secretaries started to clear the office, and as the last one exited, James came stomping through the door before it closed to stand directly before Laura.

"I don't know what that was all about, but take a good look 'cause after I've said my piece, it's the last time you'll ever see any of us again. We're never selling to you. And we damn sure don't ever want anything to do with you again so stay away from my family," James said.

Laura leaned forward, completely unfazed by what James had said. "Why you are just too precious when you throw a fit. I know that things moved a bit fast for you so I will repeat; I do not need your father's cooperation. One way or another, he will sign the papers."

James turned to leave and, once he was at the door, stopped with his hands resting on the knob. His facial expression changed from serious to the same grin that Laura had come to despise from the early years of instructing him as a child.

"Is there something about all of this that you find amusing?" Laura asked.

"Just thinking about all you'll get done with that old empty factory."

"Once I own *Daddy Cain's,* I assure you that I will make it extremely productive. And making money off of his name will be quite rewarding."

"Is that supposed to bother me? It doesn't. I'll just start over," James said.

"We are finished here." Laura motioned for an aide to contact security. "I suggest you do yourself a favor and learn a little something about business. I will not just own the factory. I will own everything associated with your father's company."

Security had made their way into the office and started to pull James along with them. Almost out of the door, James said, "I guess it's a good thing that the only thing he owns is the building and equipment."

"Wait," Laura shouted. "What did you say?"

"You heard me, Governess. I told you that everything in that factory belongs to my daddy," James said while looking at Benjamin. "But the recipes, brand name, logos, kettles we invented, patented techniques, trade secrets—shoot, everything. That's all me."

"You are lying," Laura said, unable to believe what was happening.

"Sure I am." He laughed and shook the guard off him. "You kept tabs on what Daddy owns because of what little he has to report to Georgia and Uncle Sam, but I'm not locked down like that. I learned to diversify at business school. So go ahead and buy 'im out. I'll just go back to square one and start over. And if you try to use anything I own...whew! Your bosses are gonna be pissed something powerful when they learn how much money you wasted."

Laura's eye twitched as she picked up an object from the table and threw it at James, who had already left. She let out a savage scream of anger at the implications that all her careful planning had been in vain. She could not make James sell, not after her grandiose yet premature victory speech. Everyone was ordered out of the conference room, and even with the door closed, she could be heard in the office.

WHEN BENJAMIN RETURNED to his cubicle, he sat for a moment, trying to process what had happened and then stood and hurried into Clinton's office.

"You wanna tell me what the hell that was?" Benjamin shouted before even entering completely.

"I'm as lost as you are," he said while taking a small flask from his desk. "I've never seen Ms. Harvington like that. It was almost—"

"Vindictive," Benjamin finished for him. "There's no doubt about that." He sighed and sat, rubbing his forehead. "I should go talk to Jimmy."

"For what? What would you say?" Clinton asked. "It's no one's fault. You win some, you lose some."

Benjamin didn't say another word as he left Clinton's office and bolted toward the exit. They were located on one of the upper floors, so he hazarded that he could still catch up to James. Instead of the elevator, he ran down the stairs, taking them multiple steps at a time and even jumping down to lower landings over the rail. When he reached the first floor, he could see James finishing up a conversation with his father and then closing the door on his vehicle.

"Jimmy." Benjamin gasped, winded from his exertion.

Bryan approached, looking angry, but James took them to a nearby street bench and they sat down. "We gotta stop meeting like this." James offered a soft smile.

"It's definitely not a good sign," Benjamin agreed.

Benjamin didn't say any more, so James crossed his arms and waited. "Did you wanna tell me something?"

"That...I don't know what that was in there. I've never held a negotiation like that."

"I know." James sat back and spread his arms along the back of the bench.

"You do?"

"Sure, I do. I saved my daddy's tail back there so the least he could do was be straight with me. He said you and that other guy were pretty much blindsided."

"I still feel bad about the meeting, though," Benjamin said, feeling he should have been more prepared.

James stood up and offered his hand. "Then how's about you come watch me and my family do something that'll make you feel good."

"LET'S SEE SOME hustle," Bryan screamed to the children on the field. As he stood, he spilled popcorn on James while trying to balance his drink.

"Is he always like that?" Benjamin asked while staring at James's excited cousin.

"He takes all sports seriously," James laughed. "Even if it's peewee football."

Benjamin smiled at the fact that an adult could show such passion for a game that was primarily meant to build self-esteem. The young children ran back and forth on the large field as the parents clapped. Off near one of the concession stands, Kenneth-George wore a bright reflective vest, picking up trash, while Charles was off in another part of the complex serving food that his company had donated. This small slice of Southern living almost seemed too good to be true, but for the first time since being in his new location, Benjamin found something he liked.

"You know, we had field meets and block parties like this back home in Chicago," Benjamin said.

"Oh yeah?"

"Yeah. But they weren't nearly this big. I guess it's because the sports complex down here is so large, or you guys have more money...which is odd for such a small town. Either way, Calloway is lucky."

"Luck didn't have anything to do with it. I like being active but didn't wanna stay cooped up at my place in my gym. Had to get on my old man's nerves for almost a whole day before he opened his checkbook for this."

"You poor thing," Benjamin said dryly.

"Walk with me. I need to say hi to some folks," James said as he leapt out of the bleachers.

"Some folks?" Benjamin asked. "It looks like there's almost two hundred people out here."

"And a lot of 'em work for me," James said, slapping his back. "Half the events out here are sponsored by my family, so it's only polite to stop by."

Benjamin just followed as James covered the field of the complex. Along the way, many organizations and clubs showed their appreciation to the junior Cain, and Benjamin began to understand why he was so well known. He was just as famous as he was infamous. As the two made their way toward the end of the field, Benjamin could hear a familiar voice that wasn't visible until he and James made their way through the crowd.

"What do we have here?" Ellsworth said with a pleased grin. "Well, if it isn't the generous Mr. Jimmy Cain himself." With his last words, the group of women he was addressing turned to thank and applaud James.

"Thank you, thank you everyone." James stepped in front of the group and stood next to Ellsworth. "It's real nice to be part of such a good cause. And Elli—Mr. Ferguson here is a fine man to teach you lovely ladies proper self-defense."

Ellsworth didn't seem to have hurt himself too seriously from their last encounter, and Benjamin was glad he was up and about. Despite how happy James had made Ellsworth by greeting him, Benjamin was sure it would all change once Ellsworth noticed he had accompanied James. And then it happened. The two locked gazes, and Ellsworth flashed a display of anger. With his public appearance over, James attempted to leave, but Ellsworth called to him.

"Where're you off to? The ladies were just about to have a good old-fashioned tug of war, and I can use your help to demonstrate the rules."

"I don't think anyone needs help understanding those," James said.

"Maybe you're right. Ladies, let's give Mr. Cain another round of applause. Maybe next time, I'll have someone his size so he won't be scared to get dirty."

With that said, James turned around and headed to the rope. It was in an area that had been saturated with water to form a sloppy mud pit, and the small crowd followed behind them. James put on his glove and picked up one end while Ellsworth did the same at the other. As he spoke of what was not allowed and demonstrated, Benjamin spoke in James's ear.

"He's trying to start something with you again."

"Benji, we've been doing this for about twenty years now. I know how this goes."

Benjamin put up his hands and walked back into the crowd, mumbling under his breath, "No wonder he's about to explode."

WITH ALL OF the instructions given, a student blew the whistle and the rope tightened.

"Hang on, Jimmy, it's no fun unless you do." Ellsworth gained an early lead due to his size.

"Quit running your mouth so much and pull." James slid even farther toward Ellsworth and began to regret his taunt.

As the two opponents struggled against one another, Benjamin took notice of the gathering students and their hushed tones. From the way their lips parted and their hands grasped at their chests, Benjamin knew that they were more interested in the two men than the athletic endeavor. Hand over hand, Ellsworth pulled James closer. In his shirtless track suit, every muscle strained while he reeled in what he wanted to catch.

"Give it up," Ellsworth grunted while maintaining his advantage.

James leaned back but couldn't stop himself from sliding forward. He thought that Ellsworth would tire soon, but he started to take steps backward while pulling. It was then James noticed a depression in the ground behind Ellsworth.

"On a count of three, I will." James smiled at him, causing Ellsworth to pull even harder and to move faster. "One...two...three," he counted and pulled with all his might. His rival had stepped into the divot, and when he tried to regain his footing, James took advantage of his imbalance to pull him face-first into the mud.

"You damn cheat," Ellsworth shouted while the others clapped for James.

"Now don't be sore, Elli," James said while lifting the rope and twirling it lazily in victory.

James took a step forward and almost lost his balance. The rope had bundled around his foot, and he tried to shake it off. Instead of sliding off, though, it became tighter. James followed the braid to see Ellsworth holding the end, and before he could react, he was pulled down into the mud when Ellsworth snatched the braid tight.

"You're gonna pay for that—" James tried to say, but a face full of mud cut him off.

"Come on then," Ellsworth said, standing up.

James shot up and hobbled over to him, moving awkwardly in the mud.

"James, everyone is watching," Benjamin called.

"We sure are, sugar," one of the students said as they all got closer.

JAMES CHARGED AT Ellsworth, but he was ready. James jumped to tackle him, but Ellsworth caught him under his arm and pinned him to the ground. With a tight forearm against his chest, he straddled James with thick viselike thighs that ground him into the mud. Ellsworth enjoyed himself as James struggled to break free, bucking under him while receiving slaps to his head.

"Just tap out already," Ellsworth screamed once again.

His weight was too much for James to overcome. Ellsworth didn't care that James was at a disadvantage in skill level. He was about to demand surrender once again when James brought up a clump of mud to his face, which staggered him. While Ellsworth regained his vision, James knocked him back and moved away, slipping out of his shirt when Ellsworth tried to grab him again.

"Zero to one, Ellie," James said while putting some distance between the two. He crouched down to take off his boots for better footing. Once finished, James stood up straight and wiped the excess mud from his face.

"Now it's getting good." A woman lightly hit Benjamin as they all looked on.

James gave a smirk as he shoved his thumbs in the pockets of his damp jeans. He commanded Ellsworth's attention and that of the crowd when the distinct vee of his lower torso was revealed, allowing everyone to see his lack of undergarments.

Ellsworth wasn't smiling. He ran his hand over his head to slick back the hair from his eyes. He then split his track pants vertically at the buttons for better movement.

"Time to hurt." Ellsworth charged forward, and James matched his speed.

"That's all you had to say," James responded.

When the two were within striking distance of one another, James fell to his knees and below Ellsworth's reach. The mud allowed him to slide behind Ellsworth, and before he could react, James wrapped both arms around his granite stomach to suplex him to the ground. With an advantage James could finally press, he attempted to drive Ellsworth to the ground again but was grabbed by his arm, and Ellsworth pulled himself free. He didn't let go and instead pulled James in close to lift him above his head by a grip around his waist and another on his chest.

"You just don't know when to quit, do you," Ellsworth asked rhetorically.

He tossed James like a rag doll into the mud face-first. Before he could recover, Ellsworth landed on top of him and pulled his arm behind his back.

"Any time now would be good!" He breathed hard into James's ear. Ellsworth had his face so close that his nose touched James's skin and transferred a small drop of sweat to run down James's face.

"Ellie? Is that you I feel?" James suddenly asked while trying to catch his breath. Ellsworth lifted his head from James's neck, but he didn't get up. "I think it is."

Ellsworth was momentarily embarrassed and released his grip on James's arm. James turned over on his back, and the movement caused Ellsworth to grab him by both his wrists and pin them to the ground above his head.

"You talk too damn much, but you're not going anywhere until I say so," Ellsworth said, becoming angrier.

"It is you," James said finally. "You're poking me, Ellie..."

"Shut up!"

"I said you're poking me there, Ellie," James continued taunting. "Damn, and you're coming to bat with a Louisville Slugger." He sounded surprisingly impressed.

"I said shut your trap," Ellsworth yelled, bringing James's arms into the air and slamming them down without near the strength he had displayed earlier.

"That can't be too comfy. Lemme help you out." James spread his legs slightly and brought up a knee. Ellsworth couldn't help but fall in closer, with his hands still restraining James's wrists. "How's that?"

"T-That won't work," Ellsworth stammered.

James started to move his hips toward Ellsworth in slow motions. In the position he was in, Ellsworth couldn't support himself and was unable to prevent his full weight from falling onto James. Their bare stomachs met, causing Ellsworth to take a sharp breath in. He noticed too late, but with James still beneath him, he watched as James freed his arms, and his body shuddered when he felt a fingernail tracing the outline of his back. Moving lower with each passing second.

"Is this how you fight?" Ellsworth asked, his voice low and raspy.

"I don't wanna fight you," James said as his hand found Ellsworth's hips and pulled him in. "Is that why you've been acting crazy lately? Has it been that long for you?"

"Are you an idiot?" Ellsworth asked, completely serious for a moment.

James laughed. "S'okay." James now had his other hand and placed it on Ellsworth's face. His thumb traced a small outline of his lips before moving to the back of his neck as he tried to pull him in.

"Lemme go. I don't wanna do this with you anymore." Ellsworth almost pleaded. He was beet red and still angry but no longer at James.

"C'mon now, bud. It's just me," James said while slowly pulling him down to his own face. Ellsworth continued to struggle but couldn't help but comply. "Jimmy Cain, remember? Daddy Cain Jr."

"You're a brat is what you are."

"Don't I know it," James said with their faces only inches apart. "So hows about it? How's about you teach me a lesson. I can buy anything I want, but I gotta ask for you. Are you gonna make a man out of me? Make me a real boy?"

Ellsworth stopped all protest and grabbed the sides of James's face, holding him. His nostrils flared as his breath escaped his mouth.

Shaking violently with frustration, he ground into James, hard. "You're gonna beg for it by the time I'm done with you," he hissed.

Ellsworth rolled the two over so that he was underneath. He sat up and started to bring his opponent in when James rolled backward out of his embrace. James continued until he was several paces away and then stood up.

"Why do guys always have to say something and mess it all up? Too much, Ellie, that almost got weird." He turned his back from a trembling Ellsworth and walked into the crowd of women who made a path for him. "And that, ladies, is how you properly redirect momentum."

BENJAMIN WAS SHOCKED as the crowd cheered and clapped for James. He continued to walk away from them all, so Benjamin ran to catch up.

"You're evil." He laughed. "How can you intentionally do that to another guy?"

"Do what? It's just Ellie. We play chicken like that all the time. Guess he won this time, though," he said. "Besides, I got better things to do. You up to anything tonight?"

"Have you been waiting all day to ask that?" Benjamin asked, beginning to regret joining him.

James sighed. "I don't know what you folks call it where you're from, but I was just asking you on a date. Isn't that how you get to know someone? You do date, don't you?"

"Considering everything that has happened today, I don't think that's a good idea."

"So I'll pick you up tonight at nine?" James asked.

"No, you won't," Benjamin said, agitated that James had once again disregarded what he said.

Instead of another pass, James collected some of the smooth mud from his body and threw it onto Benjamin's shirt.

Benjamin could barely comprehend what was happening but found enough of himself to ask, "Why?"

"Because you're gonna go home and get ready, but I want you thinking about me as much as I have about you."

"You think I'm going now?" he asked, upset.

"Are you really going to let me get away with that?" James winked at him and ran off.

Chapter Six

"I DON'T THINK he's gonna come, Jimmy," Bryan said.

"I'm not giving up just yet," James said while dialing Benjamin's number once again.

James fidgeted with anxiety over the prospect that Bryan was right. The two stood on the sidewalk in front of Benjamin's apartment, ready to leave for his farm, but James had insisted on bringing his new courtship along. As he waited for James to give up his pursuit, Bryan noticed how beautiful the city's downtown area looked at night. The sun had just set, but a lingering amber smoldered in the clouds to the west. It blanketed the district with a soft glow as more vendors and street entertainers drew in tourists and the scent of fried dough and smoked meats filled the air. The moment was nice, but he still felt out of place.

"C'mon, even KG's getting restless," Bryan said while waving for his cousin to stop blaring the horn of his truck.

James still wasn't convinced. "I know, but I had a really good feeling about tonight."

"Sure you did, Romeo. I'm guessing he didn't tell you his room number?"

"Actually, that's on me. I made 'im mad before I asked."

"Then how did you plan on meeting up?" Bryan asked.

"I hadn't gotten that far." James walked toward the entrance to the building. "But I just got an idea."

BENJAMIN ENTERED HIS loft and threw the laundry he had just picked up over a nearby chair. He didn't feel like taking the time to put it away because of his mental exhaustion from the day's earlier events. He sank onto his couch, and just as he started to relax, his room phone rang.

"Hello, this is Mr. Rei."

"Good evening, sir. This is the front desk. I'm afraid there's an urgent matter we need to resolve regarding a payment issue for your suite."

"Payment issue?" Benjamin asked, confused. "No there must be some sort of mistake. I'm on a company account. If you call—"

"I apologize for not being more specific, sir, I meant the amenities and services you selected when you checked in. We've dealt with this before as your unit houses many temporary residents. They also were from out of state, and because of the new security features added to most bank and credit cards, we have difficulty authorizing payments over a certain amount without multiple verification steps."

"I understand but wait—how much are you trying to charge?" he asked.

When Benjamin heard the amount, he dropped the phone. No longer feeling tired, he hurried down to the lobby and toward the front desk. As he approached, a sinking feeling filled him when he spied the backs of three familiar men.

"Jimmy?"

James turned around and waved to him. "There you are. Ready to go?"

Benjamin walked past James and spoke to the concierge at the desk.

"I need to clear up some outrageous charges they are trying to make to—"

"That was Jimmy," Bryan said.

"And just when I was about to find out where he lived. Thanks cousin."

"Wait. So there's nothing wrong with my account?" Benjamin asked the concierge. "I want to see the manager. Now!"

After a few minutes passed, the manager arrived. Benjamin pointed and said to James, "Tell him."

"Tell him what?"

"About how you had the front desk say there was something wrong with my account when there wasn't!" Benjamin explained. "Do you even know how many laws you've broken? How did you even convince him to do that?"

"Jimmy?" the manager asked. "Did you really do that?"

"Wait. You two know one another?" Benjamin asked.

"Sure we do." James cupped the back of the manager's neck and, after a few soft pats, started to stroke his jaw with his thumb. "You never called me back."

"I-I didn't think you were serious about that," he said while blushing slightly.

"If I don't mean it, then I don't say it."

James moved his hand down from his neck and along his arm. When their hand's met, James took the other man's into his own and started to trace his fingers around. As angry as he was, Benjamin still took note of how sincere James was being with a former one-night stand. Again his ire returned, because James was again showing him an aspect of his personality that Benjamin liked.

"Excuse me, I'm sorry to interrupt...whatever this is, but are you going to do something?" Benjamin asked the manager. "Actually, I'm not sorry." He crossed his arms.

"He's right. I'm going to have to tell the powers that be and get a police report," the manager responded.

"For what? I was the one who had all your services upgraded, then decided to make it all complimentary. But it's a little hard to tell you when you don't answer your phone. My man at the front desk must've called while I was still trying to get ahold of you. He's really on top of his game with how fast he is," James said while smiling harder at Benjamin.

"How could you do any of that? Do you suddenly own the place?"

James raised an eyebrow.

"No... No!" Benjamin threw his head back and placed his palms over his eyes.

"Whoa, don't go all sideways on me now. If it makes you feel better, I don't own it—my daddy does. I just also happen to have access to everything he does. Including the guest list."

"Wait, then why didn't you just look up his room number?" Bryan asked.

Benjamin didn't say another word as he walked past everyone, before James could answer. He was almost to the elevator when James ran in front of him to block his path.

"Where are you headed off to?"

"To bed," Benjamin said.

"But the night's still young."

James was expecting another clipped response, but instead Benjamin grabbed him about his waist and, with no effort, lifted him like he was on a cheerleading team and set him aside.

"Benji, I swear." James clapped his hands.

"Go away please."

"But what about our date?" James asked seriously.

"Date?" Benjamin whirled on him. "You intentionally dirtied my clothes, blew up my phone like a crazy ex-boyfriend, and borderline broke privacy laws, all in an attempt to bludgeon your way into a date, and for what? Why?"

"Why what?" James asked calmly.

Benjamin took a deep, slow breath and held his hands out in front of him. "Why are you acting like this? Why are you doing these insane things?"

James just shrugged and slapped Benjamin on a strained bicep. Shaking his hand as if it hurt but still smiling, he said, "Didn't you hear me earlier? I mean what I say. And I told you, I like you."

"You're saying that you're acting like an idiot because you like me?" Benjamin asked, completely floored by his answer.

"If you think I'm lying, just ask every other boy in history what they got up to for someone they liked."

James took both of Benjamin's hands into his own. He leaned back, and after a small pause, Benjamin allowed himself to be pulled forward.

"Please," James asked while leading him to his cousin's truck. "I promise you'll have fun."

"Jimmy..." Benjamin said, but nothing else came out.

"Ah, there it is. You called me 'Jimmy' again, so you're not mad anymore."

"Who says I'm not?"

"All right, I can crawl first." James released his hands and ran over to open the door of the vehicle for Benjamin. "So lemme show you a good time, away from the city. Unless that laundry is more fun?"

"HANG ON TO your seat." James said and grabbed Benjamin tightly.

"Why? What's going on?" Benjamin asked. He turned to Bryan, who was driving, and then followed his gaze to the large creek they were approaching.

"Don't you worry none, city boy," Bryan said calmly. "We usually make the jump."

"I'm going to die," Benjamin said softly to himself.

He was neither disappointed nor regretful, simply astonished. As he sat in the passenger seat of Bryan's truck, gripping the strap that crossed over his torso, scenery sped toward the windshield. They were sailing, flying through the air, but gravity had reclaimed them and the vehicle was approaching at an unsightly angle.

The headlights only distorted Benjamin's perception more, providing the only illumination under the canopy of trees on the dark back roads that James had insisted they travel. Both James and Bryan were wailing, but Benjamin could only hear his own breathing, and his stomach felt like it was rising out of his body from the momentum just as the vehicle made contact with the ground.

"Hot damn, I saw sparks from that one," James said to Bryan.

"Shoot, if your new friend wasn't with us we probably would've took off." Bryan laughed while taking a long drink from a large insulated and covered mug. When he finally pulled it away from his mouth, he made a loud, painful noise and shook his head. "Man, that's cold."

"Is that—?"

"Sure is—peach pop. Made by the one and only Miss Sissy. She makes it into a syrup I even sell at the plant." James took the cup and offered it to him.

Benjamin was still too shocked from Bryan intentionally jumping his truck over a small creek at an abandoned bridge. He looked at the cup, which James was nudging toward him, and after calming his nerves, released one hand gripping his seat belt to take a small sip.

"So?"

"I-It's amazing..." Benjamin said, sounding less nervous as he took another gulp almost as big as Bryan's. "I can't believe I turned this down when Miss Sissy offered me one. Do you think she's interested in.... No—wrong time."

"Good man. Just wait until we get to my place. I just made some shine that'll make that taste better than Daddy Cain's Big sauce," Bryan said to Benjamin.

Before Benjamin could protest, Kenneth-George shot past the three of them in James's car. He was traveling faster than they were, something that Benjamin was no longer surprised about. Still, he thought that the low light and brush would have at least made the young boy more cautious.

James stood up and out of the sunroof. "Look at that boy go. Hey, Benji, get up here." When he didn't move, James ducked his head below and offered a hand. "Think what you want, but I can't let anything bad happen to you."

"I..." Benjamin didn't have an excuse this time.

"You know, if you're scared, just say so. I don't judge. I just didn't figure you'd be so...*plain.*"

Benjamin let go of the seat belt and set the drink down. Even in the nonexistent sunlight, he could still see the glint of taunting in James's eyes. Those incredibly green eyes. And then he saw it. It started as a small condescending huff but finished to form a ruby grin on James's face.

With that small smile, Benjamin realized that James was not acting. How many times had he taken his many conquests on such trips? How many of the same lines had he used over and over? And they worked. Not because it was a game or hustle to him, but because James Warren Cain really was an entitled rich kid who had been handed the keys to his father's business and got to slack off with his family all day.

He found ways to entertain himself, and his company. And despite all his efforts, Benjamin kept resisting. He knew this, and knew that James would continue unless he was told to stop or lost interest. *Plain* was the word that James had used, but deep down, Benjamin knew he was only being nice and not saying the one word that he actually meant. A dreaded word that he never wanted to be accused of during a date. Boring. And in that instant, Benjamin decided to throw caution to the wind, which was rapidly passing them by.

"Move over, Cletus," Benjamin said as he stood up through the roof. His larger size pushing James back as he faced him.

"Dang it, Jimmy, get your rump outta my face," Bryan screamed from below but was silenced by a soft hind kick from his cousin.

"Was that a joke?" James asked while running a hand along his neck.

"Isn't that what you're supposed to do on a date?" He smiled.

"Well, shoot, you just got all kinds of comfortable, didn't you?"

"Not comfortable," Benjamin said, leaning back toward the passenger side while he rested his arms wide about the roof of the truck. "I'm just trying to relax a bit."

"I guess we did overdo it earlier." James knelt down into the cabin to speak to Bryan, and as he stood back up, the truck slowed until its speed was practically a crawl.

"You coming?" James reached for one of the handrails and pulled himself out of the sunroof. He moved carefully until he hopped down into the bed of the truck, then reached out his hands for Benjamin. Reluctantly, Benjamin took his hand to steady himself as he did the same and joined James in the bed.

"There now. That wasn't too bad, was it?"

Benjamin almost lost his balance as Bryan began to accelerate once again, so he sat down in the bed and James joined him, both leaning their backs against the cabin.

"I'm not sure if this is better. Is he planning on jumping anymore creeks?"

James laughed. "Nah, I told 'im to take it easy. Besides, I wanted to give you the chance to take it all in."

"Take what in?"

"This, all of this." James said while stretching his arms to the sky. "Look around you, Benji. Breathe it in. I know they don't have the wild open yonder up there in Chicago."

Benjamin took in a deep breath and exhaled slowly. James was right that the open farmland and warm air of southern Georgia was much different than his hometown. He had been told that they were headed toward a more rural county and could appreciate the charm of being so far removed from it all.

"There's so much green around here," Benjamin said.

"Oh, so you guys don't have trees where you're from?" James teased.

"I meant that it doesn't look anything like this up there. Outside of the city, there are plenty of farms and plains, but it gets a little dreary and gray when the winter comes. It's nowhere near this vibrant."

"That's as good a way to put it as any."

James sat forward and removed his shirt. He tied a lopsided knot with the sleeves about his waist, then folded his hands behind his head.

"You should give this a shot, see how it feels," James said.

"I'm good"

"So you're done with relaxing then?"

Benjamin grimaced slightly but stood up on his knees. It was hard for him to maintain his balance, so James kneeled as well and placed his hands on Benjamin's shoulders to steady him.

"Don't worry. I got ya," James said.

Benjamin unbuttoned his own shirt but kept it on. The wind whipped around his body before the soft fabric of his dark shirt captured a gust, sending the back of the shirt billowing upward and to his side with a loud flap.

"Not bad," Benjamin said while brushing a licorice strand of hair from his eyes that the wind had loosened. "This does feel nice."

"If it feels half as good as you look, then I'm jealous," James said.

"Jeez." Benjamin burst out laughing. "You really don't stop, do you?"

"What can I say? I was raised to tell no lies."

Benjamin reached up and moved James's hands down from his shoulders to his waist. He slipped his shirt off and brought it to his waist as well, then waited.

"A little help," Benjamin said.

James began to tie the shirt around his waist. He was taking his time, but Benjamin didn't mind, as James refrained from touching him inappropriately. When he was done, James continued to stare at the knot.

"My eyes are up here, hound dog." Benjamin laughed. James glanced up but not into his eyes. "Up here," Benjamin repeated and crossed his arms over his chest.

"I needed that," James said. "Hey, do me a favor and don't move."

"Why?"

"Just stay still."

James reached toward Benjamin's right ear and ran his hand through his hair. He wasn't sure why until James sat back down while cradling something in his hand.

"You think it's a sign?" James asked.

Benjamin peered into James's palm to see a small blinking light that was revealed to be an insect upon closer inspection.

"Oh no damn way," Benjamin said, surprised.

"Take another look around."

The sun was setting, and along the road were small flashes filling the evening sky.

"This is incredible," Benjamin said.

"I always loved this part of coming to visit my cousin. I'm glad you gave me the chance to share it with you."

Benjamin wrapped an arm around James's shoulder, who appeared surprised by the gesture. "Maybe it is a sign."

BRYAN CAIN'S FARM was alive. That was the only way Benjamin could describe the energy and atmosphere of the guests who had joined them this evening. James and Bryan led the way as Benjamin entered a barn where the majority of the festivities were being held. On his way in, he passed many people, all of whom were occupied in their own forms of entertainment. Several teams encircled a small pool and cheered on the oil wrestlers flailing about. Another group bounced small plastic balls into a cup, determining who had to drink the contents. Between the displays of who had the best motorcycle, the small firing range where glass bottles were shot at with pellet guns, and even a bath where people were bobbing for fruit in what looked like a dark spirit, Benjamin didn't know where to start.

Various forms of lighting had been set up around the area, allowing everyone to safely navigate the festivities, and in some cases, the larger floodlights mounted on the trucks added to the illumination. But inside the barn, it was a different story. From the outside, it looked like any farm building, but inside Bryan had turned it into his own speakeasy.

The old wood smelled of bourbon, and the lights had been intentionally lowered to that of soft candles. Everyone inside found a comfortable spot to call their own between the multiple chairs, booths, and stools that had been collected or even brought to the party. When they reached the wooden bar, Bryan slid behind it and started to make them drinks.

"Try this on for size, Benji," Bryan said while pouring three shots. Before Benjamin could pick up the small glass, he also popped the tops off of three beers.

"Are you trying to get me drunk tonight?" Benjamin asked James.

"Drink first, and I just might answer that," James said and lifted his glass.

The two other men did the same, and in a quick gulp, they swallowed the clear liquid.

"God," Benjamin hacked out. His eyes were watering while he struggled to keep his stomach contents down. "What was that? Rubbing alcohol? I think I can run my car off that stuff."

"Heck no, we make it from grains," Bryan said as if Benjamin was being ridiculous.

"We sure do, so I guess you're right. It might get you a few miles down the road." James laughed and rubbed Benjamin's back.

Benjamin continued catching his breath through blurry vision and a wide smile. He sat his glass down in front of Bryan for another drink, and after a small reluctant look to James, his cousin filled the shot. Benjamin picked it up and inclined his head to drink again, but Kenneth-George dashed behind him and grabbed the potent spirit.

"I swear, KG, you'd better not take one sip," James said.

Kenneth-George made a dismissive sound that James didn't seem to like.

"I'm not playing around with you."

Kenneth-George just rolled his eyes, but James was already moving. He pushed Kenneth-George back hard, and when he was sufficiently unbalanced, James wrapped both of his arms around him from behind.

"Quit all that fussing. I said no!"

Kenneth-George struggled, but his brother was much stronger, so he started to kick and thrash about.

"Excuse us, Benji, KG here needs some brotherly love." He squeezed tightly. "Keep 'im company will you, cousin?"

James dragged his little brother out of the barn, kicking and cursing the entire way. When they were out of sight, Benjamin turned to Bryan and nervously asked, "So?"

"So what?" Bryan asked, feigning innocence.

"Well, are we going to do this?" Benjamin asked coolly.

"I don't reckon I know what you mean, *Benji*," Bryan said.

"That—the way you keep speaking to me. I would swear you are angry, but I haven't done anything." Benjamin remained calm. He stood from his stool and walked behind the bar with Bryan. He gestured with his hand, and Bryan took the seat Benjamin had been occupying. "Is there something I should know?" He picked up a bottle to fill their shot glasses.

Bryan drained the glass with a loud gulp before Benjamin sat down the bottle. "You don't have to know anything, boy," he snapped. "That there is my cousin, and there ain't anything I won't do for him. It doesn't matter what you know because nothing's gonna change that."

"Look, I realize we got off to a shaky start, but I'm trying to extend an olive branch," Benjamin replied diplomatically.

"You really think you're three-quarter slick, huh?"

"What?" Benjamin asked through a small laugh. "Look, I honestly don't know what any of that means."

"The deal that you and Governess put together went belly-up, and you're telling me that you're giving Jimmy the time of day just because he finally won you over?" Bryan accused.

"Listen..." Benjamin started with a smile. He could see the same noble traits in Bryan that he did in James. "I don't think won is the word, but Jimmy...he's nice, and like you said, the acquisitions deal isn't happening so I'll be gone soon."

"Then why're you here?"

"Because I was invited, aggressively so." Benjamin shook his head. "I don't have much time left, so it's now or never."

Bryan stood up from the stool and looked Benjamin in his eyes. He took off his hat and frowned at what was just suggested.

"So after all this, now you're okay getting laid by Jimmy?"

"You say that like it's a bad thing." Benjamin raised an eyebrow. "And besides, what makes you think I'm the one that'll be lying down?" He downed the contents of his glass.

Bryan didn't break his gaze. After several seconds, he reached out and shook Benjamin's hand much to Benjamin's delight. He would now have to hope that Kenneth-George wouldn't be as protective, yet somewhere deep down he knew these hurdles would continue to pop up. Bryan freshened their drinks, and gestured for Benjamin to follow him to the rear of his barn where a few pool tables were set up. They weren't about to start a game however, as Bryan walked to a table with several young women around it.

"Can I get you ladies anything?" Bryan asked.

"No. Thank you, though," one of their group answered. Of the four, she looked to be the most in control of her faculties.

"How about a drink then? This is my farm, so it's the least I can do for such pretty strangers." Bryan appeared to be trying to coax more than a sentence from them.

"We already have drinks, but maybe a little later," another woman answered. She glanced at Benjamin and met his eyes. He offered a soft smile and shake of his head to discourage her. She whispered something to another friend, which he couldn't hear, but they all smiled politely at him.

Bryan could take a hint, and after turning around to go outside was surprised to see James walking back in with Kenneth-George. His younger cousin looked crestfallen and slightly bruised but whatever he and James had discussed seemed to be completely understood.

"Sorry about that, fellas. Isn't that right?" James asked his brother who only huffed and stalked off toward the food tables.

"You know what, Jimmy Cain," Benjamin said while walking toward him. He sat down his drink and hooked a finger into the top portion of James's pants to pull him in close. "I think I wanna dance with you."

"Someone kick a jukebox, now," James yelled to the room.

"Oh my gosh, you're James Cain," one of the women said.

Benjamin brought his chin to his chest and laughed as James corrected her.

"It's Jimmy," he said forcefully. "And as pretty as you are, little miss, I'm kinda busy, so if you'd be so kind as to let me and Mr. Rei here have us our moment...I'm sure my cousin, Bryan can see to you."

"I'm sure he can," she said while grabbing Bryan's arm.

James only smiled but was pulled aside almost instantly. Benjamin pointed to one of the speakers mounted on a wall in the corner and no sooner than he did, the music started to play.

"Time to cut a rug," James yelled. He turned, dragging Benjamin in tow only to run into the broad chest of the last person Benjamin was expecting to see.

"JIMMY," ELLSWORTH YELLED and grabbed him by the shoulders. "I—"

"No." James cut him off.

"W-What the Sam Hill do you mean, no?"

"I mean no," James said and slapped Ellsworth's hands off of him. "Whatever it is, I don't care."

"You know damn well what *it* is. And you can't even give me enough courtesy to take your licks like a man."

"Goodbye." James started to walk past with Benjamin.

With James's back to Ellsworth, he never saw him lash out to grab his arm. The grip that he held surprised James, not just because of how fast he took hold but also because it actually hurt. James pulled away, and Ellsworth turned around, tightening his grip even more, which caused James to let out a small grunt of discomfort. Benjamin reacted instantly to the sound and grabbed Ellsworth by the arm that held James.

"This isn't any of your business, city boy," Ellsworth spat.

"Let him go, or I'm calling the police, but not before I hurt you," Benjamin threatened.

Ellsworth released James and turned his full attention to Benjamin. The two men towered over most of the people at the gathering, and in such agitated states, these behemoths practically looked as if they would bring down the entire building. Not at all concerned for his safety, James stepped between the two.

"He's not worth it," James tried to reason. "He can puff up all he wants, but he doesn't fight dirty. Right, Ellie?" James turned to face him. "Or are you gonna beat up on a man who won't fight back?"

Ellsworth walked up to James, but before he could show him how accurate his hypothesis was, another person spoke and grabbed Ellsworth's hand.

"He's right, Ellsworth. We both know Jimmy isn't much without his daddy's money behind him."

"Maynard?" James yelled. "All right, whatever the heck this is has been a hoot, but my guy is waiting on me."

"So he is a shiny new toy?" Maynard laughed dismissively as he took up a position on Ellsworth's arm.

"Better than being a rebound," Benjamin shot back.

They all became tense once again until Bryan interrupted, "Look, Ellie...Ellsworth, I know you and Jimmy have been going at it since kindergarten, and I don't care. You crashed my party, but now it's time to leave."

"And what if we're not ready to leave?" Maynard asked.

Everyone within earshot laughed at his question. Bryan and James didn't give it another thought, and even Ellsworth seemed taken aback at the question.

"Maynard, you never really lived down here so I won't mince words. That's how people get shot," Bryan finished while reaching behind him.

"Just leave us alone," James said while turning from them.

He and Benjamin were only a few feet away when Ellsworth cried out.

"This isn't over yet, *Jungle Jim*," Ellsworth said.

James immediately became enraged. He wouldn't show it now in front of Benjamin, and didn't want to cause an incident at Bryan's farm, but there was no way he could let Ellsworth call him that without ramifications.

"Do you like having egg on your face? 'Cause that's what's about to happen," James shouted.

"There's that bass in your voice I wanted to hear," Ellsworth mocked him. "You ready to get your guns up?"

Instead of answering him, James walked toward the exit with Benjamin trailing behind. Everyone inside followed them out, and as the crowd gathered, James yelled loud enough for everyone to hear.

"You got some dang nerve," James snapped. "Ruining everyone's good time."

"Why are you still talking?" Ellsworth asked while taking off his shirt.

"You know we can't fight each other, but let's make this real simple. You and me race! One on one around the old horse trail off the highway. Loser gets ghost, so the winner can enjoy these here lovely festivities that Cousin Bryan has provided."

Ellsworth didn't say a word. He walked past James with his arm around Maynard's shoulder, and they both dove into his 1969 Charger. The onyx black coat of paint reflected the moonlight perfectly as it shuddered to start. Although James would never admit it, the sleek white stripes on its side and massive blower on the hood did impress him.

"Do you really think that death trap you call a truck can keep up with us?" Maynard shouted while leaning out of the window over Ellsworth revving his engine.

James just smiled, and before Maynard could speak again, Kenneth-George blew past only inches away from his face in James's car. He didn't show off his driving skills this time, and only did one circle around James before bringing the white 1969 Shelby GT-500 to a halt in front of him.

"You wanna come again with that?" James asked Maynard.

The two drivers staged their vehicles. Many of the guests there climbed onto the roof of Bryan's barn in order to see the racers once they reached the road. The trail was also visible, but because of the trees, certain parts remained obstructed. Bryan stood in front of the racers to signal the start. He was accompanied by the woman who had now reconsidered her opinion of him from earlier.

"Jimmy," Benjamin said, opening the door and sitting in the passenger seat. "Are we really going through with this?"

"We?" James asked. "I'm not casing on you, but are you sure about this?"

"No," he said honestly. "But since day one, Ellsworth has been bothering us, and it's gotten old.... Actually, have you noticed that his timing is always perfect to interrupt us whenever we—"

"Not the time." James smiled. "I actually gotta concentrate for this one."

They both went silent and looked straight ahead. The car vibrated as James revved his own engine. Bryan had his arms up and counted down from ten, taking down one of his fingers with each second. Benjamin knew it wasn't the time, but still couldn't help himself from commenting on his current location.

"You know, if I would've known that you drive this beast, then you probably could've gotten me in your office that day."

"Five... Four... Three..."

James just smirked. "If I was that shallow, don't you think I would've just shown you my house or bank account?"

"Two... One..."

"Noted." Benjamin smiled back.

"Go."

The two cars took off, burned out with an unnecessary amount of smoke and debris. It took a moment to steady their courses, but the paths straightened out as James and Ellsworth left the confines of Bryan's farm and hit the highway. Ellsworth made it first, and drove in the wrong direction on the left lane as James stayed with him in the right. With his eyes on the road, James could still see Maynard making obscene gestures at him in his peripheral vision.

"Hold on," James yelled as the two cars made a sharp left turn onto the trail. James's Mustang drifted slightly from the wide arc of the turn in order not to lose speed.

"Give it up, Jimmy. It's not the car. It's the driver!"

"Wait, was that Ellsworth?" Benjamin asked while looking around the car.

"The CB. Turn it up and get on the mic," James said, nodding to the radio.

Benjamin did as instructed. "What do I say?"

"Anything! Just think of something to throw his game off," James said.

Benjamin keyed the mic. *"Uh...your parents are gonna be thankful it's a closed casket funeral when we scrape your pink smears off—"*

"Whoa! That got violent quick," James said, shocked. "Should I be worried?"

"What do you want from me? Why do you even have these in your cars? It's not like you guys are truckers."

"How else can we talk when we street race?" James asked.

"You ask that like it's normal!"

James looked over at Ellsworth who stole a glance before pulling forward.

James did the same but kept up with the other car only enough so that it couldn't overtake him completely. Driving down a straight and narrow stretch, it was clear why. As they came to the end of the road, it split in two, and Ellsworth had no choice but to go left, so he took the path.

"No," James shouted as he skidded to a stop at the fork.

"What is it?" Benjamin asked, concerned more about the race. "He's winning."

"I wish he was," James said as he took off after Ellsworth. "That trail is dangerous."

"What?"

"I could've ate that piece of crap Charger up for breakfast, lunch, and dinner with old Shelby here. I wanted him to think I was forcing him left so he would cut me off and go right."

"So what now?" Benjamin asked.

James took off again at an incredible speed. Each gear shift, each brake was ingrained into his muscle memory.

"Now I make sure he doesn't wind up in a ditch," James answered.

Not even a minute later, Ellsworth came into view. He was still driving fast, only not nearly as reckless. James tried calling them on the radio and, when he received no response, honked the horn, which it seemed was going be ignored as well. He leaned out of the window to call to Ellsworth, and a foam cup was thrown in his face.

"Peach soda... Oh that bastard," James yelled.

Not wasting any more time, James drove faster. Ellsworth weaved back and forth to block their path, but not fast enough. James shot past him and, with nothing in his way, took off. He had at least a thirty-second lead on Ellsworth, and when they reached another split in the road, James took it.

"I can see the highway from here," Benjamin said, looking at a break in the trees.

James didn't say anything and, instead, stopped his car. He backed it up against a fallen tree and turned off his vehicle but left his lights on.

"James?"

Ellsworth had finally made it down the path but stopped. He saw James trying to restart his vehicle, but from his vantage point, it looked like an obvious stall. Ellsworth also saw the highway, but couldn't safely navigate around James and the blockade his car had made.

"See you at the finish line, Jimmy." Ellsworth laughed and turned around to follow his original path.

Benjamin stared at James, who remained silent. After a minute, he expertly started his vehicle and drove back to his cousin's farm. It was a very awkward moment. As he pulled back up to the starting point, multiple people were congratulating Ellsworth as he brought Maynard in by his waist. The two men shared many celebratory kisses as they were sprayed with beers. This only stopped once James walked up.

"A deal's a deal," Ellsworth said smugly.

Instead of saying anything, James extended his hand. "Sure is, and the best man won."

"Jimmy Cain being gracious, now this is a surprise!" Maynard laughed, but he was the only one.

Ellsworth's triumphant grin turned into a scowl. He slapped James's hand away, which caused many people to gasp. Maynard tried to calm him, but Ellsworth wouldn't be slowed by anyone as he jumped into his car and sped off. James was walking back to his own car when Benjamin stopped him.

"Where are you going?"

"Nowhere, anywhere," James answered him weakly. "I'm a man of my word."

"I thought we were on a date?"

"You're not pissed that I ruined the night by whipping it out with Ellie? And that I lost on top of all that?"

"Do you think I'm that shallow?" Benjamin asked. James lightened so he added, "How about you take me nowhere, fast."

JAMES STEPPED OUT of his vehicle with a bottle and walked. He didn't say anything to Benjamin, who followed behind. They passed the fallen tree that James had backed his car up to and, after a few feet, came to a road block.

"What is this?" Benjamin asked as they passed the barrier.

"Something nice, just wait."

The two continued on, then broke through the brush to an old creek. The smell of moss filled the air and the low fog chilled them while rolling in from the water. James sat down at the bank and took off his shoes to let the water dance around his toes as he drank.

"You knew..." Benjamin said.

James took a long swig and handed the bottle to him.

"Yeah, I did," James confessed when Benjamin sat down.

"But... I mean, how?"

"Me and Ellie grew up in Calloway. He doesn't know these back roads like us Cains. Heck, we still come up here sometimes and sleep over at Bryan's."

"And if he would have seen the highway or that Maynard person said something, they could've run right off into this creek," Benjamin said.

"If they made it through the trees first," James said grimly.

The two men drank in silence for a while with James ingesting at a much faster rate. Benjamin didn't say anything, until James could barely hold his head up.

"Doesn't take much, does it, huh?" Benjamin asked. "I didn't think you would be a lightweight."

"I find other ways to have a good time," James hiccupped out.

"Like with that Maynard guy?"

"Don't!" James shoved him lightly. "The two of us went to business school together over at Georgia State and got close after one night of partying too hard. Thing is, though, he and I fell out. Hard."

"Oh, this'll be good, he's your ex?" Benjamin asked, not at all threatened.

"Kinda." James took another long drink and lay back. "Nah, his daddy and mine are old friends, but they moved up North when he was born. I never saw him too much except when his family would come down here for whatever reason. At school, though, I tried to be his... I don't know," James mumbled as he started to drift.

When Benjamin was satisfied James couldn't put up a fight, he took away the bottle. There was something interesting, yet oddly confounding about James's actions tonight. Protecting someone from harm was easy to admire, but doing it in the face of such taunts and jeers took control. Benjamin considered that he had grossly misjudged James and decided then to be just as sincere.

The sounds of frogs croaking and crickets chirping filled the evening air. Benjamin enjoyed the panorama as he gazed up at the full moon. Birds would infrequently cross his line of sight, but that only added to the moment. He was about to get up and wake James, but he looked too peaceful under the moonlight. Benjamin smiled, but when James began to shiver, he lay down next to him and pulled James closer.

"Hmm... Benji?" James asked groggily through his haze.

"Shhh," Benjamin calmed him down. "Nowhere fast."

James closed his eyes and rested his head on Benjamin's chest. Sleep finally took James, and Benjamin offered a soft lingering press of lips on his forehead.

Chapter Seven

"HERE WE ARE," James said after he parked his car in front of Benjamin's building.

"Yeah, so here we are..."

Sometime during his nap earlier that morning, Benjamin had taken them back to Bryan's farm. With most of his guests gone, Bryan had carried his cousin to a secluded room to let him rest while he, Benjamin, Kenneth-George, and a few stragglers helped to clean up. It didn't take long, but with nothing to do the next day, Benjamin stayed up a bit with Bryan and Kenneth-George to try to get to know them better. They had done this in the barn, so didn't notice that the sun was up until James came in through the wide doors.

James stepped out of his car and walked around to open the passenger door. When a wobbling Benjamin stepped out, James steadied Benjamin with hands on his waist and just under his arm so that he wouldn't fall. The two froze in place and took a few seconds to remember the night they had enjoyed together. The ride back had been pleasantly quiet, but with the opportunity in front of him, Benjamin saw no need to be coy.

"I had a real nice time last night, really nice," James said. He took Benjamin's hand and walked him leisurely toward the entrance.

"I did too," Benjamin answered, exhausted but at the same time excited to let James lead him into his own dwelling. "Even with all of that stuff with Ellsworth, I really did have fun."

Benjamin took his hand back only to wrap his arm around James's waist. James leaned his head on Benjamin's shoulder and walked with his eyes closed. To his surprise, Benjamin once again kissed his forehead. They reached the elevator, and once it opened, the general manager from the previous night stepped out. He muttered something profane to Benjamin in a sarcastic tone and winked at him just as the doors closed.

The ride up took no time, and by design, the elevator opened directly into Benjamin's loft. When they stepped out, Benjamin turned James to bring him against his own body. He leaned lazily into James, who laughed as he practically dragged Benjamin to an oversized couch and deposited him on it.

"Can you remind me why I was avoiding this?" Benjamin asked as he removed his shoes.

James slid off his shirt and started to unbutton Benjamin's. When he had it off, James straddled and ground against him. James's thighs clamped about his waist as Benjamin wrapped an arm around James's torso to pull him closer. Benjamin ran his open mouth over James's chest, exhaling his warm, moist breath as he palmed the lowest part of James's back and held him in place.

James released a soft breath but Benjamin didn't stop. Soon the drag of lips moving over James's bare skin turned into kisses. They were soft at first, but when Benjamin made another pass through the deep cleft that separated James's chest muscles, he used his teeth. Teeth that gnashed and a mouth that suckled, causing sounds of euphoria to come from James.

Benjamin stood them up, and buried his face into James's broad shoulders. James pulled away, but Benjamin wouldn't relent. He needed to kiss every vein and taste every sinewy muscle that strained from his contact. When James's resistance became stronger, he finally released him. James didn't move, and instead, rested his forehead against Benjamin's and looked into his eyes with a smile.

"I-I don't know, don't care, and damn sure don't wanna do any more talking." James finally answered his question.

Benjamin chuckled lightly and cupped James's face with a hand. James closed his eyes, and Benjamin took the time to kiss him on the forehead. Then on his nose. He reached out and lifted James's chin so their lips could meet.

"Ben, there you are," Clinton said as he exited the elevator.

Benjamin stopped in his tracks with his lips lightly brushing against James's and glanced behind James to see a clearly distressed Clinton approaching him. He instantly turned around, and once he felt less embarrassed, he spoke.

"Clint, what are you doing here?" Benjamin asked him, his voice raspy.

"I've been trying to get in contact with you all morning, where have you—"

"Hey! Hi," James interrupted. "Clint is it?" When Clinton nodded, James continued, "Look, Mr. Clint, I'm sure you have a whole heap of questions and such. I have a few myself, like why are you here, how'd you get in, why are you here! But me and Benji are busy at the moment."

"James..."

"No, Benji, the first time I saw Mr. Clint here, he and his boss lady gave my daddy a nasty touch of the vapors. And now he's gone and given me and my boys a case of the blues."

"How did you get in here, Clint?" Benjamin asked, genuinely curious.

"Don't forget who owns the lease. We have a key."

"I'll remember that, but it still doesn't answer the question of why you're here."

"I swear I'm gonna kill someone," James shouted to the room. "Benji."

"Right, bad timing. I'll see you a bit later," Benjamin said.

"No, you'll come with me right now," Clinton said forcefully. "Ms. Harvington just had an emergency meeting with the CEO and board of directors. I don't have to tell you that it didn't go so well, so now she wants all of the senior section representatives and special liaisons in our conference room yesterday."

Benjamin went silent to process the information. He knew that something like this would happen, but in no way did he expect to be a part of it.

"But I'm just a low-level player in our company."

"Not too low apparently. The meeting was put on hold until I found you." Clinton turned to leave. "I'll be downstairs. Hurry and get cleaned up so we can leave."

"Is anyone listening to me?" James said, walking in front of Benjamin. "Hey, you and me, the nasty." James pointed to a doorway.

"Listen..." Benjamin said to Clinton.

"Look, I can see you were in the middle of something, but it'll have to wait. I'm not asking you, I'm telling you. If you're not downstairs in ten minutes, then you can stay up here to pack your bags because I will fire you."

"Wait, you're going to fire me for being late to work on a weekend when I wasn't even scheduled to come in?" Benjamin asked angrily.

"Read your contract again. You give us a minimum of a fifty-hour workweek for your salary, and that includes weekends if need be. And it's needed. Or plain old-fashioned insubordination, I don't care," Clinton snapped.

Benjamin noticed the look of stress on Clinton's face and the telltale indications of sleep deprivation from the deep bags under his eyes. Clinton seemed to calm himself down before he spoke again.

"It's been a long morning. We all have to do this, so the sooner we get it done, the sooner I can leave you and James be."

Clinton walked back to the elevator, and James walked next to him. James smiled lightly at him while carefully keeping the shirt in his hand in front of his groin. The two entered, and as the door closed, Benjamin called to him.

"Jimmy, I'm..."

"Don't be. I run a company too, remember?" James's smile faded, and he sighed. "I should get over there right now, maybe sit inside our blast chillers for a bit."

The door closed, and with a painful tugging in his loin and knots in his stomach, Benjamin went into his room to take a very cold shower.

"MR. REI, HOW very fortunate for us that you could make time for us in what must undoubtedly be a very busy schedule." Laura chided Benjamin as he entered the conference room.

The department heads and their aides were all gathered around the massive triangular table with Laura at the peak. Benjamin didn't know why, but could tell that everyone in the room was tense. This was from the aura that their conference leader gave off but also because of the gravity of the situation they were in. He didn't know any of them personally and had only seen a few in passing, but with a name placard in front of each of them, he was able to identify the heads of their legal, sales, marketing, logistics, and of course acquisitions departments.

"Ms. Harvington, I only..."

"Spare me," she snapped. "I thought I had made myself perfectly clear the last time we spoke, however I can see that you are of the kind that needs to be told things twice."

Laura sauntered toward a large digital display and typed a few commands into a tablet, causing the larger screen to reveal multiple graphs and charts concerning her latest target. Once again Benjamin noticed how strong she looked in her suit. It was red; everything she wore currently was red, including her heels. But instead of the bright and warm color, it was a deep shade, almost maroon to the point of reminding him of blood.

"As you are all aware," she addressed the room, "Mr. Charles Cain has outright refused to be purchased by us. Now I consider myself an old-fashioned woman, which is why under normal circumstances a hostile takeover would be most prudent. However, that constant aggravation he calls his lastborn has put forth an interesting notion, one that cannot be ignored. Benjamin." She finished and all eyes turned to him.

"Ma'am, I'm not sure...that is, I don't..."

"What Benjamin is trying to say, Ms. Harvington, is that we don't think there is anything we can do," Clinton answered in his stead. The two exchanged a small glance, and Benjamin could see a small okay gesture on Clinton's hand.

"That is unacceptable," Laura roared.

"And yet it doesn't change anything, Laura," the logistics leader spoke up. He had just as much seniority as Laura, which gave him little to fear from her.

"He's right," the woman representing legal added. "We can press them all we like, but if what Mr. Cain's son said is true, then the only option we have is to get him to sell to us."

"Have I been speaking to myself?" Laura asked the room. "I have already informed everyone here that is not a viable option, so find another."

"Maybe I'm not making myself clear, Ms. Harvington." The woman from legal stood to make sure that no one would put forth any more moot arguments. "*Daddy Cain's* is a private company. That means the only people he has to speak to about his business are the state, federal, and local regulators. As long as he is in compliance, then we cannot get information about them." She paused to let that sink in. "There is no way for us to verify if what he said is true unless we purchase them."

"But without the brand, the company is useless. We would just be buying property and equipment," the sales representative said.

"Not to mention, I won't have anything to promote," a member of the marketing team noted, to which everyone agreed.

Laura crossed her arms and then reached up to pinch the bridge of her nose with her free hand. She had been placed in charge of this project by their headquarters, and although that gave her a wide latitude, even she couldn't make her peers do anything that went against the best interests of their company.

"Let us start again..."

"For the third time, Laura?" It was the logistics leader again.

"Did you ever consider that if you put as much effort into trying to solve a problem as thinking of reasons not to work—?"

"How dare you!" He shot out of his chair. "I wasn't the one who wasted millions of dollars and botched a basic purchase! Even worse, you're increasing their profits!"

"Excuse me?" Laura asked.

"The vendors you purchased. Without *Daddy Cain's* they don't have enough business to remain open. We either sell off what you just bought, or crawl back to them for substantially cheaper contracts. Which do you think we were approved for? All of which could have been prevented if—"

"All right enough," Benjamin yelled, surprising everyone including himself. He hated when senior employees argued, mostly because they had forgotten what it was like to climb up through the ranks and make a mistake.

"You have our attention, Mr. Benjamin, so please use what little time you have left to speak your mind before you are escorted out of here." Laura didn't even look at him as she buzzed her intercom.

"Let him talk," the logistics representative spoke up for him. "You made us wait around for the man, so he must be valuable or have something to contribute."

Laura looked at everyone and saw them nodding in agreement. "Very well. I requested you here because, despite your limited experience and your...colorful outburst, you were the only one to whom Mr. Cain responded to."

Benjamin paused to gather his thoughts. All eyes were on him, and it was then he realized that this could be his make or break moment. He quickly ran through all of the information he had committed to memory and then thought of all the complications that they would have to deal with going forward. None of that mattered now. The only thing that they could do, that he could do, was to come up with an alternate plan that somehow resulted in his company purchasing both parts of *Daddy Cain's.*

"I think I may have an idea," Benjamin said finally.

"My word, the child is positively a savant," Laura yelled.

"What I meant, Ms. Harvington, is that you all are coming at this from the wrong angle. We have to assume everything that Jim...James said is true." Benjamin fought down a blush at his unprofessionalism but continued. "With that in mind, we can't call his bluff because there is no way we would get approved for the funding. Not to mention if we use anything he owns, he'll sue us."

"Is that something we should really be concerned about?" a different marketing representative asked. "Can't we tweak it just enough to be different?"

"Not if we want to keep our jobs."

They all looked at the speaker from the legal department.

"Assuming we did go down that route, and let me reiterate that I strongly advise against that, then best case scenario, we all get fired and possibly face civil suits as well since it's against company policy. Worse case, James takes us to the cleaners and the company goes bankrupt."

"That doesn't seem right," the sales leader said.

Benjamin tried once more. "Again, we're going off what James said. Trade secrets are serious business, not to mention the patents that they own. And it's per count or violation. Clinton and I were there when James warned us, so if we go ahead anyway, that's intent. A jury will be very sympathetic to the Cains for all they have done for the local community."

"So what is your idea?" Laura asked, this time listening intently. He had just impressed her with his offhand legal knowledge.

"We get James, the son, to sell."

Clinton asked, "And how are we going to do that?"

"I don't know." Laura grimaced again, but Benjamin kept speaking. "But I do know that is the only avenue we have. That or give up entirely."

"I will not allow that to happen," Laura said to the room. She noticed the clock on the wall and let out a small sigh. "It is late in the morning. We will adjourn this meeting for two hours for everyone to collect themselves. As distasteful as I find it, I agree with Mr. Rei. You will all have something to contribute as to how to get the young James to sell when you return."

Everyone started to leave, but as soon as Benjamin stood, Laura shot him a glance that made him retake his seat. He wasn't sure what her motives were, but with the room empty, they became clear.

"Pack your bags, child. You are on a one-way trip back to Chicago."

"Ms. Harvington..."

"Benjamin, just stop. You are finished here. Your assignment was to get Charles Cain to sell. You failed. You are a failure." She emphasized each word. "The only reason you still have your job is because the others have seen our interactions. But make no mistake, you should not be expecting a warm welcome once you are home." She shook her head. "And I had such high hopes for you."

Benjamin exploded. He could put up with many things, but not this.

"I'm not the one who failed, Ms. Harvington. You are. You can try to make this my fault all you want, but at the end of the day, it was you who made it damn near impossible for us to buy anything from the Cains!"

"And that was all I needed. You are fired, Mr. Rei! Clear out your things."

With a quick snap, Laura had her back to him. Benjamin promptly stood, so angry he didn't trust himself to speak, but he did.

"I can't wait to tell Jimmy about this," he spoke to himself.

"There is no point in trying to get on my good side. Your employment has already been terminated. Using me to try to persuade him is inventive, but ultimately childish."

"Who said anything about you?" Benjamin asked with thoughts of anticipation forming in his mind. "I'm just going over to get something that you've obviously been without for some time."

Laura was about to yell until it registered what he had just said. Her eyes darted back and forth as a wicked grin spread on her face. She heard the door open, and before Benjamin could leave, she called out to him.

"Wait," she said forcefully. It caused Benjamin to stop, and she approached him. "Come back in." He continued walking. "Please."

Everyone peeked over or out of their cubicles to ensure that they had heard correctly. Benjamin also stopped but was so intrigued he returned to the conference room.

With his arms crossed, he immediately asked, "What?"

"Have a seat, please." She gestured to a chair.

"No. Now what do you want?" he asked again.

Laura placed a hand on his shoulder. When he stared at it, she removed it and crossed her arms in front of her. "These last few weeks have been stressful, shall we say?"

"Spare *me,* Ms. Harvington," Benjamin spat. "We both see through bull for a living, so what do you want from your ex-employee?"

"It is like looking into the past," she said with a grin that unsettled Benjamin. "Very well, you just said that you were on your way to see James—for a personal encounter, may I assume?"

"Why do you care?" Benjamin asked reluctantly.

"I think we both know why, my child." Laura picked at his clothing and dusted his shoulders. "My, my, are you not a handsome one? I am sure that a strapping young gentleman such as yourself could be of great influence."

"You can't be serious?" Benjamin asked, appalled. "You want me to seduce Jimmy just to try to convince him to sell?"

"I did not say that. I just said that you could be of influence."

"There is no way..."

"Think about it this way, child. You get him to sell, and you will have made it," Laura said gleefully while patting two open palms on Benjamin's shoulders. "You will finally be a part of the boys' club. And do not tell me that does not matter to you. Trust me when I say I know very well how badly you want it. Being the officer that got *Daddy Cain's* will put you in between the crosshairs of every major firm in the country. Not to mention on the fast track for promotions and bonuses, of course."

Benjamin remained silent and looked down as he listened.

"I am just asking you to do what you have always done in this white-collar jungle, Benjamin. What we have always done—be smart. Smarter than them. Because while they have had everything handed to them on a platinum platter and have been oblivious to the advantages of their privilege, people like you and me have had to work for it. You did not get to where you are right now by playing it safe."

"I'm not lying to him!"

"Why do you insist upon saying words that have never been uttered?" Laura laughed. "I do not care what you do or how you do it. Just get it done." She put a hand on each of his shoulders to square him to her. "There is an old saying about when opportunity knocks, do you know it?"

"I-I do…"

"Then I suggest you listen closely because this is your chance, and at such a young age. A self-made man who came from nothing, only to rise to the top via hard work and perseverance."

Laura walked past him and out into the hall without another word.

"CHARLES… CHARLES…" CECILY bellowed as Charles walked past her. She turned and barely matched his pace as she tried to keep up down the long hallways of his home. "Charles, have you lost your damn mind?"

"Not now, Cecily," Charles said and kept moving, not breaking his stride in the slightest.

Charles was furious, something that was becoming a common occurrence as of late, and it was once again because of the actions of James. At such a late hour in the morning, his son was expected to perform many of the ancillary duties that he usually put off until the weekend when most of their employees were not scheduled to work. As it was now, Charles had not seen nor heard from his son all day, and he was beyond livid.

Wall-mounted intercoms would chime every so often to give him a status update from the house staff Charles employed. Everyone had been dispatched throughout his home to find James, but no one had been successful. Tired of waiting, Charles had taken it upon himself to search the premises and the many places that he knew his son utilized to stay hidden. After searching every level and many rooms, Charles had finally ended at the west wing of his home where Cecily had found him.

"Are you ready to tell me what's bothering you this morning?" Cecily asked when she finally caught up to him. She steadied a hand on his chest, and when Charles realized she would not move, he led them over to a large window with a perfect view of his lake.

"Cecily… I didn't mean to—that is to say…" Charles stammered out.

"Oh you're never a bother. I'm actually used to it after all these years." She chuckled. Charles joined her in laughter and started to dab at his forehead with a cloth. "So what did Jimmy do this time?"

"My word, you need to stay out of my head," Charles said while taking her hand into his own and patting it.

"You know I wouldn't dream of going in there. They don't make water hot enough to clean that filthy place," Cecily said. "I've helped you with your children since Lucile went on home to heaven. Talk to me now. I know that look."

"I wish the answer to my troubles were just as easy for you to see." Charles stood and ran a hand through his hair before he spoke. "Jimmy is one straw away from breaking my damn back!"

"Charles..."

"I mean it this time. I have tried with that boy. Lord knows I have. But every time, every single damn time that boy takes a step forward, he *runs* at least ten back."

"So what else is new?" Cecily asked him while shrugging her shoulders.

"Are you even listening to me?" Charles snapped. "I swear that I would strangle that boy if I saw him right now."

Cecily stood up before he could react. She walked toward him, to which he stood his ground and bowed his head slightly as Cecily smacked the back of his head.

"Did you get it all out?" Cecily asked patiently.

"Thank you," Charles said sincerely.

He turned to face the window and gazed out over the lake. The sight of the still water and small animals scurrying about calmed him. Cecily didn't interrupt, and Charles was thankful that she let him speak when he was ready.

"I should not have said that about Jimmy. It's not something any parent should ever say."

"Mmhmm..." Cecily rolled her eyes. "Don't even start that way of thinking. You're not the first parent, and believe me when I say you won't be the last." She rubbed his back.

"I have just had so much on my itinerary as of late," Charles said

"Is this about you and Mayor Ferguson?"

"Him, the company," he said. "I even took on the role of planner for the ball later this week. And what has that boy of mine done? Nothing but add to my grief."

"Does he know that?" she asked.

"Know what?"

"Does Jimmy know what you're planning?"

"Of course not. Why would he?"

"Why would he, indeed?"

"Well?"

"Well what?" she asked back in a mocking tone. Cecily took off her glasses and cleaned them so Charles knew he was in for a lecture.

"Go ahead." He motioned her to continue.

"Joking aside, you know what level of work and the amount of time he spends at the plant you want, but he doesn't. All he knows is that Big Daddy Cain has suddenly decided to bring down the hammer. You're demanding everything and even more."

"I practically gave him the company," Charles nearly shouted.

"And what does that mean to someone so young? He may not do the job in the manner that you want, but it still gets done. The employees are happy, business is booming. What more could you possibly want?"

Charles didn't have an answer to her question. It was true that his son's job performance was more than adequate despite his methods. And James did have a natural inclination toward business. He tried to think of another way to express the frustrations he was feeling, but every thought that came to his mind was rendered moot from Cecily's logic. Why couldn't James run a company that was practically his the way he wanted as long as the work was completed?

"I think I need to finally discuss my plans with Jimmy," Charles said.

"Not just him, Charles, talk to all your boys." Charles remained silent, so Cecily asked another question. "When was the last time you all did something nice together?"

"Jimmy and I?"

"I meant your family, Charles, but if you have to think about it—" Cecily said while shaking her head.

"Do not," Charles chided her. "Have you even the slightest idea of how difficult it is to raise four, actually five teenagers at once?"

"Did you forget that my three children are barely a year apart?" she asked.

"My point is, at that age, with all of them coming into their own, it was difficult to keep up while running a company. I tried so very hard to spend as much family time with them as I could, but that did not stop them from pouting or sucking their teeth at me with every question or attempt to reach out." Charles shook his head. "We drifted."

"Then find your way back," she said in a matter-of-fact way.

Cecily's solution was simple. They always were. Charles turned from her and smiled as he looked out the window once more. There was no reason he couldn't spend more time with his children, and with as much stress he had been putting on himself lately, it would be a refreshing change of pace.

"Will I have to pay you your normal retainer for such sound advice?" Charles joked.

"There is a first time for everything, I suppose."

"You know, I really do appreciate every—"

Charles cut himself off when he noticed smoke in the sky. It was extremely close, and he followed the trail back to the haze of heat rising from one of his cedar gazebos.

"What is going on down there?" he asked aloud.

"It's just Jimmy," Cecily said and turned to walk away.

"Boys," he shouted, but not entirely in anger.

"HERE'S THE LAST of it," Bryan said as he stepped up to James with an ice chest in his hands.

"Thanks, just set it off to the side by that table."

Kenneth-George hurried over to help his cousin. They were all outside under an oversized pavilion where James was working while they waited for the rest of the family to join them. Although he wasn't over-extended, James had several projects going on at the moment.

"Let's see, jumping rope, volleyball, radios, and now balloons?" Bryan asked.

"Wait until they get here. I want those kids so tuckered out that they won't be able to make it to the dinner table tonight," James said.

"I can't believe you got stuck babysitting, but I guess you gotta be nice to your sisters sometimes." Bryan's eyes became hooded. "But that doesn't mean we gotta be nice to you."

"Huh?"

Bryan opened the chest that had been filled with ice and water. He and Kenneth-George both reached in and pulled out partially frozen but completely filled water balloons.

"Ah shoot," James said. Outnumbered and outgunned, he dove behind one of the pine chairs that furnished the area. "I guess it's my fault for asking you to grab 'em, right? Right?"

James didn't hear anything from them so he stood up. His brother and cousin were motionless, and he followed their gaze to see Cecily, covering her mouth while she approached the structure. Beside her, his father was drenched in cold water after the impacts of several of the balloons.

"Uncle Charles..." Bryan said.

Charles held up his hand. He attempted lighting his pipe but couldn't start a flame, so blew the wet tobacco out along with a small spout of water and shrill whistle before saying, "With you three, it never rains but pours, I see."

"Hey, Daddy," James said while passing him a towel.

James led his father past the large smokers of dry meat and portable ranges where pots simmered, which he had set up. Cecily took a seat and began preparing other items while Kenneth-George and Bryan finally settled enough to wash the many vegetables.

"What is all of this, son? Is there something wrong with your kitchen inside?"

"Hm? Oh nothing, it's just such a nice morning, so I called up Miss Sissy to let her know I could help her get started on her Sunday specials." James sounded even more enthusiastic.

"I do not know what to say," Charles said, perplexed. "Wait, Cecily, you knew where he was? Why did you not tell me?"

"You didn't ask," she answered without looking up and began humming to herself.

Charles appeared to be prepared to ask another question, but James cut him off.

"Get over here, old man. I've got something for you to try." When his father came near, James dipped a spoon into a pot and gave his father a sample of his latest concoction. "So?"

"Jimmy," he said. "What is...is this a new recipe?"

"Not just a new recipe. *My* recipe. I'm hoping this will be my Big sauce. The Big X."

"You mean you are already working on your own? Son, this is delicious," Charles said after tasting another spoonful of the golden orange sauce.

"Thanks, but it's not right yet. I'm still missing something, and I can't slap our label on just anything."

"Jimmy!" Charles chuckled while pulling him into a hug. James didn't fight it but was surprised at how emotional his father was being as he rubbed his face and kissed his head.

"Everything all right?" James asked after he broke their embrace. He took a seat slightly away from his family and gestured for his father to join him. After picking up a bundle of collards and starting to separate them, his father joined in.

"Everything is fine," Charles said. "I am just happy to see you in such good spirits and working so hard."

"I'm always working hard."

"Yes, of course you are," Charles said while flicking the excess water from a stem onto James's nose. "And I thought only a boy could put such a smile on your face."

"Oh, why it is a boy," Cecily shouted.

"Miss Sissy," James said shyly while running a hand through his hair. "But she's right, Daddy, Benji is a nice guy."

"Who is this *Benji*?"

"Oh why you've already met him, Charles. That cute, big strong boy from *Filip*." Cecily injected herself into their private conversation again.

"Cecily," Charles warned.

"What?" she asked innocently. "No one is paying attention to the two of you. I'm just busying myself cleaning these vegetables." Cecily started humming louder.

James turned his attention back to his father. "It is him—Mr. Rei."

"Jimmy..." Charles wasn't sure what to say. "You saw what he and Laura were up to with our company."

"Not him. He didn't know anything about it."

"Are you sure about that?"

James looked down momentarily, but his father lifted his face back up and smiled.

"Jimmy, I am just trying to ensure that you consider all the facts."

"Well, I believe 'im."

Charles didn't speak any more about it. Soon James stood to check on the pots that were simmering on his stoves, and with all of his family in one location, he decided to inform them of his news.

"Pack your bags, boys. We are going fishing."

"Huh?" It was the only word Bryan could manage, but soon the idea excited him. "You mean like when we were kids, Uncle Charles?"

"Well, you boys can drink now...even a few for you, Kenneth-George." Charles winked to his son.

James slightly smiled and stood still while his brother and cousin jumped about in excitement.

"Oh that's lovely, Charles. It's so nice to see a father spending time with his boys." She turned to James. "Jimmy, why don't you invite Benji along?"

James beamed at the idea and asked his father, "Can I, Daddy? I promise we'll be good."

"Well...I..."

Cecily answered in his stead. "He thinks it's a fine idea, Jimmy. I told him inside that you might want some company along, and he said as long as he had his boys, he was as right as rain."

"You're the best! Wait until you meet him properly," James said while hugging his father tightly and lifting him off the ground. "I gotta tell Benji."

JAMES RAN OFF and made a phone call. With Bryan and Kenneth-George talking back and forth at the excitement over their trip, Charles walked closer to Cecily to investigate her actions.

"Why?" he asked sternly.

"Charles, I swear, you didn't hear anything that Jimmy said, did you?"

"I heard everything."

"But you didn't listen," she said calmly.

"You mean like you were when I was trying to have a conversation with him?" Charles accused.

Cecily set down the ingredients she was cleaning. Charles did not shirk because even though Cecily was like the mother that James had never known, she was not his parent. Her idea was dangerously skirting the edges of meddling.

"If you were any other man, we would be fighting," Cecily started. "But that doesn't change anything."

Charles took a breath and, in an even voice, asked yet again, "Why?"

"Because he wants him there, Charles. He likes him."

"And how would you know that?"

"He knows his name..." Cecily said in a droll tone.

It was true. And Charles couldn't recall his son calling a random tryst anything more than "some guy" or "what's-his-name." But just because he could recall it, didn't make this one was something special.

"Even if that is true, could you not have waited for a more opportune time?" he asked.

"You need a better time than now?" Cecily replied.

"And what is so special about this time? Why now?"

Cecily paused and grinned. Charles noticed this, and when she tilted her head toward him and looked over her glasses, he knew he was in for a revelation that had been beyond his grasp.

"Charlie," she said, calling him by the nickname he had outgrown long ago. "When's the last time Jimmy brought home a boy for you to meet? One that he wanted you to meet?"

"I really should start paying you," was all Charles could manage.

Cecily chuckled as Charles kissed her cheek and started to leave. Once he was at the exit, his sons and nephew surrounded him to confirm the location and time of their departure. He was headed back inside his home when Cecily called to him.

"Next time, make sure you have all of the water out of your ears before you try to argue with me."

Instead of answering, Charles walked back to the gazebo and over to Bryan's ice chest. He pulled out one of the balloons, and Cecily instantly got to her feet.

"No! Don't you even think about it," she warned. "I swear to God that if you even try it—"

Cecily never finished the sentence. Charles tossed the balloon, which she couldn't avoid, and it exploded on her chest. Most of the water went onto her face because of the position she'd tried to brace herself, but she wasn't nearly as wet as he.

"Daddy?" James asked as he backed out of the way. Bryan and Kenneth-George crept away as well.

"Don't worry. It's only a bit of water," Charles said with a mischievous smirk that had been passed on to his son.

Cecily took off her glasses and glowered at Charles. She was not amused and frightened everyone even more with a statement no man would want to hear in this circumstance.

"I just had my hair done," Cecily muttered.

The color from Charles's face drained away. He turned to look at his boys for help, only to see them several yards away with soft trails of dust behind them.

Chapter Eight

"BEN, YOU CAN'T seriously be planning on going through with this? You can't," Clinton pleaded as he followed Benjamin around his loft.

"Going through with what?" he asked while trying to find a legal pad that he had written many notes on.

"You know what I mean. God, I should've known something was up. Ever since the meeting last weekend, you've been off, distracted."

Benjamin yelled, completely frustrated with him. "I don't know because I'm not sure what I'm going to do yet."

"Can you just stop for a moment?" Clinton asked in a calm voice.

Benjamin froze. "What is it?"

"Everything. Everything about this is wrong and you know it," he said without any pretense.

"A boss and father all in one?" Benjamin said. "I really do work for a family company."

"Are you going to talk to me like an adult or continue making snide comments?"

"I don't know why I'm talking to you in the first place. What does my romantic life have to do with you?"

"Nothing, but then again, it's all about you," Clinton yelled back.

"Clint…"

"Don't. It's your turn to listen." Clint released a breath. "If you want to run around breaking hearts, be my guest. I don't care what you do. But any sly or underhanded dealings reflect on us, on all of us."

"I know that." Benjamin attempted to relax as well.

"Then you also know, or at least should have guessed, that if you do this, if you play with James's emotions like that, then it won't end well and it will affect a lot of people."

"I know that too."

Benjamin turned from him and headed for his kitchen. He poured two drinks and handed one to Clinton before gesturing for him to sit.

"You don't have any coffee?" Clinton asked.

Benjamin let out a soft laugh before he spoke. "I appreciate you trying to give me advice, but respectfully I didn't ask for any."

"Then why did you tell me about your conversation with Ms. Harvington?" Clinton asked.

"I guess that is a valid question," Benjamin said and gathered his thoughts. "It was practical."

"Practical how?" Clinton continued to pry.

"Okay, fine," Benjamin said with a sigh. "It's because I trust you, and you've always tried to help me out. Happy?"

"I would be if you reconsidered."

"How? What am I supposed to do?" Benjamin asked with a look of dismay. "Clint, she fired me. And after the last time you were here, I took your advice and looked over my contract. She had every legal right to do so."

"Gotta love at-will states," he said while shaking his head. "Sorry about the interruption by the way. It was a long morning before you got there."

"I can imagine." Benjamin ran a hand through his hair before he started to speak again. "But she was right. I was only transferred down here for *Daddy Cain's*. I didn't get the account so there's no reason for me to be down here anymore."

"And what will you tell James when he asks that question?"

Benjamin couldn't think of a response for that.

"Do you see what I'm getting at?" Clinton stood from his chair and motioned for Benjamin to join him at the recently repaired center window. "What do you see out there?"

"Downtown? The city?" Benjamin answered.

"You're right, Ben. A city that Charles and his son are heavily invested in." He stomped a foot to emphasize the building that they were standing in. "You don't want to make an enemy of the Cains."

"Are you saying that they would blacklist me, the company?" Benjamin asked with a slight edge in his voice. "Can they even afford that? Would they?"

"Money talks, Ben. Especially when it's *old money* like their family," Clinton said flatly. "And in case you haven't noticed, James is very close to his father. If he found out that someone intentionally and knowingly hurt his son... What would you do if you had the capability?"

Benjamin chewed his bottom lip.

Clinton rose and headed toward the elevator. He was almost to it when Benjamin repeated his question. "You still never told me what I'm supposed to do. If I don't use my access with Jimmy to even try to bring up him selling, then what option do I have?"

"*Access*? Is that what you kids are calling it these days?" Clinton asked and flashed him a suggestive smile.

"We're not in a relationship if that's what you're getting at."

"Then that morning, you two were just about to...what?" Clinton asked.

"Right, like I'm the only business traveler who plays while on assignment."

They laughed. Benjamin knew full well how to take advantage of the distance between states and sometimes continents.

"It's not like there's anything wrong with him, and I figured I wouldn't be here much longer anyway," Benjamin said.

"Ms. Harvington had other plans."

"Don't I know it. But no matter what happens, I'm not lying to him."

"Okay..."

"I mean it," Benjamin said strongly. "I would never do something like that just to get ahead."

"Okay, Ben, I get what you're saying." Clinton continued to the elevator and waited for it to return once he called it. He was stepping in when Benjamin called to him.

"Clint..."

"What?" he asked, not even hiding the disappointed expression on his face.

"Just say whatever it is you're thinking, so I can have third and fourth thoughts on this."

Clinton held the door while considering what to say. Every time he brought up the ramifications, Benjamin always had an excuse.

"I believe you, Ben, but why does it sound like you're trying to convince yourself?"

Instead of answering, Benjamin turned from him, and Clinton let the elevator door shut.

"ARE WE THERE yet?" James asked his cousin and brother yet again.

Bryan sighed and Kenneth-George inserted his earphones. While Bryan was driving, Charles trailed closely behind, being chauffeured in his classically restored Rolls-Royce. It was still very early in the morning, but that had not dampened the energy or spirits of the trio as they rode down the long forested road to their first destination before reaching the lake.

"Hey, where's Benji at? Why didn't we stop by and get 'im?" Bryan asked.

"I sent a car..." James answered in a quiet tone.

"Jimmy?" Bryan asked.

"It's nothing, Bryan... At least I hope it's not." James glanced over to find Kenneth-George wasn't paying attention.

"Did that boy do something to you?" Bryan reached under his seat and brought up a crowbar. "Because if he did, I swear I'll—"

James grabbed his shoulder and said, "Don't start beating your chest. He hasn't done anything wrong by me."

"Then what the heck just got into you?" Bryan asked.

James let a smile tug at his lips but suppressed it from fully forming because of his anxiety. He hadn't spoken to anyone about how he was feeling lately or what he was going through with Benjamin. He didn't know how. His entire family was always available to him, but James was officially charting new territory with his continued interactions with Benjamin.

"I just haven't seen 'im in a while is all," James said.

"What?" Bryan asked, confused.

"It's been a few days."

James turned to the passenger window but continued to speak in a voice that both Kenneth-George and Bryan could hear.

"The day Daddy told us we were taking this trip, that morning was the last time I saw 'im. We haven't talked really either. When I called 'im up to ask if he wanted to tag along, he texted *yes*."

Bryan and Kenneth-George simultaneously made a painful groaning sound. James didn't say more, so Bryan tried to lighten the mood.

"So it's been almost a week since you two last talked? It must've been nice with all that time to play."

James didn't answer.

Bryan let out a disgusted sound. "Wait, you haven't been with anyone since you started chasing that boy?"

"No," James said.

"Dang it," Bryan yelled. He took his hands off the steering wheel, which Kenneth-George instantly grabbed, and went into his wallet to once again give Kenneth-George his money.

"You know there's help for gambling addiction." James laughed at them.

"We'll sign up for a program later," Bryan said, "But don't try to change subjects. You're sweet on that boy, aren't you?"

"I'm sweet on all boys, cousin," James deflected.

"Why, though? I mean why are you putting in so much time and work? Didn't Ms. Sissy tell you about him? He was only here for Uncle Charles, and he said no. Won't he be leaving soon?"

James had considered that, knew that it would happen. The idea had come to him the moment Benjamin became much more social and keen to the idea of spending the night with him.

James had chalked it up to Benjamin wanting to have a simple love affair, but Benjamin's distance had made James think that he had done something wrong. It wasn't until Benjamin had accepted his invitation that a small glimmer of hope of picking up where they had left off entered James's mind, but he didn't want to be disappointed again.

"Even if he is, I'm not leaving this business unfinished." James grinned.

Bryan nodded, and Kenneth-George went back to listening to his music. James was about to focus his thoughts on Benjamin once more until Bryan reached behind Kenneth-George and pulled on James's shirt to signal him. They had done this before, but mistakenly it had been in front of Kenneth-George, who was still not emotionally mature enough to discuss such issues. James didn't want to upset him on a day they were all planning to relax, so he turned on the radio.

"Everything all right," Bryan asked while keeping his eyes straight ahead. "With Uncle Charles, I mean?"

James took out his phone and lazily went through some of the functions on the device. "Truth be told, I dunno."

"You don't even gotta clue about what he wants to talk to us about then?"

"I wish I did."

James doubled forward and pretended to laugh when he noticed Kenneth-George's eyes lingering on him. He intentionally started to take up more space than he needed and his little brother pushed him back in an annoyed manner.

"You think it's about his health?" Bryan asked as he glanced at James.

"That's why I'm worried. I know he's is hard on me, but if he isn't being a fuss box, then something just ain't right."

The two went silent. James continued on his phone, but Bryan broke in after they had traveled a few more miles. "Maybe it's nothing. Nothing serious anyway."

"What makes you say that?" James asked while perking up.

"Benji." James furrowed his brow, so Bryan explained. "Uncle Charles let 'im come along. Suppose it was serious, he wouldn't want anyone else there. At the very least, he would've waited until Melinda and Brittani were here."

Relief instantly washed over James. He looked to his cousin and almost jumped across his brother to hug him. Whatever his father had to tell him, he knew that if it was serious, Charles would have all of his children present, Cecily as well. None of them were here, and even though there was a possibility that Charles could have told his daughters already, James highly doubted it.

"That's a load off," James said. "Thanks."

"Think nothing of it, Uncle Charles is the daddy I never had. I care about 'im too."

"You don't need to tell me," James said proudly. "I guess you do use that head of yours sometimes."

"That's all the time, as a matter fact," Bryan corrected but then became somber again. "Look, I know you know I don't like talking about these things and all that but..." Bryan didn't seem to be able to finish as his voice cracked.

"I'm gonna always keep you in the loop," James said with certainty. "I know you and KG don't think about such things, but me and Daddy have been having this talk ever since I was knee-high to a duck."

"Really?"

"We had to," James answered him seriously. "I won't get into it deep or anything, but we have that talk at least once a year after his checkups. I talk to my sisters about it, but I'm talking to you too from now on."

Bryan nodded. Even though he was driving, he took his eyes off the road to look into James's eyes. Bryan stretched out his right arm across Kenneth-George, and before he had his headphones out, James took Bryan's hand into his own.

"OKAY, HERE WE go." Benjamin exhaled.

Bryan and Charles had just pulled their vehicles into the parking lot of a small general store where Benjamin had been waiting. None of Benjamin's chauffeurs had known when Charles would be arriving, but they knew not to keep him waiting. While Bryan and Kenneth-George practically leapt out of the truck to see Charles, James took a slower approach toward Benjamin, who hadn't moved.

"Jimmy," Benjamin shouted and ran over to him.

He was wearing a loose-fitting T-shirt, which James had suggested, and wrapped his arms around James before picking him up. James was tense at first, but once he was suspended in Benjamin's embrace, he seemed to relax. Benjamin set him down, keeping his hand on James's waist. He leaned in quickly for a kiss, but James broke away from him just as fast.

"What...what's wrong?" Benjamin asked.

"Ahem!" Charles cleared his throat loudly.

Benjamin and James turned to see Charles finish lighting his pipe. He took a deep puff and patted his stomach before an aide brought over his cane so he could walk closer. Once he reached them, he took another puff while appearing to appraise Benjamin.

"Mr. Cain," Benjamin started but received a small clunk on his head from Charles's cane that silenced him.

"Daddy, this is Benji, um Benjamin," James said, looking embarrassed.

"My word, Mr. Rei, you most certainly are a persistent young man, I see," Charles bellowed. "First the bar, then your office, and now my son's bed!"

Benjamin blanched. There was nothing he could say, but his mouth had fallen open. He had never imagined that Charles would see his job as the reason for spending so much time with James.

"Daddy," James chided Charles, while taking Benjamin by the arm and addressing him. "He's just trying to put the fear of God in you. He did this every time either of my sisters brought home one of their boyfriends."

"So this is your boyfriend now, son?" Charles asked. His eyes met Benjamin's, who felt as if he would pass out at any moment.

"We're just trying to get to know each other a little better is all," James said.

Bryan joined them. "C'mon, Uncle Charles, let's leave 'em to get dirty. We need to head on to the cabin and make sure the boat is ready before it warms up anyway."

Charles cocked an eyebrow and turned his back to walk with his nephew and son. When they all got into Charles's car, he shouted for them not to be long. As they left, James took Benjamin's hand and hurried into the general store.

"Hey there, Mr. Miller. How have you been?" James asked as he ran toward the section of the store with a large sign of Bait & Tackle above it.

"Jimmy Cain," Mr. Miller shouted. "As I live and breathe, son. It's been too long."

When they reached the area that James led him to, he abruptly stopped and pulled Benjamin into a hug. Slightly winded, Benjamin could feel James's chest as it expanded against his own and the soft trail of air along his neck as James exhaled onto his neck.

"Sorry about that. He's the protective type."

"Don't be. You can't be too careful these days," Benjamin answered as sincerely as he could.

James lifted his head. "I guess you're right." He scanned the area, picked up a large Styrofoam chest, and handed it to Benjamin.

"Fill it up," James said while taking Benjamin to a large, raised white wooden box.

"With what?" he asked, confused. "This is just dirt."

James laughed, and in the background, Mr. Miller chuckled as well. "Boy, I tell you...just fill it up for me."

"Where's the scoop?" Benjamin asked as James walked away to continue shopping. He was slightly irked when James just put up his hands.

"Use the tools you have. Besides, you don't wanna hurt 'em."

Benjamin didn't put much stock in James's last comment but was still not looking forward to dirtying his manicure. He shoveled both hands into the soil to pick up a large clump, but almost fell when he instinctively retracted in disgust and fear. After taking a closer look at the soil, he could see movement and ran to find James.

"What was I just touching?" Benjamin asked, almost out of breath.

"Worms," James answered while holding a large paper bag filled with groceries. He pulled out a stick of dried meat and tore a piece off with his teeth, chewing loudly before offering it to Benjamin through loud smacks.

"No, I don't think I can eat right now," Benjamin said while waving a declining hand. "Why are there worms in there?"

"Where the heck else would earthworms be?" James asked. "Didn't you grow up on an island?"

"Yeah, but we didn't use worms as bait. Most people don't," Benjamin said while trying to smile.

James handed him the bag and went back to collect the bait for later on, so Benjamin headed to the counter. Benjamin felt slightly ill and Mr. Miller had brought him some water.

"Are you all right, son?" Mr. Miller asked.

"Just a bit unnerved. I really don't like the way those things feel."

James joined them. "You know, if you're trying to get on my daddy's good side, then you'd better get a stronger stomach."

"I was surprised is all," Benjamin said.

They left the store and climbed in Bryan's truck. James drove a bit before he finally asked, "Have you ever been fresh-water fishing before?"

"No, not really. I took a class field trip when I was little and caught crabs with my uncles, but books were more interesting to me."

"And the weights," James said and took Benjamin's hand. "Still, I can't wait until you gotta bait one of these night crawlers on a hook."

James was smiling, but Benjamin knew he was serious and was not looking forward to it.

"MY WORD, JIMMY, something smells quite enticing," Charles said while entering his cabin.

"Thanks, it'll all be ready soon. You want me to call 'em all in to set the table?"

"No, not just yet," Charles said. "It has been quite a day."

James smiled, agreeing with his father. The entire day had been dedicated to spending time as a family, and it was something they had all sorely needed but hadn't realized it. Once James and Benjamin reached them, Charles had launched his yacht to spend the entire morning on the private lake that his cabin bordered, fishing with his family. After showing off his skills at one of man's oldest methods of gathering food, they had returned to hike through the pristine trails and try their hand at archery.

None of them had been as good as Charles in the classic sport, so he finally gave in and they all enjoyed swimming in the lake, even over the protests of Kenneth-George and Bryan at having to keep their shorts on. When the late afternoon sun had come, Charles made it a point to find each of them individually, except for Benjamin, and speak to them privately about their lives and how they were. After they each returned, James was expecting to go next, but it didn't come until he was preparing dinner for them all right now.

"I'm glad we did this," James said, feeling slightly nervous. He turned off his burners and joined his father at the table.

"As am I. You know," he started and lit his pipe, "these last few months, I have been especially hard on you."

"Don't you worry about it. I'm gonna clean up my act," James replied quickly, forcing a smile across his face.

"Be that as it may, I think that you deserve the true reasons behind my actions." He took a long pause. "I have decided to retire from the company entirely."

"W-What?" James asked, relieved. "Daddy, you can't retire. That means..."

"That the entire company is yours," Charles said warmly.

James wasn't sure what to say. His father had already placed an enormous amount of trust in him so far, and he had worked hard, if not unconventionally, to prove that he was worthy of such an honor. The men who would become *Daddy Cain* usually didn't do so until much later on in their lives, and as it was now, James was just shocked.

"Why? Why now?" James asked. "Is this about your health?" James's voice cracked.

"What? Of course not. Why would you think—Jimmy," Charles said and brought his son in close. "Is that what you thought, son?"

"Damn right I did," James yelled while laughing. "You scared the pants off me."

"I am not going anywhere for a long time," Charles reassured. "It is just that I have other plans is all."

"What plans?"

"I will explain it to you later. But I'm impressed. That Benjamin boy has been most respectful this entire day. I believe I told him at least twice not to call me 'sir,' but I suppose he cannot help himself." Charles smiled deeply and patted James's cheek. "You should run along now and find him."

"What about dinner?" James asked.

"Believe it or not, I still remember my way around a kitchen," Charles said.

James didn't give it another thought. He dashed across the room and, once he exited, bounded down the steps of the cabin, looking for Benjamin. When he couldn't find him immediately, one of the concierge staff silently pointed toward the lake, and James took off. He reached the trail to the dock as Benjamin charged down it and jumped into the water.

"I'm off kitchen duty," James said when he reached the end of the dock.

Benjamin swam toward him. "Then what are you still doing up there?"

James got the hint when Benjamin spread his arms. He jumped in, taking them both underneath the water.

Benjamin released James, but even under the surface of the lake, it didn't take long to find each other. Benjamin glided through the clear water and swam between James's legs to make him tumble slightly in the weightlessness of their surroundings, but James quickly recovered.

Unable to speak, James grabbed Benjamin and eased into his embrace. He lightly pushed Benjamin's free-flowing hair out of his face and nuzzled his nose against Benjamin's cheek before closing his eyes. It was silent, cold. But James was pulled in close, and he opened his eyes to greet Benjamin's.

James smiled as a group of small fish pecked at Benjamin's ear and even more gathered around him. He tried to swat them away along with the bubbles that were blocking his view of Benjamin.

The pressure in his lungs was building, so James pointed to the surface where the sun's rippled image was distorted by the water. He moved to swim up, but Benjamin gently took hold of his arm and exhaled, sending him to the floor of the lake. James didn't fight him and followed along. When they reached the bottom, James was startled when Benjamin brought him in for a kiss.

With his lips on Benjamin, James pushed off the lake bed for all he was worth and took Benjamin up with him. He kicked for extra speed, and once they breached the surface, Benjamin lifted him even higher and threw him to the side to fall back into the water with his arms outstretched.

"FINALLY." BRYAN SIGHED. "You almost had me worried."

James resurfaced and swam over to a panting Benjamin. They stared at one another so Bryan cut them off. "Aww c'mon, guys, not now."

"Keep your shirt...off, cousin. Me and Benji were just about to leave," James said.

"We were?" Benjamin asked, panting.

"Oh yeah, time to add you to the ranks," James said.

The two swam back to the dock where attendants were waiting for them with dry clothes. When they finished changing, James jogged off with Benjamin in tow. Bryan wasn't sure what James had meant and ignored his cousin who kept splashing water in his direction

"Wait," Bryan shouted. "You can't take him there. That's our place."

"Watch me," James said and made a quick call to his father.

Bryan looked at Kenneth-George and the two swam for all they were worth. They reached the dock, and after pulling on their clothing, started to chase after Benjamin and James who had a sizeable lead on them. Kenneth-George pointed to a pair of house staff who were driving toward them fast in a golf cart, and they altered their direction to intercept him.

"Perfect timing, we need you to—"

"You need to come with us, Mr. Cain, and you too, Mr. Cain," the golf cart driver said as he and his counterpart exited the cart.

"What the heck are you talking about? We're not going anywhere," Bryan said. "Did you forget who you work for?"

"I have never forgotten, sir," he said, emotionally dispassionate and completely professional, "I work for Mr. Charles Howard Cain, and he wishes to speak to you both. Something about the rules not changing and 'letting the streetlight come on before being inside.' if I recall correctly."

Bryan looked at his cousin as they took their seats. They knew they would be in for an earful once Charles started to yell at them, but nothing about that was terribly unpleasant. They had all needed this and no matter what he and Kenneth-George thought, their 'place' would soon be inducting its newest member.

"WHERE ARE WE going?" Benjamin asked after they had been hiking for a while.

"Don't worry, we're almost there," James said without turning around to face him.

Benjamin was being guided by the hand as they walked. When they got closer, James picked up the pace. They started in a light jog, which almost became a full sprint as the two moved through the forest. Initially they were on a trail, but James soon veered off once a tree came into view with an unnatural and clearly intentional marking on it.

"Oh shoot, hang on," James shouted and stopped abruptly, causing Benjamin to almost run into him.

"What is it?"

He turned to Benjamin with a mischievous grin. "Close your eyes," James said.

"You know, I could sound like a broken record, but sure, why not?" Benjamin shrugged. "Just promise me it won't involve worms or anything that has more than two legs."

"You got it," James said and took Benjamin's hand. "I'm gonna take good care of you. Just you wait and see."

Benjamin stopped talking and let James lead him. As he made contact with the large tree, Benjamin was surprised at how hollow the core was with barely any internal leaves. They continued to prick and tickle his skin, but soon he felt nothing.

"Can I open my eyes now?"

"Not yet," James said. "All right, now."

Benjamin was baffled at the sight. James had led him to a pristine glade that was secluded from every other area of the forest. In one corner was a fully grown weeping willow tree that was only a few feet away from a small stream, which carved a path around its roots. The overgrown thick leaves looked like long plaits that reached the ground and dipped into the water.

That wasn't what had confused Benjamin. Around the tree there was a raised deck that had been built. It reminded him of the porches that encircled the majority of the homes in this region, only this one was not nearly as professional. James was still posing in front of it, and as Benjamin came closer, he could see several chairs, buckets, and other makeshift furniture. Even on the deck, a row of car batteries had been attached to what looked like a simple power source. He stood right in front of James, but looked up at the multiple handholds, wooden steps, and ropes that went up to the highest portions of the tree.

"So?" James asked expectantly. There was a light in his voice that conveyed how happy he was to share this.

"Jimmy..." Benjamin started while trying to suppress his laughter. "Did you just bring me to your tree house?" The last words did it. And Benjamin couldn't stop himself from laughing.

"Of course not. This here is Fort Cain."

"It gets better," Benjamin said while laughing harder.

Benjamin climbed up the deck with James. When he stood, he was reminded of his own childhood by the posters of decades-old movies and band posters on the branches. A classic stereo system and collectible one-of-a-kind toys and action figures were also positioned strategically in addition to old furniture that had somehow been transported up to the hideaway.

"What is all this?" Benjamin asked curiously.

James motioned for him to join him at a corner of the deck. He sat down and hung his feet out of a break in the railing, and soon Benjamin joined to sit beside him. The structure overlooked the small stream, and with the sun setting, fireflies twinkled as the croaking of toads and cawing of evening birds filled the air.

"You like the way my voice sounds or something? I told you, this is Fort Cain."

"Tree house..."

"Fort!" James returned.

"We're in a tree, there's furniture, and even a small fridge. It's a tree house." He laughed. "Now if I can only find the No Girls Allowed sign."

"Oh hush up. You act like I'm the only guy who has one," James said.

"No, just the only adult that I've met."

James stood up and crossed his arms. "I think you're telling me a story."

"Fine, what other adult male do you know with a tree—with a fort?"

James sat back down and pulled Benjamin into his lap and kissed his ear lightly.

"I call mine a fort. You call it a tree house. But they call 'em fraternities, lodges, yacht clubs, golf courses, and my favorite, a dang man cave. And guess what. Most of the time no girls are allowed in those places either."

Benjamin sat up, slightly chagrinned at poking fun at James's sanctum. He stood and took the place in, picking up a random football and throwing it to James who expertly caught it and returned it with much more speed and force. Benjamin dove for it but missed and the ball came to land in front of the tree that was in the center of the deck. After he recovered, Benjamin noticed carvings in the bark that soon became clear as names. A list of names.

"Who are all these people?"

"Who, them? You're looking at the troops of Fort Cain," James said.

"But there's so many." Benjamin shook his head.

A few names Benjamin recognized like those of James and Kenneth-George, but he was surprised to see, of all people, Ellsworth's name carved in too. There were several more, but as he got closer to the bottom of the list, he also saw Maynard's and Bryan's. Benjamin took another look at the area, and it was then that he noticed the different decorations and styles that clashed. The only answer was that each person had added something personal.

"Well, yeah," James explained. "We used to come up here every summer. Sometimes it was just us and Daddy. Other times people like Mayor Ferguson would come, so Ellsworth would be up here too. I thought you figured it out that we grew up together." James let out a deep laugh. "Shoot, we all used to hide from Governess here."

Benjamin's smile vanished. He had been having such an amazing time that he had forgotten his secondary reason for joining James. Silently he turned and climbed down from the deck. He didn't know where to go, so he walked over to a tire that had been suspended by a rope from one of the tree branches and sat in it. Benjamin crossed his feet, and the motion caused him to swing slightly.

"Was it something I said?" James asked after joining him.

"It's not you," Benjamin said, defeated. "I just...I..."

"Whatever it is, tell me. I'll help you out."

"Really?" Benjamin asked, surprised.

"Sure I will," James answered and beat a hand on his chest. "Me, KG, Cousin Bryan, shoot, even my daddy and Miss Sissy, if you ask nice."

James stopped and turned to Benjamin. He walked close to him and, when he was within reach, jumped up and pulled himself on top of the tire. It spun uncontrollably for a while, but Benjamin didn't fall out nor did James let go. He reached down and grabbed Benjamin's forearm.

"I just forgot, you haven't been initiated yet," James said.

"Initiated?"

"Repeat after me: Put me through hell and all kinds of pain, I'll give up my life, but never Fort Cain."

"Seriously?" Benjamin laughed.

"Say it. If you don't, then I can't let you live. You know our secret."

Benjamin shook his head. He grabbed James's forearm just as tight and repeated the oath. When he was done, James pulled him out of the tire swing and onto the ground, but Benjamin didn't let go. Instead he pulled James on top of him, and they rolled in the dead foliage while kissing. Benjamin stopped them once he needed air and pulled James's head to his chest.

"I have to tell you something," Benjamin started while kissing the top of James's head.

"Can't it wait?" James pleaded.

"Sure," Benjamin answered and pulled James in harder. "I wish we could stay here forever, you know?"

"Actually you just reminded me of something," James said. "Every year, my daddy puts on this fundraiser at our house. Everybody who's anybody this side of the Mason-Dixon line comes. I've never done it before, but I would be real pleased if you did me the honor of accompanying me as my date. I know you don't have much time left down here, but I thought maybe you just might be able to make it."

"I think I can swing that," Benjamin said, relieved to switch topics. "But I'm not sure I'm the upper-crust type to bump elbows."

"Shoot, not even my daddy could make me do that." James shook his head. "Don't worry, though. We can cut a rug all night long."

"It's a dance?"

"You know it. It's the *Sugar Cain Ball*."

Benjamin was thrilled to be James's guest and even happier that he was his date. They had shared such a beautiful time together, and it kept getting better. If nothing else, James did trust him, and Benjamin would need to show James that his trust was well placed by telling him everything. There was nothing he wanted to do more and would find the time when the moment was right.

Even through his excitement, Benjamin still asked James, "No, seriously, what's it called?"

Chapter Nine

"I DON'T CARE if they looked up and down for them, try looking left and right," James yelled into the phone on his desk before pressing the button to disconnect the call.

"Guess who's...why so glum?" Bryan asked as he entered the office.

"I'm not sad. I'm ready to chop someone in the damn throat," James grumbled.

Bryan headed for one of his sofas while pretending to wipe tears from his eyes. James was still upset, but with his attention divided between his company, his family, and Benjamin, it was comforting that Bryan was trying to remind him, in his own way, not to take things too seriously.

"It's those dang reports again, right?" Bryan asked and sat down. He was about to ask another question but jumped up from his seat, a bit afraid.

"What is it?" James asked.

"If I stay on a couch you own for too long, I'm gonna get pregnant."

James took Bryan to his desk and placed several folders in front of him.

"You know, some days I really wanna throw a pot of hot grits on you," James said.

"We're still not allowed to fight," Bryan said and picked up a folder. "If Uncle Charles found out..."

"And after he told Miss Sissy..." James shook his head and let out a deep breath. "All right, take a look at these."

"What am I looking at?" Bryan asked as he studied the reports.

"Flip over to the summaries in the back," James instructed. When Bryan was on the correct page, James pointed to a section with a pen. "Those right there."

Bryan studied the page for several seconds. "I still don't get it," Bryan said with frustration. "It's just a bunch of times and dates. And is that how hot it was that day?" He pointed to a number that wasn't followed by a unit of measurement.

"That's what I'm saying." James placed several more folders in front of Bryan and walked around his desk. He leaned in close to examine the documents and gestured for his cousin to look as well. "These are my activity reports."

"Hold on. I've seen those before. And these don't look anything like the normal reports. Eugene would've shown 'em to me by now," Bryan interrupted.

"You have 'em mixed up," James explained. "Eugene showed you the action reports. That's all the operational stuff like equipment, shipping, accidents, and so on. These are for the products." He pointed to the header of the document that displayed the specific name of one of the many sauces that his company made.

"I've never seen these," Bryan said as he studied the different documents in an attempt to understand the new format.

"It's a whole other can of worms," James said. "You gotta go to all kinds of classes for food safety and such. Get certified, rattle off a bunch of common sense stuff." James shook his head. "And I gotta send these up to the state, so Eugene just showed you the stuff to get ready and take over his job."

Bryan remained quiet as he looked over the documents with James.

"This one says nine o'clock," Bryan said.

"I already fixed that. Daddy always uses a twenty-four-hour clock. Had to track whatever-his-name-is down and figure out if he meant night or day."

"How about that lonely one hundred right here?"

James grimaced as he studied the document. "Can you beat up someone for me?"

"Huh?"

"It's the dang temperature they cooked that at," James said.

"I can't even smoke a rack of ribs that low."

"Wait...oh I see it," James said, looking relieved but still agitated. "It's metric."

"A what now?" Bryan asked and scratched his head.

James closed the folder and stood up straight for a long stretch. When he finished, he gestured to his door and exited with Bryan to take a short but slow walk to the cafeteria. James warmly greeted and shook the hands of his employees, and it was in that moment that he realized they really did work for him, and him alone.

"Look at me," James said to Bryan. "I'm just as rude as all get out. Did you need something?"

Bryan stopped James from selecting food items and led him to the rear exit of the cafeteria and out to the parking lot where his truck was parked. "I came to spring you."

"But I have work." James stopped walking with him. "You just saw how bad those reports were."

"You have the time, cousin," Bryan said. "I got it on good authority that Maynard's the one we have to deal with for inspections this month."

"Maynard? I figured as much," James said.

"Yup. But like I said, you're fine."

"You sure it's him?" James asked. "It could be anyone. I mean I've never had the same guy or gal twice in a row."

"Quit your yapping."

Bryan picked James up to throw him over his shoulder. James tried to break free, but Bryan spun very fast and then made his way to his truck. Once he was at the passenger door, he released James who tumbled against the vehicle to support himself from his vertigo.

"I'm gonna be sick," James chuckled out.

"Look, dang it," Bryan said while catching his breath. "You've been working your tail off ever since we got back from the lake. But we got the ball tonight."

"Trust me. I don't think anything can stop me from being there."

Bryan pointed a finger at him as he walked around his truck to the driver side. "What do you think Benji is doing right now?" Bryan climbed in and started the engine.

"I don't know," James said and blushed.

"The same thing you and me should be doing, so let's shake a leg and go get ready."

"But I can't. I can't let Daddy down any more," James said.

"Who do you think sent me to come and get you?"

"MR. BENJAMIN, IN my office—may I have a word with you in my office, privately?" Laura said, strained and not at all used to asking her subordinates to do something.

"Of course, ma'am," he said.

As they walked to her office, Laura recited information to Benjamin that had already been given to his department head—his new office assignments and report deadlines that he would need to meet. It all sounded pretty standard, and that was the intention. She needed him to have an official reason for extending his stay in Georgia.

"Where are we?" Laura asked as soon as they were in her office.

"I don't have anything new to report, ma'am," Benjamin said.

Laura brought up a hand that she balled into a fist. She counted silently before snapping her head back up. Taking in a sharp breath and in a strained voice, she asked, "Can you be more specific?"

"Jimmy hasn't given me any indication that he wants to sell."

"What were his exact words when you approached the topic, Benjamin?" She no longer offered him opportunities to be obtuse.

"I-I didn't..."

"Enough of this," Laura shouted. "Is this some sort of game to you, or is it that you simply enjoy hearing me repeat myself?"

"Ms. Harvington, I know what you want me to do."

"Then see it done. I am not keeping you on the payroll just to send you gallivanting about the countryside with your...taste of the South."

"Don't call him that," Benjamin yelled.

Laura was stunned. She opened her mouth to yell back, but instead, a soft laugh emerged. She tried to suppress it, but the laugh became deeper, and her voice higher. After the outburst Benjamin had displayed, she turned from him and the laugh rose even higher, becoming a cackle as she held her side with one hand and waved Benjamin away with the other.

"Excuse me, Benjamin, but I do believe that you have become much too close to your client," Laura said and wiped a tear from her eye. "I suppose the rumors are true of James's skill for you to be so smitten."

"Go to hell," Benjamin shouted.

"You two have not? Oh that is positively adorable," Laura said. Her desk phone chimed, and she answered the receptionist, instructing her to send in her appointment. "This meeting is concluded. I will not waste your time any longer. You are unwilling to do what is necessary, so you may leave for the airport."

"Ms. Harvington..."

"Show some dignity and do not beg," Laura said.

"J-Jimmy owns *Daddy Cain's*," Benjamin blurted out.

Laura looked up. "I am aware of that."

"No, I mean all of it. He told me that his father was retiring soon and that he would be in charge of everything. That was on our first night up there."

A smile snaked its way across Laura's face. Benjamin had just confirmed for her that James did, or very soon would, own all of his company, but the information of Charles retiring was completely new. Even if Benjamin hadn't done exactly what she wanted, he had just become an important source of information.

"Well, well, Mr. Benjamin, it seems that you have yet again dodged a bullet." Laura stood up and walked over to him. "But let me be clear—I grow tired of this back and forth. So if you could be so kind as to do your damn job so that I can stop these...distasteful threats, I would appreciate it."

"Ma'am..."

Laura held up a hand and looked at the clock on her wall. "The afternoon grows late, and I am afraid that this conversation must be postponed." She contacted her receptionist again and confirmed the time of her salon appointment. When Benjamin stared at her in surprise, Laura said, "Not that it is any of your concern, but I have to attend a social function tonight."

"The *Sugar Cain Ball*?" Benjamin asked while being ushered out the door.

"How did you...you will be accompanying James tonight? Oh you are good."

Benjamin ignored her comment and started to leave. He opened the door and paused when he came across Maynard and Ellsworth waiting outside. Laura noticed the three exchange cold glances, and then Benjamin continued on.

Laura called out to him, "See you tonight."

BENJAMIN WASN'T SURE how to feel as he wandered through the many cubicles until he reached his own. He had just told Laura very privileged information and was starting to feel physically ill from betraying James. But as soon as the wave of sickness would come, it would vanish almost instantly at the idea that James had no intention of selling. He decided not to dwell upon it because he planned on telling James everything soon, so he decided to check in with his supervisor.

"Hey, stranger, where you been?" Clinton asked. He got up from his desk and came around to shake Benjamin's hand with a warm smile.

"Now if I were to tell you that I spent the last few days at the most luxurious and secluded log cabin with a private lake, all to be initiated into a clubhouse, would you believe me?" Benjamin asked with no hint of sarcasm.

"I would, and I'll admit that I'm slightly jealous as well." Clinton went back to his desk and grabbed his hat and coat. "What do you say we get out of here? I could use a small nip."

"Lead the way," Benjamin encouraged. "It might help to calm my nerves."

Clinton nodded, and the two left the building. It didn't take long for them to reach Clinton's favorite pub, and once they had ordered, Benjamin told Clinton about his time away. While most of the time Clinton laughed at Benjamin's tale, there were parts where Clinton became silent and looked away from him.

"I'm glad you had a nice time," Clinton said.

"Thanks, but I also took you up on this offer because I wanted to say sorry for acting like such a jerk. You were only trying to help."

"Nothing to apologize for," Clinton said and stared into his drink. "I'm not saying that I've been in a similar situation, but I haven't always been the perfect angel with my clients either."

"Thanks, that helps," Benjamin said and ran a hand through his hair.

"So what are you nervous about anyway?" Clinton asked.

"It's Jimmy."

"Of course it is, Mr. Obvious." Clinton teased. "I meant why are you suddenly nervous? You said you were going to tell him about Ms. Harvington."

"And I am. I was just waiting for a better time." Benjamin sighed. "But with the ball tonight and the fact that Ms. Harvington will be there, I'm worried is all."

"Wait! You're going to the ball tonight? Now I am jealous." Clinton laughed.

"I am. Jimmy invited me. But you're not?"

"It's a fundraiser. Those plates start at twenty thousand dollars."

Benjamin almost spit out his drink at the information. Clinton remained calm, but the expression he wore displayed how serious he was.

"I'm going to be so out of place." Benjamin groaned.

"You'll be fine. Just think about it. James won't let you out of his sight."

"I guess you have a point." Benjamin nodded.

Clinton looked Benjamin over and finished his drink. He stood up and offered his hand to him. "Let's go, Ben. We've gotta go shopping. Something tells me you don't have the wardrobe for this."

"Renting a tuxedo isn't hard at all," Benjamin protested.

"Tuxedo, huh?" Clinton snorted. "Yeah, okay, come with me."

"DADDY, PLEASE," JAMES shouted. Bryan and Kenneth-George were literally dragging him by his feet down a hallway while Charles strolled lazily in front of them.

"It is for your own good, son," Charles replied without looking back.

"Stop all that bellyaching, Jimmy. Dang, when'd you get so strong?" Bryan asked when James grabbed a railing and wouldn't let go.

"How can you two help him go through with this?" James shrieked. "Please don't do this!"

Kenneth-George dropped one of his brother's legs to wrestle his hands from the railing. When he had both free, he grabbed James's wrists and nodded to Bryan who grabbed both of James's ankles and they proceeded on.

"You don't love me," James accused his father.

"Why? I love you with all of my heart, son. Don't I, Eugene?"

"Um, y-yes, Mr. Cain," Eugene answered. "Why am I here again, sir?"

"I mean the nerve of Raleigh," Charles said angrily. "What were his exact words again, Eugene?"

"T-That..." Eugene swallowed hard. "That Ellsworth, 'would be the star of the ball' and that his boy 'would shine brighter than the ones in the sky,' sir."

"Exactly! I mean I have never," Charles said as he turned into an open door.

All of them entered a large bath that rivaled the public ones of ancient Rome. Several attendants were waiting and, with a snap of Charles's fingers, descended upon James who tried to escape once again. As soon as he reached the door, several large men from Charles's security detail blocked the exit, and James felt several sets of hands begin removing his clothing.

"You set me up, Bryan."

"Do not blame your cousin. This was my doing." Charles turned from his son and to the attendants. "Into the tub."

"Don't do this. It's not right!"

James didn't get a response. Instead he was grabbed by his shoulders and dragged backward. Before he could try to persuade his father again, he was released and fell into the warm pool. The bath itself was built into the ground and deep enough that James wouldn't be hurt, but the slightly acidic liquid still burned his sinuses.

"There now, that isn't so bad, is it?" Charles smirked.

James stood up and wiped the stinging buttermilk from his eyes. "I hate this so much."

"Nonsense, you loved these baths growing up," Charles said.

Charles snapped again and several attendants went to the sides of the bath. James pouted for a second and then held up his hands for them to start cleaning his nails. They moved methodically as they applied a mud mask to James's face and wrapped his head in a tight bind to prepare his hair to be cut later.

"The last time you gave me a bath, I didn't even have two numbers in my age," James grumbled.

"Now that will be enough," Charles boomed. "You will be presentable for the ball tonight, and that is final."

"Yes, sir." James exhaled in defeat.

"Good." Charles nodded. "It is only an hour or so of soaking. In the meantime, I have called ahead and your tailor will be here soon."

"Thanks." James chuckled to himself and looked up at his father. "This is worse than prom."

"Do not remind me of that debacle," Charles said while grabbing his cane to leave. "No son of mine will be outdone at his own ball. Rest assured, Daddy Cain's *debon-heir* will sparkle tonight."

"Your ball..." James mumbled under his breath.

"What was that?" Charles turned to him.

"I said my feet hurt. Must've stepped on something."

"My word," Charles said, concerned but clearly angry. "I forgot to call your shoemaker. And I am positive Raleigh has one for Ellsworth. Eugene," he bellowed and searched for his assistant.

James turned from his father and back to his cousin and brother. They were making faces at him, so he splashed large amounts of the milk on them until they stopped.

"Are you gonna bake us something later on?" Bryan asked.

"Why not? You heard of johnnycakes. Well, get ready for 'Jimmy cakes.' Can you guess what makes 'em taste so special?"

"Yuck." Bryan shuddered. "So you're not mad that I had to kidnap you?"

"Why would I be?" James grinned at him.

Charles walked back in, looking angry. "Apparently he needs more than four hours to do a proper fitting."

"I'll be all right, Daddy."

"That is not the point!" Charles gestured his cane behind him. "And what are you still doing there? Run along now and make yourself presentable."

Bryan and Kenneth-George turned to leave, and as they did so, Charles rapped his cane on the floor. Without hesitation, the security detail walked in and grabbed Kenneth-George. They stripped him over his protest, and before he could yell at his father, he was thrown into the bath with James. He slowly popped his head above the buttermilk, his bangs hanging heavy over his face.

"You really didn't see that coming?" James asked his brother.

Instead of answering, Kenneth-George slowly spat out a mouthful of sour milk into his brother's face.

"BENJI, THIS WAY, sweetheart." Cecily took his hand.

Benjamin was just exiting the car James had sent, and Cecily was kind enough to receive him as James would be busy with his father. As Benjamin was lead in from the driveway, he took in how beautiful the Cain plantation looked at night. The home lit up the night as ushers and valets took the beautifully dressed guests inside. There was even a small news crew outside. The winding staircases were adorned with garlands of blooming flowers, and all around, classic bronze lanterns had been polished to perfection and lit.

When they entered, Benjamin almost let go of Cecily's hand because of how overwhelmed he was. The main entrance hall of Charles's plantation was more like a palace than a home. The crystal chandeliers twinkled softly as the servers moved among the guests, offering hors d'oeuvres and champagne. Benjamin was thankful that Clinton had taken him shopping. His suit might well have been the least expensive there, but it was much more appropriate with its classical accents for the overall theme.

"Snap out of it. We don't have time for this," Cecily said. Her own violet evening dress more stunning than many of the guests'.

Cecily took the two of them to the base of a large marble staircase and motioned for Benjamin to look to the top. "Any second now," she said.

On cue, the band stopped playing and several trumpeters sounded a call for attention.

Eugene, looking extremely relaxed and professional for once, cleared his throat and spoke. "Good evening, ladies and gentlemen. May I present to you our honored and most gracious host, Mr. Charles Howard Cain."

A violin started to play as Charles regally descended the steps. Benjamin was entranced as Charles walked with such confidence that he almost felt he should kneel. To Charles's immediate left and right were two beautiful young women who were only slightly older than James. While one was very close in appearance to James, the other had dark hair and more gentle features.

Kenneth-George had his arm interlocked with the dark-haired woman, his tuxedo making him finally look mature, while James had his arm interlocked with his other sister. As they descended, murmurs of approval and surprise could be heard throughout the hall and Benjamin understood why. They looked like royalty.

"Good evening, everyone," Charles began. "You humble me and my family by gracing us with your presence at our one hundred and forty-seventh Sugar Cain Ball. Now I have been known to be long-winded on occasion, but to see all you beautiful ladies, handsome gentlemen, and honorable officers of our police and military—well, I know you wish to get back to the festivities. Mayor Ferguson." Charles stretched out a hand.

"Thank you, Charles. Ellsworth, please join me, son," he said, and Ellsworth immediately approached his father's side. "I too can be long-winded and don't wish to take anything away from this beautiful evening." He turned from Charles and to the crowd. "As many of you know, Charles and I have been friends practically since birth. I don't know a more honest or decent man, and one who has done so much for our fair city." He paused until an approving round of applause subsided. "It is because of this dedication that I am confident to support him in his run for mayor once my term is completed."

There was more applause, even whistling at the idea of Big Daddy Cain running Calloway more so than he already did. There were approving nods from many people who were clearly wealthy and most likely ready to donate to his campaign. Charles was shaking hands with the mayor as pictures were being taken. James made his way into the shot as well, flanking his father as Ellsworth did the same with his.

"I knew it." Cecily continued to clap. "Why I just knew that Charles had something big planned with Mayor Ferguson."

"He really is impressive," Benjamin said.

"I suppose it puts everything in perspective. Why sell your company when he can let Jimmy make the choice? Charles really does have the foresight with these sorts of things."

Benjamin clapped more slowly. No matter where he was, he kept being reminded of his goals to convince James to sell.

"LOOKS LIKE WE'RE finally done. At least for the moment," Ellsworth said to James.

"They're making the rounds so now's as good a time as any to escape," James said.

James and Ellsworth broke from where their fathers were taking pictures and moved to one of the bars. They were both used to public appearances such as this, but the flashing lights, with long handshakes and having to hold even longer smiles, was tiring.

"Thanks for having us," Ellsworth said and handed James a drink.

"The honor is mine." James leaned into his ear and spoke softly. "So you can play nice?"

Ellsworth coughed into his drink and stepped back. James had only been kidding but noticed how flustered Ellsworth had become. He didn't want to cause a scene so James changed topics.

"Got you too, huh?" James said and touched the foundation on Ellsworth's cheek.

Ellsworth's posture relaxed. "Y-yeah...you know it. Gotta be Dad's fancy boy. At least they didn't paint our cheeks rosy like when we were kids."

"Remember when they hauled us off with 'em to that new port that opened up?" James asked. "I thought my daddy was gonna pull something when he saw us wearing the same sailor suit."

"And we both had matching caps with the same ribbon." Ellsworth groaned. "You still had me beat with that big ol' rainbow sucker that covered your whole face, though."

James snickered but stopped. "I didn't mean to bring up the other day, here in front of all these people, Ellie."

"Naw, it's fine," Ellsworth said with a smile that formed and disappeared quickly. "Look, about what I called you that night at Bryan's..."

"Remember this special evening?" A photographer interrupted Ellsworth and held up a camera.

James shrugged. "We better get used to this, what with our daddies going hand in hand with his race."

"Good idea," Ellsworth said. He faced James and took his hand while staring at the camera with a poised smile.

"Oh, you boys can do better than that," the photographer urged.

James turned his back to Ellsworth. He felt him slowly wrap his arm around his waist, and James placed his hands on top of his. Even in the stiff suit, James could feel Ellsworth shaking, so he stroked the top of his hand with his own.

"Smile," the photographer shouted, then took their picture. "Nice."

The photographer left, but Ellsworth didn't release James.

"Jimmy, can we go somewhere not too far from here?"

James gently removed Ellsworth's arms and turned to him. "Sure, let's just get through all the elbow-rubbing first." He scanned the area and found the person he was looking for.

"Benji," James called and waved him over.

Benjamin headed over but stopped short. "Jimmy...you look...wow!"

"Really?" James asked.

After cleaning up, James did, in fact, look quite dashing. The pleated shirt fit tightly and a large and intricate pendant hung about his wing-tipped collar. While Benjamin had a tailcoat, James finished his entire ensemble with a thin cane similar to his father's.

James brought him in and wrapped his cape around them as they kissed. Ellsworth, to his credit, didn't move or seem uncomfortable. But when James and Benjamin parted, Ellsworth looked directly into Benjamin's eyes as if only to acknowledge his presence.

"You don't look half bad yourself," James said when they broke apart.

"He certainly does not. My, what handsome young men you all are," Laura said as she approached them with Maynard at her side and Bryan cautiously trailing to observe. Her white evening gown flowed behind her and her bare shoulders sparkled softly in the light, almost glowing.

"How are you, Jimmy?"

"I'm fine, Governess," James said neutrally. "But I'm surprised that you're here. Daddy didn't mention it, and you haven't attended one of these in forever."

"This is all for charity," Laura said in a tightly controlled voice. "And while I may not have been on the RSVP list, I am sure Charles will be delighted to know that he has raised more for the cause."

"That he will, ma'am," James replied, just as controlled. "You have yourself a nice evening."

"Oh I intend to. Your father is so generous to do this every year. The money he collects has been a safety net that many have needed in these hard economic times," Laura said, sounding genuine.

"He is," was all James said.

Laura turned her attention. "Why, Benjamin, is that you? I had no idea you would be attending this evening. I suppose that I am paying you too much." She giggled.

"Not nearly enough...ma'am," Benjamin answered nervously.

"Oh, but where are my manners? We should not be discussing work at such a lovely event. It can wait until Monday, and you can inform me of every single detail of your wonderful time here."

"Of course, Ms. Harvington."

"Excellent." Laura turned once again. "Ellsworth, please come with me," she said and walked past them.

"Y-yes, Governess," Ellsworth answered to ensure she heard him.

James frowned at Ellsworth's retreating back, slightly concerned over the way Ellsworth had acknowledged Laura. Maynard followed closely behind but returned a much less pleasant stare. With the small crowd dispersing to enjoy the party, James turned to his cousin.

"You wanna take a stab at that, cousin?" James asked.

"That's all on you," Bryan said while adjusting his bowtie. "I'm gonna go mingle, Jimmy." He left after shaking Benjamin's hand.

Now alone, James turned to Benjamin. "So what were you saying about how good I look?"

"I was saying"—Benjamin brought him in close—"that you still owe me a dance."

James didn't fight it as Benjamin led them deeper into the hall toward the sound of the band.

"THIS PLACE JUST gets bigger, doesn't it?" Benjamin asked in awe as he entered James's room.

"Not yet it doesn't." James smiled. "Come take a look at this," he instructed and hurried to open the doors that accessed his balcony. James went outside, and after stepping to the ledge, stood up on top of the railing to let the wind catch his coat. "What do you think?"

"I think," Benjamin said, "that you should stop trying to impress me. You've succeeded. But I also think we should get back downstairs."

"What for?" James asked. He came in from the balcony and walked over to take Benjamin's hands. "I already told my daddy I wanted to show you my room." He dragged Benjamin closer to his bed.

"You did not tell him that. How could you?" Benjamin asked, slightly anxious.

"'Cause I'm the new Daddy Cain and can do whatever I want," James said. When he reached his bed, he grabbed Benjamin by his broad shoulders and tossed him onto the raised mattress. Benjamin started to get up, but James placed a firm and surprisingly strong hand on his chest. "My house, my rules, boy."

Benjamin stopped protesting. Instead, he fumbled at his neck as he removed his tie with nervous anticipation while James removed his shoes and pants. When Benjamin no longer had any clothing remaining, he stood and pulled James in for a kiss. After they broke apart, Benjamin tugged at James's own vest but was once again pushed onto the bed.

"What?"

"Hush up now. I've been waiting on this for a while. Damn." James breathed out heavily as one of his eyebrows arched.

James took in Benjamin's statuesque form as he lay on his bed. He could barely focus on removing his own clothing while Benjamin continued to move seductively as the moonlight poured in from the balcony onto his completely hairless skin. When James had his last garment off, he wasted no time leaping onto Benjamin.

Benjamin spread his arms when he saw James coming and then rolled in the silk sheets while kissing James. He pulled him closer and felt the soothing and breathtaking heat of James's body against his own. It didn't take any time, and soon Benjamin felt James's erection grow and press against him as he did the same.

"Jimmy..." Benjamin said softly when they broke apart.

"How about I water this and see if it grows more?" James asked.

James didn't give him time to answer. He nibbled lightly but quickly at Benjamin's thick thighs before traveling higher up his body. Benjamin reacted with forced restraint, grabbing the sheets of the bed with one hand and James's hair with the other.

A needy sound came from Benjamin's open mouth. Instead he closed his lids over eyes rolled back due to James's onslaught. From James's crimson lips, Benjamin received the perfect balance of pressure and heat and slight scrapes of teeth. He reached to place his hands on James's cheeks, but his lower body was pulled higher. "Jimmy...Jimmy, slow down," Benjamin pleaded. "Is your tongue part typhoon?"

James lifted his head and gently lowered Benjamin. He lay on top of him and kissed his way up his torso, bit at his chest, and lapped at his neck before reaching his eyes. "I can't help it. You taste like honey."

When Benjamin smiled, James took both of Benjamin's hands and interlocked fingers with his. He straddled Benjamin's hips and kissed Benjamin while pushing his arms down against the bed and grinding into him. James was about to let him up, but Benjamin pulled his hands away and grabbed him about his waist.

"No more waiting," Benjamin responded in a deep voice.

James turned his head and Benjamin followed his gaze to a side table with a small open jar and a condom packet lying on top. He reached over and dipped his fingers in, then applied the slick oil to James. Benjamin passed the condom to James and waited while James rolled the sheath down his cock before entering him.

James ran his hands along Benjamin's chest and threw his head back while on top of Benjamin. He moved his hips fast and hard while driving

Benjamin closer to the edge of his bed while riding him. When they were close to the edge, James took in a sharp breath of air and Benjamin grabbed around his neck with one hand and pushed him back.

"My turn," Benjamin grunted.

He had broken James's stride but picked up from him. Benjamin was sitting up as he continued to push James backward. When he was completely on his back, Benjamin pulled James's legs up to wrap them around his waist as he delved deeper into him at a much faster pace.

James forgot all about talking when Benjamin clapped a hand behind his neck. It stung, but James just clawed at his back while pulling him in. He had stopped his smooth, rhythmic strokes and replaced them with hard thrusts. James's breathing became labored, and he found release in Benjamin's grip.

Benjamin shuddered. The spasms and tightening of James's muscles caused Benjamin to lose himself in the feeling. He kissed James quickly and looked right into his eyes. Benjamin's grip on the back of James's neck became tighter and he finished, surrounded by James. After a few moments of disbelief, Benjamin pulled James back up into a sitting position and kissed him while still inside of James.

"Where the heck has this guy been?" James nuzzled Benjamin's face after he released his embrace and moved to lie next to him.

"I'm not really sure, but I will be kicking myself all night long for waiting this long," Benjamin said. He lay back and pulled James into a light cuddle. "Your dad is going to kill me if he finds out."

"Nah, he won't, just kick your head in or something." James snickered. "You really gotta bring him up now, though?"

Benjamin shook his head. "Sorry about that."

"Ahh c'mon, don't you go getting all bashful now. I was just saying." James smiled. "You're not feeling bad or anything about us doing this, are you?"

"What?" Benjamin asked, shocked at the question. "If I was, then I would have a lot to explain when we go for round two and three."

"What makes you think we're doing this again? As a matter fact, I already gotcha. Why the heck are you still here instead of making me a sandwich?"

Benjamin laughed and hit James with a pillow. James was still grinning so he moved an arm lower on James's back and pulled him in harder, bringing them closer. "You were saying?"

"Oh, now I see what you mean." James wiped the grin from his face but still looked happy. "I'm having a real nice time with you."

"Me too. Tonight was amazing."

"I didn't mean... I'm saying I like that you're around," James said softly.

Benjamin didn't say a word. He pulled away from James, rose from the bed, and walked out onto James's balcony. He lowered a heavy head into his palm and leaned on the marble railing.

"You okay?" James asked cautiously.

Benjamin sighed. "I'm fine...no, I'm not."

"Is this about what you had to tell me up at the lake?"

"It is." Benjamin turned from him and shook his head. "It's just that...I don't even know where to start or what to say."

"Then don't say anything." James shrugged his shoulders.

"No, you don't understand, I-I..."

"Hey," James said warmly as he hugged Benjamin, having gotten off his bed to join him on his balcony. Benjamin was shivering, which was odd because it wasn't cold, but James said nothing.

"I need to be honest with you."

"Is it bad?" James asked.

"It is to me."

"Did you hurt someone? Steal something or anything I need to call the sheriff about?"

"What? No, it's nothing like that," Benjamin said.

"Well, then excuse the heck outta me if I really don't care at this particular point in time."

"*Point in time*?" Benjamin smiled, feeling slightly better. "You're starting to sound like your father, James."

"I take that as a compliment. We all gotta grow up some time, and since I'm the new Daddy Cain—"

"You like saying that, don't you?" Benjamin accused.

"I just became worth nine doggone figures. Yeah, I like saying it."

Benjamin hugged James. "I need to get this off my chest."

"No, you need to take a shower to get something of mine off your chest," James teased. "But later. I don't wanna mess this up. Can't we just enjoy tonight?"

Benjamin took James's face into his hands and kissed his forehead before holding him tightly.

"Sure thing. Anything you want."

Chapter Ten

"RISE AND SHINE, Jimmy." Bryan wandered into James's room. He did a quick scan of the area and didn't find his cousin but instead, Benjamin was there, just finishing tying his shoes.

"Oh uh, hey, Bryan," Benjamin said warmly. "He's still in the shower."

"Yup..." Bryan said dryly. "And you didn't join him?"

"What? No." He chuckled, "I mean I have to get on the road soon back to Savannah. Plus I'm trying to avoid running into Mr. Cain."

"Just buy yourself a helmet. Your head and Uncle Charles's cane are about to become real good friends," Bryan said.

Benjamin rolled his eyes and finished dressing. When he was done, Bryan snuck behind and restrained his arms while Kenneth-George approached, cracking his knuckles.

"Hey, I'm not done with him yet," James said. He laughed at the sight of his family wrestling with Benjamin. "Need some help?"

"I just need one more minute," Benjamin choked out when he removed Kenneth-George's arm from around his neck.

In a swift movement, James took off his towel and snapped it at the three of them until they all stood still and looked at him. He didn't say anything, but quickly dressed as they waited.

"I'll be free later on. Late lunch?" James asked Benjamin. He took Benjamin's hands into his own.

"Wouldn't miss it. I'm probably just going to see if Clint is up to anything, but I'm free all day."

"Good," James said and pulled Benjamin in for a tender kiss.

"Guys, we're right here," Bryan groaned. He pointed to Kenneth-George, who was covering his mouth and pretending to look ill.

"Uh-huh," James mumbled.

Benjamin turned James's face back to his own and rested his forehead against James's. He held James's gaze and gave him a light peck on the cheek before backing away. "If I don't leave now, I don't think I will."

Benjamin headed to the door with a warm smile and then left with a lazy yet cocky stroll, his coat held over his right shoulder. When he was in the hallway, he glanced back and James smiled.

"Sorry about that, KG. Show 'im how to get out before he gets lost."

Kenneth-George didn't rise from his brother's couch. Instead, he pulled out his phone and started to page a staff member.

"Move it," James said and pulled his brother up to push him toward Benjamin. When his brother left, he turned to Bryan. "Got any plans today?"

"Maybe. What's it to you?"

James left his room with a spring in his step, and Bryan followed him toward the wing of his house that contained the garage.

"Dang, man, we haven't spent much time together. Just the two of us, I mean."

"Well, shoot. Why're you fussing at me?" Bryan asked. "I just didn't wanna get between you and Benji."

"Blood's thicker," James said.

The two reached the garage, and James started to climb into Bryan's truck but stopped when he had one leg in.

"What is it?" Bryan asked.

"I wanna have some fun." James had a glint in his eye.

"Didn't you do that last night?"

"Yeah, a few times actually. And right before you came into my room this morning," James said and wiped his brow. "But I'm talking about stuff we can all do. Wanna open up the cafeteria later on?"

"You don't have to ask me twice. I'm anywhere I get to grub." Bryan slapped James's back. "Is Uncle Charles okay with that?"

"How many times I gotta say it? I'm—"

"The new *Daddy Cain*. Yeah, we get it." Bryan laughed at him. "All right, so get in and let's mosey on over there."

"Nah, I think I'll head on over to see Benji."

"But you just said you wanna open up the cafeteria. He just left and if you charge after 'im like this, you're gonna scare 'im off."

"Leave it be," James warned. "You let me worry about 'im. Besides you can handle all that. Just yell at Eugene. It makes things easier."

"And how the heck am I supposed to let everyone know that the new Daddy Cain has his kitchen open today," Bryan asked and looked at his watch with skepticism.

"Make it free," James said quickly. "Everyone gets a free plate, and send 'em all home with something nice. All you gotta do is tell KG, and he'll put the word out. You know that boy can't shut up."

"True enough." Bryan nodded. "So what do you want me to send 'em all home with?"

"I dunno." James thought of past items that had been gifted to his employees and community. "We already got 'em gift baskets and such. And those certificates are done to death."

"You wanna just give 'em cash? That always makes people happy," Bryan suggested.

"Nope." James looked down and bobbed his head to his side. "I just want it to be something nice but different too."

"How about your barbecue sauce?"

"Everybody in town can get that, and my workers get it for free," James said.

"I meant the Big X. We did just make a batch a few days ago," Bryan corrected him. "Uncle Charles liked it. I like it. Heck everyone who tried it likes it."

James paused before answering. "I don't know. It's not right yet."

"Even if it isn't, it's still good. And it's new. We can smoke up a whole heap of slabs for it and give everybody a bottle to take home," Bryan said. "Think about it—free product testing. Or your debut as the new head honcho."

"Make it happen," James said.

"You got it." Bryan took out his phone to make a call. "Who do I talk to so I can get it all bottled up?"

"Eugene can take care of all that."

"Done and done. I'm gonna take care of everything," Bryan said proudly. "Thanks, you know, for trusting me on this."

James just waved a hand at him as he left.

"FINALLY," JAMES WHINED as Benjamin approached and hugged him. "Took you long enough."

"It wasn't even five minutes," Benjamin said dryly.

"I don't care," James said. "Now c'mon. I know this nice place down here on the river walk that sells the best dang fried catfish nuggets you've ever tasted."

"Considering I've never tried them, I will take your word for it," Benjamin responded coolly.

"Hush up," James teased. He guided Benjamin to a local street vendor who greeted James warmly. After they received their food, James turned to leave, but the vendor stopped him and handed him a card.

"Does that happen often? People trying to make business connections like that, I mean?" Benjamin asked.

"Not really, but this wasn't about no business."

James held up the card and showed Benjamin the small hug and kisses symbols scribbled on the small piece of paper.

"Oh, what the hell?" Benjamin nudged him lightly. "You're flirting with other people while we're together?"

"Hey, I just wanted some food. I didn't do anything!" James held up his hands in a show of innocence.

"You're right." Benjamin passed his skewer of food to James. "Give me a sec. I forgot to leave a tip," he said and walked back toward the vendor.

"Whoa there, tank," James said as he ran in front of him. "I'm a lover, not a fighter."

"And I take my traits from both columns." Benjamin was smiling but still walking toward the vendor.

"C'mon now, I don't like it when someone beats up on people," James said in an almost pleading tone.

Benjamin stopped and turned back to James, cupped his cheek, and stroked lightly. "Only because you asked so nicely."

"You're not gonna to put that boy in the hospital," James tried but couldn't suppress his mischievous grin. "Are you the jealous type?"

"W-What? No! No..." Benjamin stammered. "Okay, maybe just a little."

"What for?" James asked, confused. He turned to walk and Benjamin followed until they found a bench that overlooked the waterfront.

"I don't mean to be, but you do get around," Benjamin said carefully.

"So what? I'm not ashamed of it," James returned sternly.

"I wasn't accusing you of anything."

"Then why'd you bring it up?"

Benjamin remained silent so James went on.

"I do my dirt, but I've never hurt anyone. I never told 'em I wanted to go steady or anything. And I damn sure have never messed with anyone who's hitched."

"Jimmy, please." Benjamin took James's hands into his own. "That is in no way what I meant."

James huffed and slid away from Benjamin. When he was at the other end of the bench, he laid down into Benjamin's lap, face up. "Then how's about you tell me."

Benjamin took a deep breath. "It's just...everywhere we go I'm reminded about your past flames or people who want you. Just now; every time I go home and pass by the manager. And when we were in Calloway, every time I went out with you."

James threw up his hands, "I already told Eddie I was sorry about that!"

"Not who I was talking about, but that's what I mean."

"My past is my past," James said.

"Not when they're staring you and sometimes me in the face."

James's brow furrowed so Benjamin said the names.

"Maynard and Ellsworth."

"Aww, you're not really gonna make me tell you about my crazy ex, are you?"

"Wait 'ex'? As in single?" Benjamin asked.

"Yeah, Maynard." James sighed and rubbed his eyes in embarrassment. "Remember when I mentioned we dated in college?"

"You're not proud of that? I gathered that he's an annoying little prick from when we were at the party, but he was all over Ellsworth. And he is kind of hot for a ginger, so what's the problem?"

"You just called another boy hot in front of me and I'm the one doing the explaining?" James smiled at him. "Naw, he was fine at first, but he is clingy. And just between you and me, that boy was a little too much for me in the sheets if you catch my drift."

"Actually I don't," Benjamin said and leaned forward to kiss James. "You mean frequency? Duration?" Benjamin started laughing. "Don't tell me it was size!"

"Keep at it." James pulled him down for another kiss and then went to his ear. "But I can tell you who's bigger if you want," he finished with a mocking tone.

"Yep, you win." Benjamin backed down. "But really what was the problem?"

"Well, he wanted to do too many things," James said. "I mean some of them were fine 'cause I never tried 'em, but he just kept on and wanted to do other stuff. Weird stuff."

"Oh yeah," Benjamin taunted. "Jimmy found a freak."

James shook his head and suppressed his laughter. "I don't have a problem with that, but something tells me that boy watched too many dang movies."

Benjamin grimaced and shook his head. "Sorry to hear that. It probably was pretty awkward having to go on after that discussion."

"You don't know the half," James said.

"And what about Ellsworth?"

"What about 'im?"

"You're telling me that you two have never been anything? Because at the ball, you two seemed close. Not to mention that he's the second name right under yours carved into the bark of your little tree house."

"Fort," James insisted.

"You're avoiding the question," Benjamin said.

"No, I'm not. I already told you that we've always just been friends."

"Friends?" Benjamin asked. "I think you need to explain that."

"I guess so, but we grew up together. Went to the same schools and such. Our daddies are best friends, so we were always around each other. Yeah, we go at it, but it's nothing serious, more like rivals. Our folks didn't help it any because they always tried to outdo each other through us."

"Friends?" Benjamin repeated.

"We are. You know, Ellie used to pick on me all the time, growing up. Mostly because I used to be a lanky so-and-so. I can't even tell you how many times he would chase me down. It's a good thing Bryan had my back."

"He used to beat you up?" Benjamin asked.

"Not really. We couldn't fight because of our daddies, but I don't think he ever wanted to hurt me. Actually that night at the barn was the only time he ever did something like that."

"Once is one damn time too many," Benjamin said, clearly angry.

"Down, boy." James patted his arm. "It's just the way we are. Shoot, if you think that's something, wait until our birthday."

"Our?"

"Same day. Our daddies said we were born less than a minute apart."

"That's improbably convenient," Benjamin said in an annoyed tone. "At least I don't have to worry about seeing him much, well at least when you two aren't on the campaign trail."

"That won't be for a long time, but don't you go puffing up if you come around and he's in my office."

Benjamin gazed down at James with a raised eyebrow.

"Nothing you or anyone can do to change it. Ellie's a partner at his physical therapy clinic, and I help pay him to treat people when he can't take the hit."

"Why?" Benjamin groaned. "I was okay with not liking him. Why'd you have to go and make him someone who helps people?"

"Actually he usually works with poorer kids and school athletes."

"Stop talking."

Benjamin pulled James up until their noses touched. They stopped when a ringing came from Benjamin's pocket.

"It's work." Benjamin said, looking at his phone.

"Isn't it always?"

Benjamin answered the call. "Do you have a sixth sense or something?" Benjamin asked after the video of Clinton appeared, looking completely innocent.

"I don't know what you mean, but sorry if I'm interrupting." Clinton let out a small laugh. *"I just wanted to know if you could stop by the office, I have your tickets and itinerary."*

Benjamin stopped smiling, and James sat up from his lap. He looked at James, who crossed his arms, and then back to his phone. "Sure, sure I can. When's a good time?"

"Can you meet me now? There isn't a whole lot going on at the moment, but I have it on good authority that your...that James is opening his restaurant today. I'm trying to swing by and pick up the family before I head over. If we can get this done before I leave for the day, it would help me out. Ms. Harvington frowns on any business off the clock."

"And every dang thing else," James said. He slid back over to Benjamin and grabbed his hand so that he could see the phone. "Mr. Clint, I'll make you a deal. You leave us alone and I'll put all of your kids through graduate school."

Benjamin took back his arm. "Be right over. We're actually only a few blocks from you."

"Sounds good, and tell James that was my last time. Cross my heart."

"Is that what you wanted to talk about? I know you're about to hit the road soon," James asked.

"I—no, it's not," Benjamin said quietly.

"I've put it off for too long anyway. After we go see Mr. Clint, I'm all ears," James said and took Benjamin's hand to lead him to his car.

Benjamin didn't object, and even though he wasn't looking forward to James's reaction once he told him of Laura's proposition, he would be thankful that he no longer had to hide anything.

"HOW'VE YOU BEEN, Amanda?" James asked the receptionist with a bright smile as he and Benjamin entered the floor of Benjamin's office.

"I'm surprised you remember my name," she said. "Tell me, is it a good or bad thing that you never called? The other interns had a good laugh when I told them I said I was looking forward to it."

"Yeah about that..."

"You two can finish this later," Benjamin said lightly. "Can you let Clint know we're on our way back?"

"Hold your horses. I'm not going anywhere." James turned to Benjamin with a sheepish smile. "Sorry, but your boss lady and me don't mix."

Benjamin shrugged and walked away while James turned his attention back to Amanda.

"For what it's worth, I actually did plan on calling. It's just that things got kinda busy."

"Wow, that line is even worse, coming from a guy who's not interested. And one who got me chewed out by my boss because you were able to get past me and interrupt her meeting."

"Aww, now I feel bad," James said. "Lemme make it up to ya. Spa day? I'll take you shoe shopping and let you drag me around to all the stores."

"I'm fine at a bowling alley with a plate of cheese fries," she said.

"Really?"

"Really. It's the only time I get to cheat," she said. "You can also sweeten the deal by bringing that other guy with you. Not the jailbait. That cute meathead that kind of looks like you." She winked.

"Oh that's what you're getting at."

James smiled and brushed a hand through his hair when Amanda smiled back. He was about to ask her questions to learn more about her, but an angry voice to his side got his attention.

"What are you doing here?" Maynard sneered as he entered the lobby.

"Hey to you too."

"Mr. Winchester?" Amanda asked Maynard, and he looked at her. "Ms. Harvington had to step out for a moment. She should be back soon."

Maynard nodded and turned his attention back to James. "You still haven't answered my question."

James rolled his eyes and crossed his arms. "My dang business, that's what I'm doing."

"Making the rounds then?" Maynard asked smugly.

"I guess we got that in common then. I don't reckon you wanna tell me when you're stopping by my plant for my inspection," James said, in an attempt to change subjects.

"You know it doesn't work that way," he said. "Oh wait, this is where that foreign boy works, isn't it?"

"He's from up North, Maynard," James said, trying to control his reaction. "But it doesn't have anything to do with you."

James was about to continue arguing when Clinton's and Benjamin's voices sounded. James thanked his lucky stars he would be leaving soon.

"Sure, like I can get away with that." Clinton laughed as he walked back out into the lobby with Benjamin. "And this is where we part ways. See, James, not long at all."

James didn't say anything. He noticed Benjamin and Maynard staring at one another with hard, angry eyes.

"Huh? And here I always heard that people trade up when they meet someone new," Maynard said.

"I said mind your business," James snapped.

"And I wasn't talking to you." He looked at Benjamin. "I'm surprised. Ms. Harvington said you were smart, but here you are with him." Maynard nodded his head toward James. "I suppose to each his own, but I prefer something that isn't so used. A snug fit."

"I'm going to enjoy this," Benjamin said as he walked toward Maynard.

JAMES AND CLINTON reached to keep Benjamin from getting closer to an angry and slightly frightened-looking Maynard. Even while being restrained, Benjamin continued to exchange insults with Maynard as James tried to calm him down and Clinton nodded for Amanda to contact security.

"What is this?" Laura shouted as she walked into the lobby past Maynard. Her stern visage cracking slightly at the distinctive tells of anger. "All of you, over here at once."

Benjamin and James walked over to stand in front of Laura, but Maynard remained behind her. "Ms. Harvington…"

"Excuse me, Maynard, but did you forget to whom you speak?" Laura asked in a voice that made everyone become silent.

"N-No, Governess," Maynard answered timidly. He walked around to stand in front of her with James and Benjamin.

"I do not know what sorts of nonsense the three of you are wrapped up in and I do not care. You will not, I repeat *not,* bring such foolishness into my place of business. Especially if you are in my employ!"

"Yes, ma'am," Benjamin and Maynard said at the same time.

"Mr. Rei, I instructed Clinton to give you adequate time off to prepare for your departure, but it seems that you are more than ready."

"Ms. Harvington…"

"Didn't you hear her?" Maynard responded before Laura could. "We don't need you anymore. You couldn't seal the deal with Mr. Cain and you're obviously not good enough to sweep Jimmy off his feet! I guess we'll have to find another way to make him sell."

Everyone became quiet and shifted to look at Benjamin. Laura's glare was filled with disappointment, but she quickly turned back to Maynard, who wore a condescending smirk. With everyone's full attention focused on him, Benjamin took the time to look at each person in turn. Amanda with her attention seemingly on her monitor, Clinton upset, and then to James, whose expression was one of disgust and incomprehension.

"What's he talking about, Benji?" James asked loudly.

"Jimmy..."

"Don't you *Jimmy* me, Mr. Rei. What the hell is he talking about?"

"Try not to look so surprised." Maynard injected himself into the conversation. "Why do think he spent so much time down here after Daddy Cain said no?"

"Be silent, boy," Laura admonished Maynard and then spoke to James. "Jimmy, what he said is not entirely true."

"Enough of it is, though, right?" James shouted at Benjamin. "Is that all I was to you? A damn mark? For what?"

"Jimmy, it's not like that," Benjamin pleaded after finding his voice. "I never had any intention of using what we have like that. I wanted to tell you when we went to the lake, but you guys were so happy—"

"You knew way back then!" James turned from him and made fists. "Is that why you didn't talk to me before we met up at the lake? You were making plans, huh?"

"No!" Benjamin turned James around while holding his shoulders. He tried to soothe James by rubbing his arms, but James violently slapped them away. "I wanted to tell you. Those days after you first left my place, at your tree...fort, that night at the ball."

"Well, doesn't that just make it all better?" James backed away from him. "You knew all that damn time but figured you'd wait until I laid on my damn back for you!"

"I'm not lying," Benjamin shouted.

"Then why didn't you say anything?" James asked with an eerie calm. "You keep saying that you aren't lying, so why didn't you tell me? If you didn't have anything to hide and knew you weren't doing anything wrong, then why?"

"I-I..." Benjamin stammered.

"And you—" James turned to Laura. "—why'd you do this, Governess? Huh? I know I was a bad kid, but you're gonna tell me what the hell I did to you that was so damn terrible to cause you to wanna hurt me like this!"

Laura didn't answer him and instead turned to Maynard. "I believe you have something to take care of for me."

"Yes, ma'am. See you at the inspection later today, Jimmy. I'll be glad once I finish this last one and never have to set foot in *Daddy Cain's* again," Maynard said.

"Are you hard of hearing, boy? Shut your damn mouth," Laura shouted. "Well, this was most unexpected. Clinton, if you are leaving for the day, now would be the time. Amanda, I need a list of all my calls." Laura looked to Benjamin and James. "I am quite sure that you two have things to discuss, so I will leave you to it. And not within the walls of my offices." She turned and walked away.

"Jimmy, I don't know what to say. I was going to talk to you" Benjamin said.

James glared at Benjamin and then walked past him. When he was in the elevator, he said over his shoulder, "Nothin' left to talk about."

"CAN WE PLEASE go someplace and get drunk?" Benjamin begged as he and Clinton drove toward his home.

"No," Clinton said flatly. "You should be thankful I'm giving you a lift. I told you this would happen."

"Right now, I need a friend, not a mom."

"And friends are honest. You screwed up, and now you get to hurt," Clinton said while not even looking at him. "I'm already going to be late meeting up with my family for this, so if you want to drown your sorrows, be my guest."

Benjamin stopped talking and leaned his head against the window. After everything he and James had been through to become closer, he was disappointed in himself at how he'd handled something as simple as telling the truth. His words with Cecily came back to him about not wasting time by lying, but that is exactly what he had done.

"Maybe I should just head over to Calloway with you. He'll be there." Benjamin spoke to the window.

"Have you ever been dumped?" Clinton asked. "You're leaving soon, and James is not in the mood to speak to you. I would just cut my losses. Besides, he's about to be busy with Maynard."

"That inspection?" Benjamin asked, grateful for an opportunity to focus on something else. "What's he looking at anyway?"

"Why do you care?" Clinton snapped.

"Humor me."

"Maynard's a safety inspector. He told me he's responsible for certain businesses in the tri-county area when we met."

"Tri-county?" Benjamin asked, confusion lacing his tone. "But he said Jimmy was his last inspection."

"Do you know how many businesses and restaurants there are in a county, let alone three? There's no way."

"Then what did he mean?" Benjamin asked.

"I don't know, probably for the day. Either way, I don't care." Clinton pulled his car in front of Benjamin's building. "Look, I know you're having a rough time right now, but focusing on other people won't help you with James. If it means that much to you, then talk to him."

Benjamin was lost in thought. There was something about Maynard's statements that he could not shake. There was a note of victory in his voice as he spoke to James, and at first Benjamin thought it was because of their prior relationship. Now, Benjamin couldn't help but feel that he was missing something, something that James hadn't noticed because of him.

"Ms. Harvington," Benjamin shouted.

"What about her? Look, I really need to get going." Clinton urged him on.

"Clint, when have you ever seen Ms. Harvington yell like that? And I don't mean when she's dressing someone down."

"At the meeting with Mr. Cain," Clinton answered as he thought over her actions. "He got under her skin."

"That's what I mean. Did you hear how she kept telling Maynard to be quiet?"

Clinton stared at his lap. "Ben, what are you getting at?"

"I need a favor," Benjamin replied.

"MAYNARD'S HERE." BRYAN walked into James's office.

James lay on his couch with an arm draped over his face and a drink in his other hand. "Thanks. Take care of it."

"But I thought you wanted me on the cafeteria," Bryan said. "It just opened up and most of the workers will be there soon."

"Just take care of it," James snapped. He set his drink down and turned over on his side, away from his cousin.

"So you're not gonna say a few words to your employees and all of the people coming here?"

When James didn't say anything, he left without another word.

"Mr. Cain?" A voice came through the intercom on the table above James's head. *"Mr. Cain, I have a Mr. Clinton Jackson to see you. He says it's urgent."*

"And I said don't bother me," James yelled at the speaker. He tried once again not to think of Benjamin but couldn't when he and Clinton burst into his office with security guards following, one bleeding from his lip.

"Jimmy," Benjamin called as two men grabbed his arms and tried to pull him away. "I need to talk to you!"

"How the hell did you get in here?" James asked angrily. He looked to the guard with the bleeding lip and understood. "So you beat my guards and you think I'm gonna talk to you?"

"We just need a minute," Clinton said. "Benjamin just brought something to my attention, and I think you should hear it. It's not about you two. This is important."

James crossed his arms and, after dismissing his guards, looked to Benjamin. "Talk."

"Okay, I know you're mad about what you think—"

"You'd better get to the point yesterday."

"I think Ms. Harvington is planning something with Maynard to ensure you fail this inspection," Benjamin said quickly.

"That won't happen."

"You told me about the reports and the problems. And he did say this was his 'last time.'" Benjamin walked to stand in front of James. "I know you want to hurt me right now, but you didn't have these problems until right before I arrived. And then Ms. Harvington failed at getting your company, so she tried to go through me."

James sneered. "And how'd that work out for you?"

"But then Maynard showed up and I saw him and Ellsworth leave her office the other day. Jimmy...James, that's way too coincidental."

James was silent as he considered Benjamin's theory. His gaze went down for a moment and then back up just as quickly. "Even if you're right, I have all my reports fixed. My factory is as clean as a whistle, so I can take some hits but I won't fail."

"Are you sure?" Clinton asked. "Have you personally gone over every report?"

"Dang right I have." James looked at Benjamin. "Even if Governess still wants my company, there isn't anything she can do to make me sell or close down. You can see yourselves out now."

"I just want to help," Benjamin said.

"And I want you to shut the hell up," James yelled. "You're lucky you're a guest in my establishment, so how's about you head on down for a plate in the cafeteria. Take it to go. I just cooked up something special—"

"What? What is it?" Clinton asked.

James didn't answer and immediately ran over to his computer. He shook his head, trying to clear away the clouds from his drink as a sinking feeling developed in his stomach. When he didn't find what he was looking for, he ran over to a cabinet to rummage through files until he found the folder he needed.

"James," Clinton said forcefully.

"It's my new sauce. I don't have a report on it," James said as he double-checked the files.

"Wait. How is that possible? Everything in here is state of the art," Benjamin dared to ask.

To his credit, James had other things to be concerned about so he didn't yell at Benjamin when he answered, "Not that one kettle I kept. It's not used in production anymore because it's too old and doesn't make enough. There isn't a network in here it's tied into so everything is done by hand."

"Don't you have people for that, though?" Clinton asked.

"No one touches my projects." James picked up his phone and tried to call Bryan, but after several rings, he gave up. "Dang, he's probably with Maynard now."

"What about the floor manager down there?" Benjamin suggested.

James called down to the production area who confirmed that Bryan and Maynard were looking at various devices and storage vats. He knew he couldn't interfere, so he instead considered another way to prevent the inspection of his personal kettle.

"I want that kettle dumped. Every last drop! Get some cleaners down there so he can't even ask what's going on," James ordered.

"Sir, Bryan already instructed us to do that. The cleaners just finished a few minutes before he walked in with the inspector," the employee responded.

James smiled, grateful that Bryan had anticipated his wishes. He turned back to Benjamin and Clinton and said, "Well, that's that. You two can leave now."

The two looked at one another and then turned to exit the office. Clinton was leading the way, and just as Benjamin was exiting, he asked no one in particular, "What happened to all that sauce?"

"Say what?" James asked, perplexed.

"The kettle was empty and cleaned already. What happened to all of the sauce that you made?"

James became silent. He turned to Benjamin and Clinton, who had reentered the room, as his fear slowly etched its way across his face. James ran past the both of them without speaking. He dodged the many staffers in the hallway and took the stairs to the lower level several at a time. He got to the ground level, where many of his workers were bottling products, but stopped when he saw Ellsworth. James didn't have time to ask why he was there, and as he tried to leave, Ellsworth called to him.

"Wait up, Jimmy! Shoot, where's the fire?" Ellsworth asked after he caught up to him.

"I don't have time. I'm busy," James shouted and turned from him.

Ellsworth grabbed James's hand, but James snatched it back. Ellsworth pointed to Benjamin, who was running to catch up to James and asked, "Up to your office then?"

"Not now." James walked around him, but Ellsworth ran around to block his path.

"Hold on," Ellsworth said.

James tried again to move around him, but Ellsworth remained in his path. He looked over Ellsworth's shoulder and noticed Maynard walking with Bryan, conducting more of his inspection. James then turned back to Ellsworth as suspicious thoughts entered his mind.

"Security," James shouted.

"What the hell?" Ellsworth asked in a shocked voice as four men flanked him.

"Mr. Ferguson's guest pass has been revoked. I don't wanna see him in here anymore," James said with a cold inflection.

James turned from them and didn't watch as Ellsworth was roughly escorted out. He started to run again, demanding that everyone make way for him to have an unrestricted route. After what seemed like hours, he finally reached the cafeteria where many workers and their families were seated and listening to Eugene give a speech.

"Oh, well, it looks like Mr. Cain could join us after all." Eugene clapped.

The entire assembly applauded, but James ran past them all and into the main kitchen. Several cooks were putting the finishing touches on trays that would serve a buffet, but James didn't pay attention to them. He ran past a cook and saw an iron skillet filled with fat for frying. James pushed the cook out of the way, and grabbed a towel and then the handle of the skillet.

"Clear out," James yelled. He tipped the skillet slightly so that the oil made contact with the lit burner and caught on fire. As the oil burned, the smoke billowed upward to the fire suppression hood above. James brought the fire higher to the sensors of the hood, and soon it violently released its chemicals and almost knocked James back.

"Are you crazy?" a cook asked. James stared at him, and the man added, "Sir."

"Didn't I tell everyone to clear out?" James shouted.

The kitchen staff started to leave, but James wasn't finished. He heard the commotion of the guests in the dining area and found a roll of paper towels. Just as he had done with the skillet, he lit the towels on fire and brought it up high to a fire sprinkler. Within seconds, water burst from the roof of the kitchen and out in the dining area where many surprised and angry workers and customers quickly left.

Chapter Eleven

"WHERE IS HE? Where is that boy?" Charles shouted to his former employees as he walked into the conference room in his home.

"Sir, no one has seen James for almost twenty-four hours," Eugene answered him. "After the uh...the *incident*, he just left the cafeteria."

"Did he say anything or speak to anyone?" Charles asked.

"Sir, the only thing he did was pick up a few bottles from the gift baskets that he was planning on giving out to everyone. And we only know that from the cameras. The only person he spoke to on his way out was the floor manager, and that was to tell him to trash everything that was edible in the cafeteria."

Charles rubbed the bridge of his nose and put his head down. He counted softly, and when he looked back up, he was completely red. "Where are we on cleanup?"

"It will still be a few days," the executive chef said. The dining hall wasn't so bad because that's just water. The kitchen is another matter entirely."

"How so?" Charles demanded.

"The fire suppression system in the kitchen is chemical-based, sir," Eugene explained. "It handles oil, chemical, and electrical fires, so cleaning it up isn't as easy."

"Give me a rough estimate. How much time?"

Eugene looked to the executive chef, and she nodded. "A week at the minimum, sir."

"It takes a damn week to clean one kitchen?" Charles asked.

"No, sir, we were referring to how long until the kitchen is operational again," the safety manager said. "After we get everything cleaned up, we have to get inspected by several departments to ensure the chemicals are completely gone. And it's on their schedule."

"We can call in some favors, sir"—Eugene picked up for the manager—"but they are always busy. And then we have to get the system resupplied with chemicals, and the hood has to be recertified as appropriate for use."

Charles let out a long deep sigh. He paced about the conference room and didn't say anything for several minutes. "That will be all."

"Sir," Eugene said angrily and then paused before continuing more calmly. "Sir, what are you going to do?"

"Since when do I explain myself to you? Especially when it concerns my company?"

"With respect, sir, it isn't your company anymore," Eugene said, not backing down. "You gave it away to, of all people, Jimmy."

"And what is that supposed to mean?"

"Mr. Cain, there is no one I admire more on this planet than you. I think I speak for all of us when I say you have made Calloway the city it is today and there isn't a person who doesn't owe you some form of debt for your generosity."

"Are you going to propose marriage to me, or will you finally come to your point?" Charles asked and crossed his arms.

"My point, sir, is that you know your son. We all do. These antics of his aren't new, and you still decided to give him the company."

"Who else would it go to?"

"Jimmy isn't the problem, sir. In time, I'm sure he would have made a great CEO. But he is still very young, and if these latest actions are any indication, he's also still very immature. He's not ready yet."

"I was only slightly older than him when I took over," Charles said.

"That was a much different time sir," Eugene replied. "Your son is a completely different person, and with the way things are going, *Daddy Cain's* will take some serious hits."

Charles looked around the room and saw the nods of agreement in the staff. He sat down, much more attentive to the conversation and addressed the room. "What is the bad news?"

"The entire town is up in arms, sir," a public relations representative spoke. "The consensus is that Jimmy called the entire town in to play a prank on them."

"He would never do that," Charles insisted.

"Be that as it may, sir, it doesn't change perception. There are so many ideas flying around that I can't even begin to address them or the community. They're angry, sir."

"And that doesn't even consider the amount of money we are losing because of the cafeteria being closed. Not just from the public when we open it but many of the employees who eat there," Eugene said.

Charles sighed and waved his hand about. "Very well, what are our options?"

"The department heads and I have come up with a three-pronged attack, sir. We need to pacify the community and our workers, and deal with Jimmy," Eugene said.

"I will take care of the last issue," Charles said sternly. "But as to the workers?"

"Something simple will work, sir. A bonus, free hours, that sort of thing. They aren't so much upset, but they did have their families there and those are the ones who are probably pushing for some sort of compensation."

"Are we sure about that?" Charles asked.

"Yes," Eugene said with no ambiguity. "Whatever you decide, it doesn't have to be big, just enough. And you speaking to them would be a nice gesture as well."

"I swear the things that boy makes me go through," Charles yelled again.

"Yes, well, we should also do something for the community-at-large, sir," the public relations representative spoke. "I suggest something that everyone will see as genuine and altruistic."

"Would you like for me to tell everyone to look under their seats for a set of keys to a new car?" Charles asked and smirked for the first time all morning.

"More like a picnic, sir," the public relations representative continued. "We would be giving the community what Jimmy initially promised only at a more neutral venue. Your church is having an outreach event soon, so maybe we could provide the entertainment and food."

"And a sizable donation, sir," Eugene added.

"Can someone remind me why we are so concerned with the public? I understand their anger, but will it not pass?" Charles asked everyone.

"Eventually, sir, but you are running for office."

Charles took a deep breath and let it out slowly. Over the years, his son had given him plenty of trouble but nothing of this scale. He couldn't understand how or why James would do something so foolish that affected so many people. Many of the kitchen workers had to be reassigned to jobs they had never worked before, and the cost of cleaning and certification was high. He thought his son had come so far, but after this, for the first time, he was reconsidering who he'd left his business to.

"That will be all." Charles waved his hand.

Everyone slowly filed out except for Eugene. When the room was clear except for him and Charles, he said, "I didn't mean to overstep my bounds, sir. If you feel I have, then you'll have my resignation this afternoon."

"Good," Charles bellowed and stood up. "That is exactly what I want."

"Yes, sir," was all Eugene said.

"But while you still work for me, find my son."

"I WONDER HOW much longer." James leaned forward with his head down.

"We've been here all morning. I think they're taking their sweet time," Bryan grumbled. Before he finished, Kenneth-George hit his upper arm hard.

"What the heck was that for?" Bryan asked.

"Not now," James said. "Look, I know you guys are tired, but I gotta be sure."

They all settled down and continued to wait in the lobby of the medical building. James fidgeted with the pen in his hand to take his mind off what he hoped was a very wrong hunch. After James triggered the fire suppression system in his factory, he had immediately found Bryan and the two drove until they found Kenneth-George. When they were all together, they headed down to Jacksonville in Florida to ensure that they wouldn't be found for some time.

"Are you all right?" Bryan asked and pointed to his hands.

"I'll be okay, just as soon as those tests come back."

"I'm talking about Benji."

"I don't wanna talk about 'im," James said weakly.

"C'mon, it's me and KG. Who else are you gonna run your mouth to? Uncle Charles?" Bryan asked.

"To be honest, I half expect him to be waiting on me with a torch and pitchfork," James said and smiled slightly.

"You know Miss Sissy will listen."

"And tell half of Georgia before I even finish." James sat up straight, and Kenneth-George rubbed his shoulder.

"Wouldn't that be something? Jimmy Cain finally on the other side of the fence," Bryan said while laughing.

"I don't know how many dang times I gotta tell you to shut it," James said and smiled. "I guess it just wasn't meant to be."

"Wait, did you really like 'im?" Bryan asked seriously.

"After all that time you and KG spent making bets and you still didn't figure it out? How many times did you ask if I was sweet on 'im?"

"That's different, though. Having a crush is one thing, but he was never gonna be here long."

James sighed and looked to Kenneth-George, who shrugged his shoulders. Bryan's assessment was correct, and James had just now realized it. He hadn't discussed with Bryan and Kenneth-George the embarrassing situation that he found himself in with Benjamin and Maynard because of his concern with his company, but with the time they spent waiting, the thoughts wouldn't go away.

"I dunno, cousin." James dropped his head. "I mean he was the first person I ever told everything to, and he lied to me."

"Don't worry. Boys like him don't deserve people like you. You're too honest. Shoot, if he couldn't be just as straight with you, then to hell with 'im."

"Thanks, I needed that."

"Don't go all weepy now." Bryan pulled him in. "Let's just hurry up and get back. I wanna catch Benji before he leaves and introduce him to my tire iron."

"Hey," James shouted.

"Fine, I'll use my hands." Bryan scoffed. "KG, you still got that chain in my truck?"

"I don't want you two to hurt 'im," James said.

Bryan and Kenneth-George looked at one another and then back to James.

"Then he should've never hurt you," Bryan said.

James was about to say something, but a technician came out and called his name. "Mr. Cain?"

"Yes?" All three of them answered and stood. James smiled and looked at his family and then back to the technician. "Yeah, go ahead."

"We have the test results back," he said. "I think you may want to come with me to talk someplace private."

James nodded and followed him back until they reached the laboratory. Once inside, they entered the technician's office, and he closed the door before giving James the bad news.

"The test were positive."

A shudder ran throughout James's body as the gravity of the situation hit him all at once and his worst fears were confirmed. "And you tested it twice?"

"Three times just to be sure. Mr. Cain—"

"C'mon, Horace, you know you can call me Jimmy," James said.

"I'm just trying to be professional. I did this as a favor to you. The scholarship that you and your dad established put me through medical training. But I need to know, was anyone exposed?"

"Naw, I made sure of that. I went over the remote security feeds and all that before I came down here. No one had a drop," James said confidently.

"Still, maybe we should contact the state agencies just to be sure."

"It's not that serious, Horace!"

"We're talking about botulism. It is serious. Finding it in one bottle is rare, but several bottles all from the same batch isn't a joke."

"I know that," James said.

Horace seemed to calm down slightly and opened a folder on a table. "I also found traces of clostridium perfringens. It's—"

"Food poisoning, I know." James was slightly annoyed.

Horace let out a small laugh and set the folder down. "I don't know why, but sometimes I forget that you know almost everything about food safety."

"Comes with the territory. I didn't know what was in my bottles, but I couldn't risk it."

"It's a good thing you didn't." Horace wore a grim expression. "Clostridium usually only causes abdominal cramps and diarrhea. People get it all the time. Botulism is something else entirely. The way it affects the nerves is scary."

"I used so much honey and garlic in my recipe it's not even funny. That sauce had a new oil I made especially for it."

"That's why I'm worried. It can take up to seventy-two hours for symptoms to appear, and I wouldn't want anyone to deal with the double vision or muscle weakness."

James put his face into his hands and wiped away nothing. "Families were there. Kids and all."

"Listen, I trust you. If you say no one ate it, I believe you. I've never heard of you guys having a problem, so I'll let you handle it."

"Thanks."

"Sure thing, but what are you going to do now?" Horace asked.

"I'm going to find out how the hell I missed that," James said with resolve.

"Good luck." Horace put a hand on James's shoulder. "You know, you shouldn't wait so long to see me next time. Are you about to leave right now?"

James turned to Horace and smiled before saying, "Bad timing, but I won't wait." He was leaving, but added, "And you should do something about that hair, it's gonna have moons orbiting it soon."

Horace reached up instinctively and then shook his head.

"THERE YOU ARE, Jimmy. Get over here and help me carry these trays," Cecily shouted when she saw James's car pull into the parking lot.

James reluctantly exited his vehicle. The morning services of his church had come to a completion a few minutes ago, and everyone was filing out to a large picnic area that had been set up. Many people were walking toward the awnings under which sat the catered food provided by Charles, but James was in no hurry to make his way over to where his father would doubtlessly be.

"Sure thing, Miss Sissy," James said. When he reached her, she piled several trays into his hand that were almost uncomfortably warm on his forearms.

"Bless your heart, honey. Where have you been?" Cecily motioned for him to walk with her.

"I took a trip to Jacksonville, had some things I needed checked out."

"Like what?" Cecily asked with apparent eagerness.

"Nothing, ma'am, but I had to take care of it."

Cecily didn't ask any more questions. She and James walked silently until they reached the servers and then handed over the trays Cecily had brought to be set up.

"Is this about that Benji boy?" she asked.

"I wish it was just that."

"Oh, it's that shower you gave everyone then? Now, why did you go and do a thing like that?"

James started to answer her question but stopped when he realized the implications. He wasn't so much concerned that Cecily would tell everyone like it was the newest gossip, but that she would feel compelled, and rightly so, to inform the proper authorities and Charles as well. James did want to let everyone know why he had intentionally triggered the fire suppression system, but not until he had all the answers he was searching for.

"You know I don't tell stories, especially not to you," James said with his head bowed.

"Good. At least you know better than to try something you know wouldn't work." She chuckled.

James smiled weakly. "I do. But I can't tell you. Not just yet. I know everyone's mad at me right now, but I didn't do it just because. And if I didn't...it was something I had to do."

"All right," Cecily said and turned back to her table.

"All right?" James repeated. "As much as you run your mouth, and the only thing you have to say is that?"

Cecily swatted the back of his hand with a spoon and said, "Watch your mouth, young man."

"Sorry, ma'am," James said in a way that made him sound like a child.

"Mmhmm..." Cecily grumbled. "Look, honey, I've been riding your tail since you could walk. And even though you made my arm tired working on your backside, you've never lied to me. Those little pranks of yours got close to it, but you have never outright lied. If you say you had to, then I have no reason not to trust you."

James teared up and hugged her. While resting his head on her bosom, Cecily gently stroked his hair and whispered soft reassurances to him. The drive to his church hadn't taken long, but the entire trip had been made uncomfortable because of the many hard stares he had gotten from people who noticed him.

"James, a word," Charles said strongly.

James looked up and saw that his father was alone. He had been expecting this but not during such a public setting.

"All right, Daddy."

Charles nodded to Cecily and took James away. He led them to the back of the church where no one else was, and after looking over the area to make sure they wouldn't be overheard, he began yelling.

"I do not care why, son," he said without pretense. "You will clear your things from that office by the end of the day!"

"But, Daddy!"

"What did I just say?" Charles screamed so loudly he turned red. "Never mind the money, and forget the hours that must be dedicated to cleanup, what you did was unforgivable. If the kitchen staff had breathed in any of those chemicals..."

"That's what I mean, you never listen to me," James shouted back.

"Why should I, son? Whenever I try to speak to you, you find someplace to be with your cousin and brother. Disappearing for almost a day? Not answering your phone?"

"I saw it was you."

"But you did not know what I wanted to discuss, nor did you care," Charles countered. "I could have had information about your sisters, the plant, but none of that mattered to you."

"It always matters, and I'm gonna set things right first thing on Monday morning," James said.

"You most certainly will not." Charles ran his hands through his thick hair and turned from his son. He took a few breaths and then lit his pipe. "Maybe you were not listening once again," Charles said through loud puffs. "But you are no longer in charge."

"You can't fire me," James said, shocked.

"I just did."

"No, I meant that as a matter of fact." James looked his father in the eyes and took in a deep breath at challenging him. "You gave me the company, all of it. And it wasn't under duress or anything. All of your lawyers were there, and I lost count of how many times they asked if you were sure."

Charles dropped his pipe, and his mouth remained opened. His eye twitched and his hand holding his cane shook.

"Are you disobeying me, boy?"

"No, sir," James said with deference. "But I'll be damned if I let someone take what's mine."

"You didn't build a thing."

"And neither did you." James lowered his voice but did not stop. "It's mine, and if you wanna go toe to toe in court, I'll be there. I just hope this doesn't distract from your campaign."

"Then pack a trash bag, son, because I want you out of my home before I return from these festivities! You should also find a replacement for Eugene. He will be running for one of the city commissioner positions after I am mayor and with my full confidence and endorsement."

James didn't say anything. He quickly turned from his father and stormed off.

"I HOPE THIS isn't too rough for you." Bryan laughed and patted the bed in a small room of his barn. "If it storms and you get scared, call KG."

"I'm fine," James said as he plopped onto the mattress and stared at the ceiling.

"So Uncle Charles really put you out on the streets?" Bryan asked seriously.

"If you wanna call it that, go ahead. I'm doing fine, though. Still in charge of *Daddy Cain's*."

Bryan whistled and lay next to James. "So what's next?"

"I don't know." James sighed. "I just wanna find out how my batch got infected."

"Ditto, I think we should..."

Bryan trailed off when the loud rumble of a vehicle's engine was carried through the open doors of his barn. He and James sat up as Ellsworth walked in. No one else was with him, but Ellsworth looked clearly upset and impatient.

"Ellsworth? What the heck brings you my way?" Bryan asked.

"Where is he?" Ellsworth hollered.

"I'm right here. What do you want, Ellie?"

Ellsworth charged at James. He was within a few feet when Bryan grabbed him under his arms and pulled him back.

"Lemme go, Bryan. This doesn't have anything to do with you!"

"If you put your hands on my cousin, then it is my business," Bryan said.

After struggling in his grip, Ellsworth finally relaxed and pushed Bryan back.

"All right, I won't touch 'im, but you owe me an explanation. What the hell was that the other day?"

"What? When you wouldn't move the hell outta my way and I had you moved myself?"

"You're goddamn right! Who the hell do you think you are? You don't have any right treating people like that!"

James looked to Bryan who walked past Ellsworth and into the room off to the side. "I'm not closing the door, so mind your manners now, Ellsworth. You're in my home now."

Once Bryan was inside of the room, James said, "I'm Daddy Cain. When you come into my factory, I'm the damn king!"

Ellsworth turned from James. He paced back and forth before punching a random oil lantern so hard that it sailed across the room, the glass shattering when it hit a support beam. He turned back to James, who still had his arms crossed, and walked to stand in front of him.

"Those guards of yours treated me like dirt, like I stole something!"

"So what? You want a hug or something? I can call Miss Sissy up," James said.

"Why do you always have to do this?" Ellsworth asked tiredly. "I thought we were getting better."

"'*Better*?'" James asked, confused. "I don't know... Wait, why are you here anyway?"

"Because I wanted to see you. Is that too dang much?" Ellsworth shook his head. "Is it that Benji boy? Is that why you don't have time for me?"

"Damn it, why can't you just mind your own damn business? You know, you gotta lot of nerve coming over here, seeing as how you and Maynard tried to set me up."

"What?" Ellsworth croaked.

"You heard 'im," Bryan said as he entered the room. "That dang inspection we just had. You're telling us that you and Maynard just happened to be at the plant right after Governess told him to take care of something for her?"

"I don't know what the two of you are talking about."

"Bullshit," James yelled.

"Call me liar again," Ellsworth warned. "Now I don't know anything about someone trying to set you up."

"So why were you there?" James asked.

"I wanted to see you. We didn't get a chance to talk at the ball, remember?"

James paused and remembered that Ellsworth did want to speak with him. It was still very coincidental that he and Maynard were both at his plant together, but Maynard had been conducting the inspection with Bryan so they couldn't have arrived at the same time.

"You're trying to be slick, but why didn't you just call Jimmy? Why walk through the plant? But I guess we know why Governess asked you to come alone with her at the ball," Bryan said.

"I already told the both of you why I was there," Ellsworth shouted back. "Governess wanted me to get my dad's attention to talk to him about something at the ball, so I did. Now I'm not putting up with any more accusations from you, Bryan. Either of you! How the hell could you think that about me?"

"Ellie, you picked on me every dang day growing up. And the last few weeks, I don't know what your problem has been! So don't ask me *how*. Come to think of it, I'll ask you right here and right now, what? What do you want from me?"

"Damn it, Jimmy. I just wanted you to be my guy," Ellsworth exploded, and James took a step back.

"Oh what the hell?" Bryan asked.

"Bryan, give us a few," James said quietly. When Bryan walked back into the room, James sighed and turned back to Ellsworth. "Is that what all that was about?"

"You didn't forget that tug of war, did you?" Ellsworth asked and chuckled softly.

"Naw, but I just figured that was because we were so close."

"You're not that cute... Well, you know what I mean," Ellsworth said.

James gestured to a couch, and they both sat down. "Ellie, I've never looked at you like that."

"I know, but you did ask me," Ellsworth said. "I'm not trying to mess up anything you have with Benjamin, but he's leaving soon."

"He is, but all these years? If you wanted to get close, then why are you always on my case?"

"Shucks, I'm not like that all the time." Ellsworth put up his hands.

"Like when?" James demanded.

"W-When you're not with some guy," Ellsworth said, embarrassment in each word. "I can't help it. That's why I kept on showing my tail and acting a fool around you and that Benjamin boy."

James wanted to laugh but thought better of it. With a wide smile, he coughed out over chuckles that kept interrupting him, "It's not like we can't go play doctor. Last I checked you do own a clinic."

"That's not what I want," Ellsworth said and then laughed himself. "I said I wanted you to be my guy. No one else." As he finished, Ellsworth took James's hand into his own.

James stared into the blue crystals that were Ellsworth's eyes. He had never known this level of honesty from Ellsworth, and the gesture was making him feel uncomfortable as Ellsworth slid closer to him and wrapped an arm around his waist.

"I'm sorry," James said.

"Don't be." Ellsworth tried to kiss James, but James moved back. "What?"

"I said I'm sorry. Sorry for accusing you and sorry because I still don't look at you like that."

"Jimmy..." Ellsworth said through a cracking voice.

"You're not a liar. I know that. But what you want, I can't give you. Maybe one day when I'm ready to settle down, but I can't even say if that's gonna be with you."

Ellsworth smiled and hugged James tightly. It was the first time they had made such intimate physical contact when they weren't trying to hurt one another. As James relaxed in his embrace, Ellsworth nuzzled his nose into James's hair and kissed his head. James was content to stay like this for a while, but when he shifted positions and looked up he saw another car pull up and Benjamin step out.

"It's the one I'm not," Ellsworth whispered.

Benjamin approached, so James stood from where he sat next to Ellsworth. "Don't worry. This won't take long," James said angrily.

ELLSWORTH STOOD AS James went to meet Benjamin. He wasn't sure what was happening, so he called over to Bryan. "Did I miss something?"

"Oh yeah. You missed a whole lot. Short story, though, is that Benji was getting close to Jimmy to try to make 'im sell. Orders from the Governess."

"He did what?" Ellsworth asked. He motioned for Bryan to join him as they walked toward James and Benjamin. When they were close enough, Ellsworth heard Benjamin trying to apologize.

"Just wanted you to know that," Benjamin finished.

"Sure thing, but you're a day late and a dollar short," James yelled back.

"You know what, forget it. I told you that I wasn't planning on using you that way because it's the truth. I may be an idiot for not telling you sooner, but I'm not what you're trying to make me out to be."

"It just takes one time," James said.

"And that's it? You're not even going to try to work things out?"

"What the heck do we gotta work out?" James asked. "This was supposed to be a nice little affair. You're leaving soon, so what are we supposed to work on?"

Benjamin grimaced but didn't shout back. James was right. "Then why did you call me here?"

"I wanted to thank you. In person at least." James nodded. "I appreciate what you and Mr. Clint did for me back there. If you hadn't... It's a good thing you did, so thank you."

"It's no problem," Benjamin said lightly. "Can I ask what the issue was?"

"That batch was poison, Benji," Bryan yelled at him. "Shoot, you probably knew the whole time. Wasn't that the plan that you and your boss lady cooked up?"

"What? N-no, Bryan," Benjamin pleaded. "If I had anything to do with it, then why would I have warned Jimmy?"

"Bryan..." James said and tried to take his cousin away.

"No, he doesn't get off that easy." Bryan took off his shirt and nodded to Ellsworth who did the same. They started toward Benjamin, and Bryan continued, "That boy tried to get your company and then played with your emotions, and now he's lying to our faces." He turned to Benjamin. "You know damn well what the hell you did!"

"How?" Benjamin asked everyone. "How could I do anything to affect any product that's in there? I was with Jimmy most of the time, and I don't have unrestricted access. I still have to get a visitor's pass when I stop by."

Ellsworth stopped moving forward, but Bryan said, "Then you got Maynard to do it for you!"

"Hold up," Ellsworth said. "If Maynard isn't at work, then he's with me. I don't know what you meant by poison, but Maynard doesn't set foot in Calloway without me knowing. He actually doesn't really like it there."

EVERYONE STARTED TO talk over one another as James thought about everything that had been said. His security was very good and no unusual reports had come across his desk in a very long time. Except for those dealing with the items that he sold. As James contemplated how someone could tamper with his kettle, he remembered the traits of the contaminants found. They weren't chemicals, and when he remembered how they formed, a wave of nausea almost consumed him.

"B-Bryan?" James said. "It was you?"

Everyone stopped talking, and Bryan looked to James. "What are talking about?"

"My kettle, cousin. You and I are the only people who touch it. We made a batch a few days ago."

"I always help you make stuff," Bryan said.

"And you're also the only person with unrestricted access to the plant. You're Jimmy's right hand," Benjamin said as he took up a position next to James.

"Just wait a second, guys," Ellsworth said. "It's Bryan we're talking about. I mean, if Governess really was two-faced enough to order Benji to cozy up to Jimmy, then who's to say—"

"How do you know about that?" James cut him off.

"B-Bryan just told me," Ellsworth answered.

"I ain't told 'im about that," James said with heat in his voice. "And I didn't bring it up when we went to Florida." He looked to Bryan. "Well, speak up, Cousin Bryan!"

Bryan looked to everyone and then sneered while taking slow steps back. "All right, Jimmy, you got me."

"What the hell," James shouted and tried to jump at his cousin. Benjamin and Ellsworth held him back as he thrashed about, trying to reach him. "Do you have any idea how many people you could've hurt?"

"Oh quit all that damn crying. You sound like a damn gal," Bryan said. "Your whining ass always has."

"Bryan," Ellsworth shouted. "W-what... Wait, what the hell is going on?"

"Why?" Benjamin asked the question that no one could.

"You two really can't see it, huh?" Bryan spread his arms and spun around. "I'm tired of being broke!"

"You're a damn Cain, Bryan! My cousin," James shouted.

"No! I'm 'Cousin Bryan,'" he said. "Your damn lap dog. Always running your errands, watching out for you, and for what? For someone to snap their damn fingers and I jump!"

James took a deep breath. He wasn't sure what was happening but proceeded as calmly as he was able. "You work for me. It's your damn job to do what I say."

"I'm not Eugene, and you're not Uncle Charles. You act like you're doing me a favor, but I'm just a joke to everyone. You only come over when you're bored because you're so busy with all your money friends like Ellsworth here. Shoot, even at my own party, I can't get the time of day from a girl unless she knows I'm related to Jimmy Cain!"

"A joke?" James asked with his legs feeling weak.

"You're damn right, a joke. It's always been that way. They only called you *Jungle Jim* when we were kids because you kept your poor redneck cousin around all the time. Like I'm some damn charity case."

The room was spinning. People had been angry with James in his time, but no one had displayed this level of hate. "I had you around because I never wanted you to leave," he said over a lump in his throat. "I thought you liked your farm."

"You mean this damn sugar shack?" Bryan yelled. "The one you come around and mess up all the time?"

"Bryan..." James said as warm tears fell from his eyes.

"Don't try that," Bryan said with a wavering voice. "You always sent me away. Even Uncle Charles when he got tired of me. You didn't want me around. That's why he went and got you KG."

"Don't talk about my brother," James shouted.

"He's not your damn brother," Bryan yelled back just as forcefully. "He's not blood, like you and me. But who gets to live with you? Who gets made up all nice for the ball? You wanna know why? It's 'cause Governess was gonna pay me a lotta damn money! Hell, I can't believe you didn't notice I turned off that kettle, but then again, I'm just your *do* boy. The boy that shadows Eugene and makes sure your company is running so you can play around all day!"

"The reports... you messed with 'em?" James barely got out.

"Just enough to keep your mind off the kettle we use. A different one every so often and you were too damn worried about your conquests to stay long enough to talk to your people. You always had me or Eugene do it."

James looked down. He was trembling at the realization of his cousin's true feelings. Arguing was pointless, so James said the only thing he could.

"No."

"What?" Bryan asked.

"You're not going to make me and my daddy the bad guys." James looked into Bryan's eyes. "How long? How long have you hated me? A year? Two?"

Bryan remained silent.

"Oh what five then, ten? Stop me anytime you want, cousin, 'cause now we're getting to when we were kids!" James walked up to Bryan, who didn't move. "You can blame us all you want for your troubles, but it's not our fault your daddy is a drunk who pissed away his inheritance! All of your life, you never went hungry or without. And you were always loved. You wanna be mad at someone, then look in a damn mirror! I never put anyone before you, and you can't stand my guts. Did you always hate us? Was it always pretend?"

"I already said my piece," Bryan said. He turned from them all and walked into his barn. "Get off my property."

JAMES WATCHED HIS cousin close the door to his barn. In the deafening silence, Benjamin and Ellsworth turned to James with shocked and consoling expressions as James took a small step and swayed unsteadily.

"Jimmy?" Ellsworth said softly. He walked up to stand behind James when he didn't get an immediate answer.

"I wanna hurt 'im. I wanna hurt 'im bad!"

"I know you do," Ellsworth said.

"You don't know nothin'! Not a damn thing," James shouted. He lowered his head to stare at the ground. "All his life, that man sat in my daddy's house and lied to us. Hiding behind his smiles when he's just as ugly as sin on the inside."

"I'm sorry. Sometimes you only see the real face of your family when it comes to money," Ellsworth said and placed a hand on James's shoulder.

"That's all right, though. I got something for 'im! I'm gonna... I-I swear I'm gonna..."

Ellsworth listened intently as James tried to finish his threat. Instead, he heard the unmistakable sigh of anguish as James started to cry. James crumbled to the ground and he immediately knelt behind him and wrapped his arms around James as he lost the ability to hold himself up and fell back against Ellsworth who cradled him. James's crying soon turned into deep, painful sobs.

"Jimmy," Benjamin said and hurried to console James.

"Get away from me!" James pushed him away as he tried to comfort him. "I'm tired of people lying to me!"

"Hey, it's gonna be okay," Ellsworth said while letting James cry. He looked to Benjamin who stepped back and waited.

"I can't," James wailed. "I just can't!"

"You can't what?"

"I can't say a damn word to anyone, Ellie. If I tell my daddy or anybody else, they'll lock 'im up."

"Isn't that the point, though?" Ellsworth asked. "Bryan almost put people in the hospital, and that boy has no love for you left if he ever did."

"I know that. I do. But I can't. He's my blood, and I know he's done so much wrong, but that doesn't change anything. He lied to me all my damn life, but I still love 'im and I just can't!"

Ellsworth pulled James in closer. He rocked him slightly as his muffled protest became inaudible and his trembling became violent shakes. Ellsworth looked to Benjamin, who nodded his understanding that nothing was to be said to Charles or the authorities about what they had just learned. As Benjamin left, Ellsworth caught something akin to defeat in Benjamin's eyes but was too concerned about James to give it much thought.

Epilogue

"AH, MR. BENJAMIN. Please come in and have a seat." Laura waved her hand for him to enter.

It was early in the afternoon, and Benjamin wanted to get home to complete his packing. After leaving the bizarre situation at Bryan's farm, he was glad to go back in Chicago where things weren't as complicated, at least to him. As he had gotten ready to head to the airport much earlier than his flight was scheduled, he'd received a call from Laura instructing him to meet her at her office.

"Ms. Harvington, I hope you don't mind if I get right to it. Why did you call me here?" Benjamin asked cautiously.

"Nothing unpleasant, I assure you. On the contrary." She handed him an envelope. "I think that you will be most pleased."

Benjamin opened the envelope and pulled out a settlement of funds that were to be deposited into his bank account. He was momentarily surprised at the value and even more shocked that the money would be made available to him within hours.

"I don't understand. What is this?"

"Your bonus, Mr. Rei. Although you may not have been successful in acquiring *Daddy Cain's,* your work went well above and beyond what was required of you."

"Ma'am, I..."

"I know that you may feel reluctant at accepting this, especially with the compromising position I put you in with James. It is why you have earned this, in addition to a glowing recommendation from me that you are eminently qualified for promotion and that you should be at the company's earliest convenience."

Benjamin felt himself smile for the first time in Laura's presence. He considered that he might have misjudged her but then remembered what Bryan had said. How she had concocted the entire plan to bring down James's company from the inside. He stopped smiling and glared at Laura.

"This won't go beyond me, but I know what you did. You and Bryan," Benjamin said.

Laura smiled and leaned back in her chair. "Why I am absolutely positive that I have no idea what you are talking about."

"I'm not fishing, I already know...wait! This doesn't make any sense! None of it does," Benjamin shouted.

"Oh?" Laura smirked.

"I'm thinking of a business scenario, Ms. Harvington—a hypothetical one. If someone worked with Bryan to taint a recipe, one that only he and James knew about, why would they try to buy Daddy Cain's?"

"Well, that is a good hypothetical question," she said.

"If people would have gotten sick, died, then the brand value would've been useless. It could have been sold off, but why sink so many resources into buying it?" Laura remained silent, and it finally dawned on Benjamin. "You never wanted *Daddy Cain's,* did you? You went through all of this, brought me down here, and pushed me toward Jimmy, for what?"

"My word. You are smart, child!" Laura laughed. She stood from her desk and walked over to stand in front of him. She crossed her arms and said, "I suppose it is a good thing this discussion is only hypothetical then. However, I will say that I am not entirely ungrateful. You helped me to achieve my objectives, Benjamin, and I like to pay it forward by putting out a bit of good Karma into the universe every so often. It is why I brought you down here, to give you the honored and unique opportunity of being my protégé."

"You're not serious?" Benjamin backed away, appalled. "All of this was a way to get me down here to mentor me?"

Laura laughed dismissively. "Well, you certainly have a high opinion of yourself, but no. I also needed James distracted."

"What?" Benjamin asked angrily.

"Enough," Laura snapped. "I do not care if your feelings are hurt or if you are angry. Because at the end of the day, you did what you had to do, just as I did once. Regardless of my methods, I get results as do you. Now it would be in your best interest to walk out of my office."

"You used me," Benjamin said in shock.

"And in exchange, I plan on taking you with me to the top." Laura walked back to her desk and picked up a stack of papers before heading to the exit, clearly about to leave. "That will be all, take some time off to enjoy your bonus, Benjamin. I expect you back to work with a clear head. Speak with Amanda if you wish to change where your flight is headed, but I assume that you will need to make moving arrangements."

Benjamin was so angry he could feel his palms sweating. Everything about his reasons for being in Calloway was a lie. And he had indirectly helped Laura to hurt James. He couldn't stand it and knew what he had to do.

"I don't want your money!"

Laura looked at him with a quizzical expression. "Are you saying that instead of six figures and a promotion you would prefer to be fired? Because that is where you are headed, Benjamin," she said in a professional tone and started to walk toward the elevator.

"Not fired, I want to quit. Release me from my contract with no penalties," Benjamin said while following her.

Once they were both inside and the elevator started to move, Laura let out a small giggle and said, "You cannot be serious, child."

"I'm not your child, and I'm dead serious!"

Laura cocked her head and crossed her arms. "Such passion. Very well. I will release you from your contract. But now it is my turn to ask why?"

"No one uses me! And I'm not leaving Calloway until I expose you for the person you are."

The elevator reached the ground floor, and Laura exhaled. "Morality is so overrated. I suppose my son learned his father's charm well."

"W-What are you talking about?" Benjamin asked.

"Why, Jimmy of course," Laura said. "It has barely been any time at all, and yet you seem completely smitten."

"Are you saying—? Wait, he's not your—he doesn't have any features of—"

"I may not be a geneticist, but I know who my son is, Benjamin. And so does Charles. Mayor Ferguson, Cecily, practically all of the older adults in Calloway. But James does not." She smiled wickedly.

"Why are you telling me this?" Benjamin's head spun.

"Because, Mr. Benjamin, you believe yourself to be so morally upright. And I am sure that you plan on trying to repair your relationship with my son. I saw how he reacted to you lying to him, and now you know another secret. One that his father and all his loved ones have gone to painstaking labors to keep quiet. So will you tell him and destroy the love he has for all of those people? Or will you continue to lie to his face every time you see him?"

LAURA WALKED AWAY from Benjamin before he could respond. She strode purposefully through the lobby and outside to a small group of people who had gathered, some of whom had cameras. As soon as Laura cleared her throat, the crowd focused their attention on her and several microphones came close to her face.

"Good morning, everyone, and thank you all for coming on such short notice," Laura said pleasantly. "As you all know, the city of Savannah has been very good to me. And as much as I love this city, my home, my heart, will always be in Calloway. Now I know that you are all aware of the recent...shenanigans that have taken place there, and I, for one, think it's appalling. Appalling that a young man with so much power can affect so many. Appalling that a man thinks that it is okay to be chauvinistic toward women in this day in age."

"I suppose it is true that the apple never falls far. And though these are not my sole motivations, I find it appalling that the citizens of Calloway have been bamboozled into thinking that they only have one choice for mayor. Well, not any longer, because as of this moment, I would like to officially declare my candidacy for mayor of Calloway!"

Laura smiled as her senses were assaulted by the bright lights and loud shutters of the cameras. She answered a few quick questions very briefly, but soon made her way toward a car she had called ahead for. Once inside the vehicle, she placed a hand over her chest and took in an exhilarating and triumphant breath before releasing it slowly.

As the driver waited for the media to clear a driving path, Laura couldn't help but caress a large jeweled locket she felt with her hand over her heart. She brought the expensive jewelry out from under her blouse and took a moment to collect herself before opening it. Looking down at the single picture of her decades-younger self wrapped in the arms of Charles, Laura reverently skimmed a finger across his face.

"Your move, Charles," Laura said in a low voice full of longing, as a genuine smile spread across her face.

"Ma'am?" the driver asked and looked into the rearview mirror. He stole a glance at Laura and immediately regretted it when he noticed the unshed tears in her eyes.

"What the hell do you—?" Laura shouted but stopped to collect herself. "Give the road your undivided attention." She angrily blinked back tears.

LAURA'S CAR DROVE off, and Benjamin had to force himself to break away from the spectacle as the reporters started to set up camp and ask questions of everyone in the immediate area. While walking, Benjamin pulled out his phone and looked through his notes until he found the number he was looking for.

"Hello, Miss Sissy? It's Benjamin. I need a favor. I need to speak with Mr. Cain. It's about a job."

About the Author

Thad J. is a Florida native who was born and raised in West Palm Beach. After a spending several years on active duty, he moved to Orlando to work as a pastry cook while finishing college. He has been writing short stories and fiction for as long as he can remember and just started writing gay romantic fiction.

Facebook: www.facebook.com/profile.php?id=100017680668295
Twitter: www.twitter.com/AuthorThaddeusJ

Also Available from NineStar Press

www.ninestarpress.com

www.ingramcontent.com/pod-product-compliance
Lightning Source LLC
Chambersburg PA
CBHW030304180626
46810CB00003B/907